WHATEVER HAPPENED TO

UNCLE ED?

ERIC MILLER

Big Time Books™
Los Angeles, California
www.BigTimeBooks.com

WHATEVER HAPPENED TO UNCLE ED?

Edited by Leya Booth and Julia Watson
All errors are the fault of the author

Back Cover and Interior layouts by Steven W. Booth
www.GeniusBookServices.com

Paperback ISBN 979-8-9923971-0-9
Ebook ISBN 979-8-9923971-1-6

PRAISE FOR BIG TIME BOOKS RELEASES

Whatever Happened To Uncle Ed?

"The narrative is full of developments that blend affecting emotional truths with feats of writerly imagination and deeply enjoyable plot twists—Miller manages to make the prospect of facing one's own worst nightmare simultaneously horrifying and hilarious..."

–Kirkus Reviews

"Original, skillfully crafted, surprising plot twists, memorable characters, all delivered in author Eric Miller's distinctive and narrative driven storytelling style, "Whatever Happened to Uncle Ed?" is especially and unreservedly recommended..."

–Midwest Book Review

Hell Comes To Hollywood
Bram Stoker Award Nominated

"Gorier than any PG-13 horror flick you'll see, and written better (by a mile) than any SyFy schlockfest, Hell Comes To Hollywood is worth a look."

–Dr. Loomis, Ain't It Cool News Horror

"Hell Comes To Hollywood is all-encompassing, featuring stories that span from wonderfully gratuitous, over-the-top gorefests... to tales that are genuinely haunting and linger in your mind long afterward..."

–Vivienne Vaughn, Fangoria

18 Wheels of Horror

"Filled with disturbing twists and terrifying threats, these spine-chilling stories have enough suspense to spook even the bravest of souls."
—Blake Boldt, *Road King Magazine*

"...the endless rumble of engines and wheels, the perceived romance and wearying lonely truths of the open road, the aspect of unique Americana, it's all here."
—Christine Morgan, *The Horror Fiction Review*

Hell Comes To Hollywood 2

"Miller's Hell Comes To Hollywood II ought to be required reading for anyone who has even an inkling of trying to make it in the City of Dreams."
—Scott Urban, *The Horror Zine*

"On the whole, the anthology receives a big thumbs up; it is an entertaining read with an unusually high number of good stories..."
—TT Zuma, *Horror World*

18 Wheels of Science Fiction

"...75 MPH of free-wheeling fun from cover to cover!"
—*Midwest Book Review*

"...Definitely fun."
—*Analog Science Fiction and Fact*

ACKNOWLEDGMENTS

In spite of what many people think, no writer works alone. Yes, we spend thousands of hours by ourselves, hammering away at keyboards and often cursing at computer screens. But it takes a team to get us through those often trying creative times, and once the story is done, to help unleash it on the world. So a sincere thank you to the people below for helping me bring this book to life.

Quentin Frost, for encouraging me to expand the short story. Wendy Kutzner, for endless patience while I was writing. Steven Booth, for design work and hand-holding. Julia Watson, for fixing my more egregious grammatical errors. Leya Booth, for eagle-eye editing and for laughing at the torture scene. Jenny Callahan Austin, for catching those damn typos. Shane Bitterling, for the T-shirts, Pizzas, and eternal friendship. Richard Tanne, for kicking my ass to get this done. Kathryn McGee, for being a bright light in a dark time, and for notes I really did listen to. Zelda Devon, for the perfect cover. John Palisano, for friendship and inspiration. Ron Zwang, for believing in the project. Literary agent Cherry Weiner, for insightful notes, submissions, and for giving me a shot.

And special thanks to my late friend and sometimes co-writer Patrick Shiffrar, who after reading an early draft suggested I make the story more about love, and less about hate. Those are words we should all live and write by.

Eric Miller
January 2025

To Mom and Dad

NOW

Max Brown is somewhere over forty. Average-sized, dark-haired, and pale-skinned from too much fluorescent and not enough sunlight. He is lean, though hints of wiry muscle fill out the worn fabric of his button-down shirt. And while his face is open and friendly, there is an air of mystery about him, of secrecy. It flows from the depths of his haunted eyes.

He pores over an anonymous ledger in an anonymous cubicle in an anonymous office. The cubicle is void of any personal effects; no pictures, no plants, no funny coffee mugs full of cartoon-topped pens like normal people have. This lack of decoration is not because he's new to the firm and hasn't unpacked his effects yet. Nor is it because he's been fired and has cleaned out his desk. The absence of personality in his workspace stems from far more complex issues in his life. Basically, Max doesn't have normal things around because Max isn't normal.

Focused on his job, he compares figures on the lined green paper with those on his computer screen. Now and then he reaches over his teeming collection of empty Diet Coke cans and punches a correction on the computer keyboard.

A *creak* sounds behind him.

Max grabs a silver letter opener the instant he hears the noise. He raises the sharp point and spins his desk chair around, ready to fend off an attack. When he sees the threat is not going to kill him in the next few seconds—the rolling cart of donuts and bagels and other carb-laden treats are more of a long-term danger than a short-term peril—he relaxes and covers his reaction by grabbing a stray envelope and using the improvised dagger to cut it open.

Shane the bagel guy is oblivious to the fact that the accountant was just about to stab him in the throat. To be fair, Shane is oblivious to almost everything. Everything, that is, except his last customer, the attractive brunette sitting a few cubicles over. She had smiled at his new Frankenstein T-shirt when he sold her a scone a minute ago. But *everybody* digs Frank, he reasons to himself, so he decides to wear his Lon Chaney Wolfman shirt the next day. If she smiles at *that*, well, he's gonna ask her to go out after work sometime, and for more than just a pastry, yessiree Bob.

Shane stops his cart and sees Max staring at him. He eyes the letter opener in the accountant's hand and the questioning look on the man's face. Shane knows Max isn't going to buy anything. He never does. But Shane is nothing if not persistent; he didn't get to be the #1 salesman in the Pelidyne Corporation's snack cart division by giving up. He did it with hard work, persistence, and charm. And, of course, his awesome conversation-starting T-shirt collection. So he shoves the thoughts of his future wife aside, readies his best "you can't live without a tasty treat" sales pitch, and jumps into the daily ritual.

"Hey, Max. How's it going today?"

Max smiles back. He knows all about rituals. And persistence. He plays his part in the charade and pretends to be normal. "Good so far."

Shane nods and decides on the fly to go with a common interest sales pitch. "How'd the Lakers do last night?"

"You know. Tough year."

"Bummer. But don't worry. The wins are gonna come back, you'll see."

"Yeah." Max starts to turn back to his desk.

Feeling the possible sale slipping away, Shane doubles down. "Hey, you ever think about playing hoops again? Me and some guys run on weekends over at the Y, three on three. I hear you were pretty good back in the day."

A distant memory softens Max's face, but he shakes his head. "Back in the day, maybe. But I lost my shot. So, no thanks."

"That sucks, man," Shane says, then he gets to the real point of his chatter. "Anyway, you up for a bagel today? Boiled and baked, just like in New York City. I'll toss in the cream cheese for free."

Max points toward the Diet Coke cans. "I already had breakfast."

Shane eyes the growing collection. "That stuff is going to kill you, dude."

"It'll have to get in line."

Something about the way Max says this makes it clear he's not talking about his poor diet. Shane doesn't notice. He is a pure salesman and has already spotted his next victim across the office floor, so he doesn't waste any time wondering what could be wrong with Max's personal life. He just nods and shoves his cart toward his new mark.

"Later, man."

"Later."

As the cart wheels away, Max lays the letter opener down and turns back to his job. He has lost his place in the endless morass of numbers, but soon finds it and gets absorbed in the spreadsheet again. The job is boring, but he likes it that way. He needs it that way. He buries himself in meaningless columns of numbers to give order to his life. Where the other number crunchers complain about working overtime, he asks for it, even volunteering for weekend shifts. He's management and it doesn't raise his pay, but Max doesn't care. The sheer routine of it all keeps him sane. Or close enough to fool his coworkers.

And most of the time, himself.

Another workday passes. The clock spins, the sun moves across the land, and Max makes order out of numerical chaos.

Towards the end of the shift an older, balding man pokes his head over the cubicle and breaks Max's concentration. Sam Wheeler wears a weathered London Fog jacket on his broad shoulders and carries a Halliburton briefcase in a large hand. He is Max's boss, but he hasn't always been in middle management. In his younger days, he was an officer in the Airborne Rangers and managed soldiers instead of accountants. And though the paperwork load was worse in the Army, jumping out of airplanes and shooting at bad people evened things out. He had it better than most soldiers who served and remembers it as one of the best times of his life. Now he is mundane, like most people are.

Like Max wishes he could be.

"You did it again," Sam says.

Max glances up, disoriented. He has been absorbed in the arcane formulae of the ledger without a break for hours. "Did what?"

"Six-eighteen. Long past quitting time." Sam frowns with concern when he studies the younger man. It's a familiar look; he's been concerned about Max for a long time.

"I must have gotten caught up," Max says, sliding the ledger into a drawer and turning off the monitor.

"You've been doing that a lot lately."

Max shrugs the comment off. "You know."

"Yeah," Sam says. "I know."

He walks away as Max gathers his things—a threadbare black Levi jacket and a half-empty can of Diet Coke. It's not that he's a minimalist or following some sort of trend. He just doesn't bother with things that aren't useful.

Sam stops by the door and waits for Max to catch up. When he does, Sam elbows him and grins. "Jennifer's in town."

It's Max's turn to frown. "So?"

"So, Cindy and I thought you two might... you know." Sam makes a slight thrusting motion with his hips. It is the universal, and stupid-looking, sign for sex. Universal in male locker rooms, truck stops, fraternity parties, and other such testosterone-filled places. It looks even more stupid being done by a sixty-something manager in an accounting office.

Max shakes his head at the ludicrous image. "Really?"

"Does that mean you're in?"

"I can't. I've got some stuff to do."

"She's my little sister for crying out loud. I wouldn't try to set her up with just anyone."

"You sure about that?" Max says, pushing past his boss and walking down the hallway.

"Of course. I want her to be with a nice, safe, boring guy like you."

"Thanks. I guess."

Sam persists. "It's not like you have to spend the rest of your life with her. Just a little dinner, a little dancing, then, well, maybe dessert."

"Does she know you talk about her like that?"

"She put me up to it. And you should hear what she says about me."

"Probably better than what they say around here."

"Come on. You look like you could use a night out of the house. Get out and have some fun for once. I promise it won't kill you."

Max stops dead in his tracks at the comment and shakes his head. "I'm sorry. Really. But I've got some people staying with me."

"You've *always* got people staying with you. It's like the Bates Motel over at your place. What gives?"

Max struggles to find an innocent explanation for his complicated domestic life. There isn't one, but he comes up with something he hopes is adequate. "I've got some friends in from out of town. They needed a place to stay for a while."

Sam shrugs. "Okay, then. Enjoy yourself."

Figurative bullet, dodged.

Sam takes one last shot at matchmaking as they walk into the well-lit parking lot. "She'll be here for a week..."

"I'll think about it. And say hi to her and Cindy for me."

"You got it."

Max waves and heads for his car.

℘

Max doesn't go straight home after work. He never does. Instead, he drives around town in his trusty old Chevy Impala. The body is rusted and the upholstery is ripped but he's nothing if not a practical man; it runs, it's paid for, and it's been a long, long time since he felt the need to impress anyone.

He cruises for hours, looking for all the world like a man avoiding something. Or for that matter, stalking something. Long after the sun drops from the sky and the full moon crests above the horizon he tires of the endless meandering loops and stops at a grocery store.

Inside, he wanders through the well-stocked aisles and watches people caught up in their grocery lists. He wishes he could be like them, that his only worry was which version of Hamburger Helper would please the family tonight, or how many grams of fat were in a serving of Kraft Macaroni & Cheese, or if he should buy the half-gallon of milk and risk running out by the end of the week or gamble on a gallon and hope he can use it up before it goes sour.

He stops in the pet food aisle, pretending to read the labels on the assorted brands of cat food to see which would be best for his beloved Fleabag. He almost seems like the other shoppers for a while.

But he is not like them.

Not even close.

He grabs the Meow Mix. The cartoon animals on the sack make him smile. Smiles are rare for Max, and he treasures them when they appear. He heads for the checkout lane, deep in thought as usual. The checkout girl flirts with him. She's cute in a cartoon animal kind of way, but he is oblivious.

"Hey, Max. How's it going?"

He stares at her as he comes out of his daze, trying to place her face. Does he know her from high school? From work? From a restaurant? Then he remembers; he knows her from *here*. Duh. From countless late-night excursions into the land of avoidance.

"It's going all right, Mary Ann," he says, reading her name tag and handing over some cash.

"It's Amber, remember?" She blushes and rings up his purchase. "I just wore her apron tonight. I left mine at home."

Max blushes himself. "Oh, yeah, right. Sorry, Amber. I've just been a little sick this week."

"The flu bug got you? It's going around again."

"Uh, yeah," he lies. "Really wiped me out."

"That sucks." She hands him the change. There is an awkward silence. The ancient woman in line behind him clears her throat and bumps him with her cart.

Max grabs the Meow Mix. "I better go before you catch it too. Thanks, Amber." He hurries for the door, running away from the well-lit, friendly place.

The Impala sits behind a closed motorcycle repair shop. A garage door stands open, spilling light into the parking lot and illuminating Max and a burly mechanic as they make a deal. Max holds a shiny, black, full-faced motorcycle helmet in the crook of an elbow, and with a free hand pulls out a fat roll of cash. He peels five crisp hundreds off the top and slaps them into the man's greasy palm. The mechanic grins and stuffs the money in a pocket.

He thinks Max is a little strange; the accountant could have bought the helmet during regular store hours for less money, but for some reason, he wants to keep the purchase secret. The mechanic's first guess is that Max has a wife like his own, a screeching banshee who won't let him ride his hog even though he works on bikes for a living. Then he looks at his customer again and changes his mind; this guy doesn't have a wife. Not even a psychotic one. The mechanic would bet a week's pay that Max lives with his mother. And in a way, he would be right.

Max continues his shopping spree at the counter of an Army-Navy military surplus store. The shop is closed, but the grizzled storekeeper lives in the back and always opens up for special customers like the furtive accountant.

Long ago, the storekeeper had served in the Navy in the Vietnam War. He was a gun captain on a battleship, in charge of the men who loaded huge bags of gunpowder behind the massive shells in the main guns. The weapons could shoot for miles, around the curve of the earth, and rain tons of high-explosive death on an enemy who couldn't strike back. The storekeeper's ears rang for years after he was discharged from the service thanks to the incredible detonations.

Now he sweeps the floor and stocks the shelves at his decrepit store and remembers the good old days when he had commies to shoot at.

A large box sits on the counter, and the storekeeper plunks objects into it as Max points them out. A machete, two boxes of signal flares, a bullet-proof vest, and many, many boxes of ammo. Max seems much more comfortable shopping here than he was at the grocery store. He points to a glittering K-Bar knife in the glass case under the counter and the storekeeper brings it out; Max runs a finger crossways across the blade, smiles at the razor edge, and drops it into the box.

"Going hunting," he explains.

The storekeeper nods, not caring what the items will be used for as long as the money is green and has an American president on it. Preferably Ben Franklin. Max pays cash again. His rolled-up bank gets smaller but is still substantial.

Before he picks up the box, Max lays another hundred-dollar bill on the counter and whispers a question. The storekeeper glances around to make sure no one is watching (the government is everywhere, you know) then writes a phone number on the back of a Chinese takeout menu and slides it over.

The alley is dirty even by inner city standards, but it's the perfect setting for Max's meeting with a camouflage-clad survivalist. The survivalist was never in the military, though he acts like he was. He dresses like it and talks like it, but in reality, he was afraid to go through basic training. His friends told him boot camp was a piece of cake, but he never got the courage to sign up.

Max flashes his money. The man hands him a long object in a canvas bag. Max unzips the bag, pulls out an automatic combat shotgun, and checks it over for defects. He is pleased to find the weapon to be in perfect operating order. It even has a fat round drum magazine as a lethal bonus. He re-wraps the gun in the bag and hands the survivalist a lot of cash.

The survivalist smiles, hoping the Russians or the Chinese or the United Nations hold off their invasion of America long enough for him to drink away a good chunk of his newfound wealth. If not, well, he's got more guns at home.

And plenty of hand grenades.

Cruising again, Max checks his watch. It's after ten. Time to stop avoiding things and go home. He turns off the main drag and onto a broad residential avenue. A mile later he pulls into his driveway, rolling past the crumbling stone gate pillar that sports a tarnished metal *Braun Manor* plaque hanging at an angle by one remaining bolt, and stops on the roundabout in front of the porch.

He opens the door and steps out, pausing to examine his house. The sodium-arc security light casts deep shadows as it tries to light the structure, but it is a wasted effort; the three-story Victorian mansion radiates darkness even at noon, a vacuum of light that tosses shivers to the rare person who dares walk the sidewalk in front of it rather than subconsciously—or consciously—crossing the street. It had originally been the main house of a sprawling estate set far out of the city limits. But the years have chipped away at the acreage and rendered it nothing more than the largest and most imposing structure in a crowded suburban neighborhood.

In the daylight, the house looks dangerous. At night, downright evil. The paint peels, the gutters sag, and most of the grass is dead. It's not that Max had never tried to improve the place. The white paint had turned sooty gray minutes after he slapped it on, and thousands of gallons of water and fertilizer did nothing more than make the yard a muddy mess and add a few leaves to the gnarled tree. The only things that look new are the thick metal-reinforced front door, the plain molding surrounding it, and the long wooden porch.

Max thinks the house likes the way it looks and refuses to change, carrying an angry chip on its shoulder as a reminder of its faded glory. So it stands tall and glares, dominating everything around it.

And as he does every time he sees the place (and, if truth be told, almost every hour of every day) Max remembers his mother.

THEN

Max huddled under the blankets in the darkness of his small bedroom, listening to his parents fight on the other side of the closed door. The argument was a beauty, with the screams reaching a volume he hadn't heard since Christmas the year before. Something was even broken this time. That was new. He guessed it was a lamp from the way the light creeping under the threshold dimmed after the crash.

Slight, shy, and intelligent, Max wasn't born a momma's boy. Rather, he was turned into one by fate. But who could blame him for clinging to the only good thing in his tumultuous life? His mother Maxine was kind and loving and there for him as much as she could be. Which wasn't a lot, with her working as a maid at an endless series of seedy motels during the day and waiting tables at whatever diner would hire her at night, but she *tried*, and that was important to the boy. She earned his love.

Unlike his father.

Joshua Brown earned nothing but hate.

To Joshua, Max was an accident, an afterthought, a pain in the ass mouth to feed who didn't earn his keep. He was none of those, but no matter how hard he tried to show his father otherwise, the man grew angrier and more dismissive. Joshua's constant drinking didn't help matters. Nor did the chronic unemployment that moved the family to an endless series of small towns every few months, looking for jobs his dad would hold onto just long enough to raise their hopes that *this might be the one*, only to get fired soon after starting.

Max could understand all of that. He could even forgive most of it in a surprisingly adult way and shove the rest of it down so far inside his young gut he barely knew it was there. But what he couldn't understand, what he couldn't forgive, was that his father hit his mother. That was an unforgivable sin in the boy's tiny heart and he raged that he was powerless to stop it.

Now, seven years and change after the fateful night of foolish passion that welded Maxine and Joshua together for eternity just as surely as it broke them apart, an understanding had been reached; Max hated his father, and his father hated him back.

The fight tonight was over another move. Joshua announced he had quit his five-month stint as a night clerk at a gas station because he had been offered a job as a handyman and caretaker of his previously unknown great-uncle's estate. The uncle expected them in a few days, so the family would have to move as soon as they could pack.

Maxine didn't want to leave. She was tired of the endless ritual of packing and unpacking even though they didn't have many things, and she wanted her son to start school in the fall with his friends from the previous year. Unknown to her, Max didn't have any friends. They had only been in this town since New Year's and he just had the usual assortment of bullies who delighted in beating the crap out of the new kid, and teachers too overworked to notice or care. But he didn't want to tell his mother and ruin her happy illusion. He was thoughtful, for a seven-year-old.

True to form, Joshua had declared he didn't care what Maxine wanted—she was his wife, and the Bible said she had to obey him, no matter what. He only trotted out the Good Book when he knew he couldn't win a fight any other way. And things had escalated from there.

Max cried in the dark as he listened to them yell. Hot tears stained his pillow as he wished for magic things. He wished he was big enough to protect his mother. He wished he was rich so he could take her away to the island he'd seen on National Geographic and live happily ever after. He wished his father would drop dead from a heart attack. He wished for a lot of things, but none of them came true that night.

After a while, the fight was over. Max heard the front door slam and knew his father was going to a bar to get drunk again. A few minutes later, Maxine came into his room. She sat on the edge of his bed in the darkness and touched his face with a cool hand. He pretended to be asleep, that he hadn't heard the argument, but she knew he was faking. She always knew.

"We're moving again, Max," she sighed. "I'm sorry."

His father and the Bible had won again.

"It's okay, Mom. I don't care." He rubbed his cheek against her hand and felt her rub back. It almost made everything okay.

"But your friends…"

Max pretended to be upset, then pretended to swallow it. "I can make new ones."

Maxine tried to say something else but couldn't manage without sobbing. Instead, she curled up around her son in the small bed and hugged him until they both fell asleep.

Momma's boy? Maybe so. But you take your slice of heaven when you can get it, and screw what anybody thinks.

‿

Max loathed mornings. He could never seem to get moving until lunchtime and fell asleep often at school. He was a night person, even as a child. He usually stayed up as late as he could, even after his mom or dad had ordered him to turn out the lights and go to sleep. The nighttime was full of magic and mystery to him, with the promise of secrets kept in the velvet darkness. He liked the stillness, the quietness, and the feeling of being alone but not lonely. And even if he didn't have books to read, pictures to draw, or the transistor radio turned as low as he could and still hear the distant music and voices, he would still be wide awake long after midnight, dreaming of distant lands and magical beings.

The morning sunlight streaming through the blinds didn't care about any of that as it fell on Max's face and pulled him out of his slumber. He lay there like he always did, moving nothing but his eyes as he looked around and tried to remember where he was. After a minute it came back to him and he sat up and stretched. He could hear his mom working in the living room, so he got out of bed, pulled on his clothes, and stumbled out to see if she needed help packing.

As he walked down the hallway he passed the door to his parents' bedroom. He peeked inside and saw his father face down on the bed, a late sleeper like his son. But Joshua had a different reason than Max; the empty whiskey bottle still clutched in his outstretched hand. In another of his many adult mannerisms, Max shook his head in disgust and continued down the hall.

In the living room, he saw his mom had gotten an early start and had already put what few possessions they had into boxes. She glanced up when she heard Max come into the room and smiled.

"Good morning," she said. "Are you hungry?"

"Not really. Sorry I didn't get up and help."

"It's fine. You can help me pack up your room. *After* you have breakfast."

"Okay."

Though he truly wasn't hungry, he ate anyway. The store-brand Corn Pops always tasted good, but they were even better when his mom tamped down every sweet kernel with the spoon to make sure they were soaked in milk. Little gestures like that made him love her even more. After he finished eating he washed the dish and spoon and grabbed an empty box.

"What's next, Mom?"

Before she could answer, Joshua barked from the bedroom. "You can make me some coffee and eggs, that's what."

They both looked up and saw him leaning in the door frame, glaring at them with bloodshot eyes. He was almost always in a bad mood these days, but it was even worse in the mornings.

Maxine got up and walked toward the kitchen. "Would you like some toast, too?"

"As long as you don't burn it. You always burn it."

"I told you, the toaster is broken and—"

"I don't want to hear excuses. Just have it ready when I get out of the shower."

He stomped to the bathroom. As the water started running, Maxine fixed his breakfast. She put two slices of bread in the battered chrome toaster and pushed the handle down. As the machine heated up she grabbed the last of the eggs from the nearly empty refrigerator and broke them into the pan. She threw the eggshells into the trash and noticed Max staring at her.

"What?" She asked.

"Why is he always so mean to you?"

"He just has a lot on his mind, that's all. It's not easy for him. He has a lot of responsibility."

"It's not easy for you either."

They stared at each other as the eggs cooked and the water ran in the bathroom. There was nothing more she could say. Max was right. Joshua was an asshole more often than not. But she loved him despite his flaws, and there were times when he was the sweetest, most caring man in the world. Though she had to admit to herself those times were getting fewer and further between as the years passed. She couldn't say that to Max, of course. For all his seeming maturity, he was still just a little boy. So she smiled like always and prayed everything would turn out all right. The moment was broken when the perfect golden-brown toast popped out of the toaster.

"Why don't you go to your room and get your stuff together? Your father wants to be on the road by noon."

"Okay, Mom."

Max started to walk to his bedroom but stopped when he saw Maxine push the toast back down in the toaster, guaranteeing it would burn. She winked at him and turned back to the eggs.

ᏋᏅ

Max grew bored watching the endless Midwestern cornfields pass by and fell asleep in the back seat. He woke hours later when the car slowed down. As the sun dipped low in the sky they turned off the highway onto a side road. He stared over his parents' shoulders and out the windshield, watching an average neighborhood roll by. Then the houses ended and the road passed through a thick forest. Joshua stopped the car at an intersection and shot a confused glance at the side road.

"Is this the right road?" Maxine asked.

"You tell me. You got the goddamn map," Joshua snarled.

"All right. I was just trying to help."

Joshua shook his head at his wife and gunned the motor. The car roared ahead. A minute later the trees thinned out on the left, and a huge Victorian mansion appeared. Lights glared from every window.

"That's it. Braun Manor. Uncle Edward's house."

As they pulled through the tall stone gates and drove up the driveway, Max peered out at the house. There was no way the young boy could know how important this place would be to his life, but even so, he sensed there was something alien about it, something *wrong*. He made himself as small as he could in the back seat and fought to stop his hands from trembling.

Joshua stopped the car in front of the stairs and they all got out.

Max hugged his mom's leg as they studied swirling patterns of ornate symbols and distorted images of animals, people, and plants carved into the porch and front door. The images covered the floorboards and spilled onto the steps, compelling and repulsive at the same time.

Joshua saw nothing, felt nothing. Not the fear radiating from his family or the subtle energy oozing from the carvings. To him, it was just a house. A big one, but just a house. And an opportunity. He mounted the steps and walked toward the entrance. Maxine followed, and Max stayed close behind her.

"He better not be mad at us being late. That'd be a shitty way to start this all off."

"I'm sure he'll understand," Maxine said.

"He better." Joshua glanced back at his son. "And you mind your manners, boy. If it wasn't for Uncle Ed, we could all be sleeping in the car from here on out. So you keep quiet and do what you're told."

Max nodded at his father, but his eyes shined with defiance.

Joshua turned back to ring the bell. As his finger neared the button, the door sprang open.

Light flooded from the inside in a perfect backlight for Edward Braun. His tall frame and powerful body were evident under his evening wear. His hair was thick despite his advanced age, though peppered with gray, as was his neat goatee. His eyes were deep pools radiating fierce intelligence and hinting at dark secrets. He turned his gaze to Joshua and his face lit up in delight. His voice rumbled from deep in his chest, a voice carrying the accent of a dozen different countries and at the same time, none.

"Joshua! How wonderful to meet you in person."

"You too, Edward. Always good to find out you have relatives you didn't know about."

"Especially if they are rich?"

"I, um, I didn't mean—" Joshua cowered before the man.

Edward cut him off with a laugh. "Of course you didn't. I'm just glad you decided to accept my offer to come here and work for me."

"Well, to be honest, it came at just the right time. I was getting sick of my last job anyway, and this sounded like a fresh start. And, um, sorry we're late. We had a little trouble with the map."

Behind him, it was all Maxine could do to not roll her eyes.

Edward caught her expression and smiled before looking back to Joshua. "Not a problem. Now, don't be rude. Introduce me to your family. *Our* family."

As much as he wanted to be brave, Max couldn't help but slip even further behind his mother's legs as Edward's attention turned to them. His small hands twisted in her pants and he buried his face in the fabric. He wasn't a shy child. Not yet anyway. He just knew there was something very, very wrong about Edward Braun.

Joshua turned to his wife and child. "This is my wife, Maxine. She's really glad to meet you, aren't you, Maxine?"

Maxine sensed the same thing Max did, but to a lesser degree. There was something off about Edward, something that gave her pause. But she was used to standing up to men, so she met his gaze without hesitation. "Mr. Braun."

Edward stepped forward and bowed with old-school charm, grabbed her hand, and kissed the back. "Charmed..."

She blushed in spite of herself. A surge of hope swelled in her heart, and her inner voice whispered that maybe it wouldn't be as bad this time. Maybe it would turn out all right.

Maybe.

Edward continued. "...and 'Uncle Edward' is fine. We are family, after all, if distant." He let go of her hand and peered over her shoulder, down to where Max was hiding.

"And this must be young Max."

"Yeah. He's a real momma's boy. Now come over here and say hello to your great uncle." Joshua grabbed Max by the back of his neck and pushed him forward.

Max stumbled out from behind his mother and stared up at the massive man standing before him. As they locked eyes, everything seemed to drop away except he and Edward. His vision narrowed to a glowing circle around Edward's head, and even the night sounds warped in some strange way he couldn't understand. It felt to him as if time had stopped, and they had been standing there staring at each other forever, even though it couldn't have been more than a second or two. It was more than his small mind could comprehend, and even years later as an adult when he thought back to this moment he would have a hard time processing it. But in that terrible instant, a great wave of familiarity passed between them and Max felt he and his uncle had somehow known each other for longer than either of them had been alive.

"Sorry, Uncle Edward," Joshua's voice warbled from somewhere, breaking Max out of his trance. "The boy's a real scaredy-cat."

Edward smiled again, and only Max could see it wasn't the expression of a friendly man, a kindly uncle. At first, he thought it was the same savage grin of the tigers he had seen on Marlin Perkins' TV show *Mutual of Omaha's Wild Kingdom* as the big cats chased down stray antelopes and tore them to bloody pieces. Then he realized the man was more like the great white sharks on the same show. It wasn't the carnivorous expression that made him think so, but rather Ed's cold, dead eyes.

Max glared back at the man with all the fury a child could muster.

Edward saw the hatred and chuckled. "There's nothing to be afraid of here, young man. Nothing at all."

Oh, but there was.

And Max knew it.

NOW

Max steps onto the porch, trying to shake off the past. He hears the sound of children at play echoing through the night air and glances down the street. The happy noise fills his ears and for a fleeting moment he thinks about throwing the box down and running away from the house forever. Then he looks up to the full moon hanging in the sky and the moment is gone. The brief glimpse of freedom was just a cruel illusion. He has a job to do inside the house, and he will never leave until it is done.

Max barges his way through the front door, balancing the package in his arms as he kicks the door shut with a free foot. He steps into the wide hallway on the main floor. Rooms branch off on either side, and a wide staircase rises in the middle. Antiques litter the place, not because somebody sought them out, but because no one ever bought anything new. Shelves full of dusty knick-knacks cover the walls. Age blankets the house, thicker than the dust.

He walks into the kitchen, flips the switch with an elbow, and turns on the overhead light. The old floorboards creak under his feet. He sets the box on the wooden table then heads for the refrigerator and grabs a can of Diet Coke from the near-empty interior.

Dinner.

He leaves most of his purchases in the box but takes the sack of cat food out and opens a cabinet. The shelves inside are already filled with twenty different brands of kibble. There is barely enough room for the new sack, but he finds a spot and stuffs the new purchase in. He feels something rubbing his leg and looks down to see the object of his pet food fetish staring up at him.

"Hey, Fleabag. You have a good day?"

The grizzled tomcat meows a response and jumps up on the counter. Max leans over and nuzzles the animal, nose to nose. It is a rare tender moment for him, a quiet time spent with something he loves. He found Fleabag one morning years ago, a starving stray dumped in the ditch across the road by some callous driver, and he had to feed the tiny kitten from a bottle until it was old enough to eat solid food. Max is certain the cat still thinks of him as its mother even though they are from completely different species. He is perfectly okay with filling the role, though he does draw the line at licking the cat's fur.

With the greeting over, he picks the purring animal up in his arms and leaves the kitchen. He crosses the hallway and walks into the enormous living room. An ancient wind-up grandfather clock sits on the mantle, ticking unnaturally loud in the quiet room. A small fire crackles in an ornate fireplace. The furniture is old-fashioned and well-worn. A large television sits in an antique cabinet, the kind with doors that can be closed to hide the screen. The TV is a rare nod to the present.

Two men are slouched in chairs.

Max, you see, has a thing about strays.

Walter is taller and thinner than his host, with sunken eyes and a balding head of white hair. His haggard condition makes him look older than his age. He stares into the fireplace, watching the flames dance and twitching when the logs crackle. If there were such a thing as a poster child for a pending nervous breakdown, he would get the job, no questions asked.

The other man is, in a word, huge. Tommy could have been a pro wrestler in another life, his bulging arms and bull neck sticking out of a half-buttoned shirt. A scowl paints his beefy face. A size sixteen Red Wing work boot taps on the carpet, the only outlet for his pent-up anger. Tommy's poster would be of rage.

"What's up, guys?" Max asks. He comes off relaxed and casual, but underneath he's coiled tighter than usual. The tension hovering in the air doesn't help. Fleabag senses the strain and jumps to the floor, disappearing under the couch.

Tommy's face brightens at Max's arrival and he sits up. He is a child in a man's body, and a child with a story to tell. "Walter won't let me turn on the fucking TV."

Max recoils from the venom in the giant's voice.

Tommy continues, intent on telling his side of the dispute before the other man can defend himself. "He freaked out a little bit ago. Broke the remote."

Max sits down on the couch and stares into the fire. He glances over, trying to gauge just how angry the man is. Walter ignores the fact that the others are talking about him.

Max decides Tommy is on the far side of pissed and uses his most soothing voice. For a reclusive, anti-social corporate accountant, he has amazing people skills. "You know he hates the TV."

"It was only *Magnum P.I.* The one where Magnum has to tread water with the shark, and he shut it off right before the shark was gonna attack!" Tommy yells at Walter.

Max tenses, ready to fight if he has to, though he's not sure what he could do if Tommy wanted to throw down.

"We've been through this before. You'll just have to wait until Walter goes to bed. That's how we do it here."

Max speaks as if to a child. A three-hundred-pound child who has been trained by the United States military to be a killing machine. The soothing voice seems to calm Tommy, and he sits back in his chair with a *creak* of old springs.

Max continues. "I like Magnum too. Maybe we can watch it tomorrow night."

Tommy's thoughts turn back to his hero. "Magnum was in Vietnam. I saw it. Rick and T.C., too. I wish I woulda run into them over there." He talks like he was in the Vietnam War, but that's impossible; the conflict was over decades ago, and he's far too young for this to be true.

"That would have been great. You guys would have kicked ass together."

"Yeah. Kicked Higgins' ass. He's a fucking jerk," Tommy says.

Max relaxes, thinking the argument is over.

Then Walter speaks up with a vaguely upper-crust accent made harsher by his condescending tone. "He's a fictional character, you simpleton. They all are."

Tommy jerks back up in his chair. "What the fuck did you say?"

Walter stands up, then turns toward Tommy and stares the man down. "I said, there is no Thomas Magnum. Just an over-emoting thespian with a ridiculous mustache."

Tommy jumps to his feet and looms over the smaller man, poking a meaty finger into his chest. "You take that back! Magnum was a hero!"

Max moves to stop the confrontation. "Both of you stop."

They relax.

A little.

Walter collapses back into his chair before breaking the silence in a pained voice. "We're going back down tonight, aren't we?"

"It's that time of the month," Max says.

Tommy sneers and cracks his knuckles. "I'm gonna get me one this time."

Walter gives Max a conflicted look. "Have you ever considered skipping a round like you did in the beginning? Even Edward let decades pass without playing."

Max shakes his head. "He had other games to play. And no. That was before I knew what the stakes were. I won't pass up a chance to save somebody now. And I know you wouldn't either."

"Of course not. I was just speculating. And besides, they might be able to take one of us if we didn't participate."

"There's a lot of things about the game I still don't understand, but I don't think it's possible."

Tommy pipes in, the malicious tone back in his voice. "Maybe they can do any fucking thing they want. Maybe they could climb up the stairs and slip into your bed and chew your fucking toes off if they wanted to."

Walter sinks lower in his seat, pulling his legs up into a protective position as Tommy gets more aggressive. His eyes blur with tears. "Fuck you."

"No, fuck *you*. I'm tired of you being such a baby. You should just leave and let the real men take care of this."

"I can't leave." Walter looks sick at the thought.

Tommy bores into him. "I ain't gonna stop you. Go on. Take a hike. We're better off without you."

"No..."

Max jumps back into the conversation. "Tommy, leave him alone."

Tommy ignores him, delighting in torturing the man. "You still think you're gonna rescue Elizabeth?"

As the cherished name is mentioned, Walter comes out of his fetal pose, shaking with pent-up rage. "You shut up about her! Just shut up!"

"Why? Are you gonna start crying again? Was she really that hot?"

"You don't know anything about her."

"Maybe I do. Maybe I met her in the basement last time around when you were hiding. Maybe I shot her and left her for dead—"

An inhuman wail bursts from Walter's throat as he leaps up and attacks Tommy. He lands a few blows to the side of the bully's head, but the larger man quickly gains the upper hand and throws him to the floor. Tommy jumps on top and twists his arm behind his back. Walter screams in pain.

"Let him go, Tommy!" Max jumps forward and grabs a huge arm, trying to pull it back, but the thick cords of muscle don't move. "Stop it!"

"Fucking little worm." Tommy yanks the arm again, and the man howls.

"*Let him go!*" Max's booms. The angry parent has lost his temper. Tommy flinches at the sound but ignores the command and tightens his grip. Max beats at his wrist to break the hold, but the man is locked on like a Rottweiler.

Then the grandfather clock chimes.

Max stops hitting Tommy.

Tommy lets go of Walter.

Walter jumps to his feet.

All three tense up in a Pavlovian response to the sound. As they count out each of the bells they move closer to each other, the argument forgotten. Fleabag bolts for the door. After the eleventh chime, the bell stops. They stand back-to-back in the silence that follows, waiting for something. There is nothing for a moment, as if the night knows they are waiting and is teasing them.

Then it happens; a deep groan rumbles from beneath the mansion's foundation, a thrumming, dark pulse that works its way through the floor and up the walls, to the upstairs rooms, and out through the roof. As it passes, a cacophony of parasitic creaks and pops echoes through the house.

The foundation settling?

No freaking way.

They exchange frightened looks, then move apart.

"One hour to midnight," Max says quietly. "Time to get ready."

Tommy shoulders Walter aside as he walks by, his bravado returning. "I'm ready. Bring it on. And I hope I run into your pretty little girlfriend."

Tears flow from Walter's eyes and he buries his head in his hands. "Bastard. Goddamn bastard."

Max slumps on the couch. He has had a long day, and there is a longer night ahead of him. He studies the sobbing man, then glares at Tommy through his fatigue.

"I don't need this shit. Especially tonight. We're supposed to be a team. We need each other to survive."

"Do we?" Tommy snorts. "You should just get rid of him, Max. We don't need him. Make him leave." With that, Tommy stomps out of the room.

His comments linger, though, and cut through the churning thoughts clouding Max's head. He leans back and searches the shadowy ceiling for answers to questions he spends most of his waking hours trying to avoid. But sometimes, like now, they jump out at him like coyotes leaping on frightened rabbits and demand his attention. He hates dark thoughts like these, but forces himself to think them anyway: Is Tommy right? Does he need Walter? Is keeping the man around more dangerous than letting him go?

He sighs and looks at Walter. "I hate to say it, but Tommy might be right. You can leave if you want to. There's no shame in it. A lot of people have walked out the door since I inherited this mess."

Walter's face twists in agony. The words hurt more than Tommy's wrestling moves. "I can't."

"I won't hold it against you. God knows I'll understand. I can help you get set up on the outside."

"Are you saying you don't want me around anymore?"

"No. I need all the help I can get. But I need a team, and if you can't handle the pressure it might be best if you got out."

Walter looks at the floor, ashamed. "He's the one who can't handle it. Anyone can see he has a mental imbalance."

"He's fast and strong and a hell of a shot."

"And I'm not." Walter isn't stupid.

"Try to see my side."

"You think I'm falling apart."

"You *are* falling apart. We all are. The last three months have been hell on all of us. Losing sucks. But it's how we keep going that counts. I need to know I can count on you to hold it together."

The clock ticks away the maddening moments. It is far past eleven—and in this house that means midnight is coming like a flaming freight train from hell and they are standing in the middle of the tracks with their clothes soaked in gasoline.

Walter looks up. "I won't let you down. I give you my word."

"Are you sure about that?"

"I have to get her back."

Max nods. Walter is nothing if not a man of honor, one who would do anything for a friend. And beyond anything for the woman he loves.

"Then you *will* get her back. And I'll talk to Tommy, get him to lay off the bully routine. I don't like it any more than you do. Just don't let him get to you so easily."

"I won't. And Max? Thank you."

Max stands up and stretches. "Don't thank me. I might just be sending you down to die."

"At least you're giving me a chance."

Max was never in the military, but at times like this, he knows what officers must feel like when commanding soldiers. The good ones love their troops, but at the same time give orders that can get them maimed or killed.

Max sighs at the thought, and with a final glance at the clock, walks out of the room and leaves Walter crying by the fire.

Max walks up to Tommy in the hallway. They stand a foot apart, the large man looming over his benefactor.

"You let him stay," Tommy growls.

Max stares up at the giant with no trace of fear. "Yes. And you're going to lay off him as of right now, or *you're* out of here. Do you understand me?"

"I don't like it."

"I don't care. This is my house, my show. You play by the rules, or you don't play at all."

Tommy grits his teeth in defiance, but after a moment his great shoulders slump. "Okay. You're the boss."

Max lets out a relieved breath. "Thank you. And think of it this way—he's another gun, and that can't help but even the odds a little. And speaking of guns..." He points toward the kitchen.

Tommy's face lights up—the little kid is back. "Did you get the stuff?"

"Happy birthday."

Tommy pushes him out of the way and makes a beeline for the kitchen. He bounds into the room and goes straight for the box. Max follows. Tommy pulls items out and lays them on the table, grinning as he examines the lethal presents. The helmet, boxes of ammo, and other supplies make a growing, sloppy pile.

Max opens a sack of cat food, watching Tommy as he fills Fleabag's bowl. He thinks the giant is like a little kid opening presents on Christmas morning. Except he's a grown man. And these definitely aren't toys.

Tommy unwraps the shotgun. He roars with delight as he sees the blackened metal. "Yes! Full auto. Extended mag. Fuck yeah!"

Popping the breech, he examines the gun from all angles, works the trigger, then whips the gun around, pointing at imaginary targets. He makes shooting sounds like any average six-foot-six, musclebound eight-year-old would. "Bada-bada-bada-bada-bada!"

Watching him, Max changes his mind about the toys. "I figured you'd like that."

"You figured right."

"Enjoy it. And keep it hidden. It's illegal as hell."

"Probably cost a bundle, too."

Fleabag digs into dinner as Tommy beams. Max smiles. "Yep. It's a good thing I inherited more than the house."

"I'll keep it out of sight. I don't want you to get thrown in prison."

A low voice sounds from across the room. The two men turn and see Walter leaning in the doorway.

"He's already there."

Forty-watt shadows flow from the three men as they walk down the narrow wooden stairway to the mansion's basement. The details of their bulky outfits are obscured by the darkness. They reach the bottom and fan out in the first chamber of the cellar. One of them hits a light switch and a brighter bulb's glow illuminates the group.

It's militia heaven.

Max is a dangerous vision in black fatigues, with a bulletproof vest covering his torso and pants bloused into combat boots. A .45 Colt pistol hangs low on one hip, a machete is strapped to the other, and a sawed-off shotgun in a holster is slung on his back. He cradles an AK-47 with a modified grip and extended magazine in his arms. A wide dog collar with long sharpened spikes wraps around his neck.

Walter has added the motorcycle helmet to his basic combat ensemble, as well as an Uzi machine gun on a sling, a 9-millimeter Beretta pistol in a shoulder harness, knives, and extra clips strapped wherever there is room. The weapons and body armor have put some stiffness in the man's back, but his eyes still dart nervously around the room.

Tommy's giant frame is made even more imposing by a pair of football shoulder pads and a ceramic-plated ballistic vest strapped under them. The automatic shotgun dangles from a sling, while multiple pistols and knives hang from various spots on his body. Camouflage paint stripes his face. His muscles bulge more than usual, pumped up by homicidal anticipation. Rambo would think twice before getting into a fight with Tommy, and he'd have to fight dirty to win.

It's a tough call whether to laugh at the ensemble or be afraid.

The mad gleam in their eyes says be afraid.

Max walks toward the back of the unfinished basement, past the looming octopus of an old-fashioned metal-bellied furnace. Ducts thick and thin stretch from the sooty monster, following the roof and floor joists to all corners of the house. Water pipes and electrical mains converge here as well, making a huge tangle of tentacles in the shadows.

The others follow him to the back room, their faces strained. Even Tommy seems scared. They stop in front of a large oak bookshelf sitting against the far wall, shelves loaded with dusty junk. Max moves to one side of it.

"Give me a hand with this."

Tommy moves to the other side. Together they scoot the bookshelf out of the way to reveal a large door. Rotted dark wood, corroded brass bindings, and a mottled covering of mold describe it, but the sum of the parts is greater and more terrifying than mere adjectives can define.

The sound of dripping water echoes around them. Max looks at his troops. They return his nervous gaze. He struggles to keep his voice steady.

"Check 'em out, guys."

With practiced ease and oiled metallic *clicks* the three check their weapons. When he is confident everyone is ready for combat, Max grabs the door handle. It feels cold, slimy, almost reptilian, and even though he knows it is metal, *alive*.

He opens the door. It swings out to reveal a tunnel cut into a rocky wall. A clammy wind moans from the dark opening and buffets the group. Noses wrinkle at the dank smell. A luminous yellow mold covers the walls, casting a soft light on the procession. It's not the clean color of sunlight, but a paler, sicker hue.

He leads the way into the tunnel. Walter follows close behind him, and Tommy brings up the rear. Max doesn't want to be in front. A large part of him would rather be in the back, hiding behind Tommy, or even be upstairs in bed with the blankets pulled over his head. But he's the leader of the group and that's how it goes. Good leaders, he knows, act calm and confident no matter how scared they are. So he stands up straight and marches ahead even though he is petrified.

After twenty feet the tunnel slopes down and to the right, and the stone floor gives way to a rickety wooden staircase. The steps creak under the party's weight. Walter's voice comes from behind as they descend.

"Your uncle was a genius, Max," he says.

"My uncle was a fool."

The stairway drops out of the ceiling of an immense cavern and angles down to meet a rough-hewn stone landing ten feet wide and twenty feet long. A plain wrought-iron railing separates the landing from the rest of the cavern. The immense sunken room is hundreds of feet wide and about a quarter mile long. The cave has a rough ceiling and a level, smooth floor. A short set of carved stone steps leads from the landing down to the floor. Near the top of the steps, by the railing, sits a rotten, overstuffed leather chair. A tarnished telescope mounted on a tripod stands on one side of the seat, and a small writing desk is on the other. One of the legs has been broken off of the desk. Dust and mold cover the unused furniture. A crack zigzags across the telescope lens.

The company stops on the landing and stares into the cavern.

Max grabs the plain metal railing to steady himself as a vision drags him to the past. He sees himself as a small boy, playing with the telescope. Someone grabs his shoulder from behind. He glances back to see who is there, but only sees a dark figure with glowing eyes glaring down at him. Max tries to back away but the hand pulls him closer and—

"This is new," Walter says.

"What?" Max says, snapping back to the present. He reels from the intensity of the fading memory.

"The railing. I don't remember it."

"Me neither."

Tommy raps on the iron rail a couple of times to make sure it is real. "Who gives a shit? It's here now," he says, and walks to the head of the steps. He shoots a questioning glare back at the others. "We gonna do this, or what?"

Max checks his watch. It shows 11:59, with the second hand sweeping toward midnight. As he counts off the seconds the spring inside his gut winds tighter and tighter. And at exactly midnight he looks out at the cave.

"Show time."

A thick blue mist forms from nowhere, covering the floor of the cavern to the level of the landing. Tommy stomps down the steps and wades into the azure soup. It swims around his legs, three feet deep. Ripples move away from him as he walks. He scans the blank expanse of the cavern, then bellows a challenge to the air.

"Come on, assholes. Let's play!" Tommy's words echo off the stone walls.

As if taking his challenge, the soothing blue mist rises, obscuring the extremities of the cave. The color turns darker and black tendrils swirl through the cloud as it sweeps toward the landing. Tommy's bravado falters and he grabs the smooth stair rail and pulls himself back up the steps to join Max and Walter.

The mist rushes forward and blots out the entire cavern, stopping like a curtain at the edge of the landing. It boils like a thunderstorm and the dark swirls coalesce into objects obscured by the blue. The maelstrom reaches a crescendo, with dark, sparkling reflections flickering through the air. Then the mist fades to reveal the interior of the cave has been transformed into a country field. A rutted road stretches from the bottom of the steps along one side of the cavern, leading to a small farm shed and a smoldering trash pile. Around the shed, a sea of dying corn stretches into the distance. A decrepit wooden fence marks the boundary of the actual cave, but the illusion is so perfect it looks like the field goes on forever.

And maybe it does.

The men stare at the vista with awe.

"They're getting pretty fucking good at that..." Tommy says.

Max searches the faces of his companions. "Anybody?" he asks.

"It... It's mine," Walter moans.

Tommy rolls his eyes. "Great. Pick on the fucking weakling."

"Where is this?" Max asks. He wishes Tommy would shut the hell up.

Walter pulls off his helmet and studies the land of his memory. "It's Kansas. I grew up here. This is the field behind my parents' house."

"Momma's boy."

"Not now." Max hisses. Then, "Walter, what happened here?"

Walter swallows the lump in his throat. "It was the great drought. Year after year, it was hot and dry and dusty everywhere. The crops died first. Then the animals. And then—and then Dad died during the third summer. Heat stroke, the doctor said. From digging a well deeper and deeper to find water. M-Mother tried to keep ahead of everything, but there was just too much to do. And... and there wasn't any rain. It all dried up and died. Everything died. There was nothing I could do. Death was everywhere. It snuck up on you and there was nothing you could do about it because it was everywhere and everything died and died and died and there was nothing—"

Tommy smacks Walter across the face, stopping his hysterical rambling. He snaps out of his daze, cheek reddening. He slides to a sitting position against the railing. He puts his head in his arms and cries. "I'm sorry. I'm so sorry."

Max tries to soothe the frightened man. "It's just an illusion. It's not real. You know that. They're just getting in our heads, pulling stuff out of our subconscious to scare us."

Tommy flushes red with rage. "I warned you. He's gonna fucking get us killed. We gotta send him back up." He moves to grab Walter.

Max steps between the two. "Not happening. Everybody fights. Nobody quits. House rules."

"Fuck the rules!"

"We need all the guns we can get. Otherwise, we might lose. Do you want to lose again, Tommy? Do you!?"

"No." Tommy snarls. He pushes past Max and grabs Walter by the shoulders, hauling the smaller man to his feet. "Get up, you fucking coward. We got a game to play."

Tommy pushes Walter down the steps, onto the dirt road. Their feet crunch on broken stalks of corn. Max follows them into the nightmare illusion from Walter's youth. He wants to chasten Tommy, but deep down in a dark corner of his soul, he agrees with the man. Walter has heart and desire, but it's buried under a cloying layer of terror. And as Max knows all too well, if they want to live through the night they have to push past the fear and leave it behind. They can always go back later and have a drink with it and cry about how much they missed each other.

For now, they have to fight.

The three men search the cornfield. Max and Walter walk in front, while Tommy covers the rear ten feet back. Their guns are drawn, and every sound makes them jump. They act as if they are in a scene from a war movie and hordes of blood-mad enemy soldiers are waiting in ambush. Max wishes he was searching for something so benign.

Sweat drips from every pore on his body; the illusion is perfect down to the oven-dry air. His shirt is soaked, and he pulls at his bulletproof vest, trying to get some air under the thick material. He considers taking it off, but after a quick mental inventory of the consequences he drop-kicks the idea into orbit.

Max brushes a sagging corncob with his gun barrel. "I feel like a bag of popcorn in a microwave..."

He glances over at Walter. The man looks as sick as ever, but his eyes have stopped darting around.

"How are you holding up?"

"I'm fine," Walter whispers.

They walk for another ten feet and come up against the fence, and by extension, the edge of the cave. But the field seems to stretch to the horizon. Heat waves ripple the view.

"End of the road," Max says. He reaches out a hand toward the top of the fence, then pulls it back before it crosses the magical line.

"It seems so real..." Walter says as he squints into the distance. "Like we could climb the fence and keep going."

"I wouldn't try it."

There was a time when a younger Max took a running leap over a similar fence just to see what would happen. That time is long gone. He keeps the memory to himself. He keeps a lot of memories to himself. He feels there's no sense distracting the others from the mission at hand, and some things he just plain wants to forget. Like, for instance, what is on the other side of the fence. So, the older, smarter, but decidedly less adventurous Max turns back toward the center of the field just as Tommy catches up.

"This way's clean. You take the point for a while and we'll try the other side."

Tommy nods. "You got it."

He walks off toward the center of the cavern, brushing aside cornstalks with the shotgun. Max starts to follow, but Walter grabs his arm.

"I'm sorry about losing my composure at the landing. Being back here again just caught me off guard."

"It's all right. I'm surprised any of us can handle it. I may not act like it, but I'm one step away from falling apart every time I come down here." Max is not kidding. He is surprised at how he can have a calm conversation in the middle of a magical cornfield when the more appropriate behavior would be sitting in a corner of a sanitarium blubbering like a fool. But the dueling human survival mechanisms of denial and acceptance are in perfect balance on the razor's edge of his mind and that somehow manages to keep him walking and talking like a normal human being most of the time.

The whiskey helps.

"If we get back safe tonight, I'll pack up and leave, if that's what you want," Walter says.

Max shakes his head. "What I want is for you to get Elizabeth back and you two move to California and have fifteen kids—and name them all after me. Even the girls. That won't happen if you quit now."

Walter struggles with his emotions, then says, "Thank you. For everything."

"Don't mention it. Now let's go find us a demon."

Tommy inches through the rows of corn in a new section of the field. A fly buzzes around his head. He ignores it. Sweat rolls down his neck. He glances back and sees Max and Walter prowling close behind, their eyes constantly on the move, searching for danger everywhere. It is dirty, slow work, but it beats rushing ahead into unknown dangers. Or so he's told; if he had his druthers—whatever those are—Tommy would much rather take the offensive any time he can. But since Max is the boss, he continues creeping.

A tiny cracking sound comes from behind them. Tommy whips around, pointing the muzzle of his shotgun toward the sound. Max ducks under the swinging barrel and rolls to the dusty ground. The barrel of his AK-47 covers the patch of corn to the right of Tommy's shotgun. Walter spins and covers the left field of fire with his Uzi. Amateurs or not, they are very good at what they do. A Navy SEAL would have trouble finding flaws in their form.

Max whispers to the giant towering over him without taking his eyes off the corn. "See anything?"

"No. But watch behind us. It's an old trick from the 'Nam. Get you looking one way and attack from the other."

Max follows his advice. He twists around and sticks his gun between Tommy's legs, aiming behind him. He sees nothing but more rows of corn. They hold position. Listening. Waiting. After a tense moment, Tommy exhales.

"False alarm," he says. "It must have run off."

"No way," Max grunts, unconvinced. "I can still feel it out there."

Tommy starts to argue, but Max puts his finger to his lips. Tommy and Walter glance back to the corn. They have learned through painful experience to trust their leader's gut feelings.

A flash of movement to the side catches Max's attention. He whips his head around and sees a hulking shape tearing through the rows. The shape is indistinct at first, hidden by the stalks and blurred by speed, but the way it moves—and the fact that it is not one of the team—screams danger. It takes another step and then launches itself at the back of Tommy's head like an organic missile. There is no time to shout a warning or aim. So

Max slams his machine gun into the back of Tommy's knee, and the huge man's leg buckles.

"Hey!" he grunts, then crashes to the ground and woofs out a lungful of air.

The men catch a glimpse of a demonic creature with rippling muscles and flashing teeth vaulting over them. Jagged claws hiss through the air where Tommy's head was an instant before, and the bundle of death hits the ground and scrambles away through the corn in a flurry of churning legs.

Max swings his AK around and lets off a long burst of gunfire. But he is too slow; the bullets rip through the air half an inch behind the shape. It crashes into the rows of corn and scuttles away with a chilling growl.

Tommy rolls to his feet and gives chase.

"Tommy, no!" Max yells.

But Tommy is past following orders, past reasonable thought. He has the enemy in his sights, a way to put the anguish of a month of tension and years of torture to rest. He is Death and he must Kill and nothing can be said or done to tear his simple-minded focus away from his quarry. He chases after the tornado of teeth and claws and leaves the others behind.

Corn stalks slash at Tommy as he runs, cutting red lines on his hands and face. He ignores the pain, hot on the trail of the creature. It zigs and zags in front of him, dodging the continuous hail of buckshot roaring from the flaming barrel of the shotgun. The sound is much the same as the one he made in the kitchen when he was pretending to shoot, except now it is a hundred times louder.

Bada-bada-bada-bada-bada.

"Stand still you fucker!" he screams.

The demon screeches something unintelligible in return as it cuts sharply to the left ahead, into a thicker patch of corn. It leaves a ragged trail Tommy follows until he breaks into the clear and sees a shape standing in front of him and he grins savagely as he raises the shotgun and pulls the trigger—

And shoots Max in the chest.

The impact spins Max around and tosses him backward. He lands face down on the ground. As he gasps for air a dim part of his brain analyzes the pain and finds it intense and yet dull at the same time, like getting beaned with a fastball when you lean a little too far into the batter's box during a baseball game, except this heater is made of multiple double-aught buckshot pellets scorching along at over eight hundred miles an hour.

"No! It's us!" Walter screams and he dives for cover beside Max.

Tommy jerks the shotgun barrel up and gapes at his fallen friend. "It was right in front of me!" He whips his head around, searching for the shape, but it is gone. He starts crying. "I didn't see him! I swear! I thought he was the monster!"

Walter ignores him and rolls Max onto his back. He gasps when he sees the holes ripped through the outer fabric of the bulletproof vest. Walter feels around, searching for signs of blood, but finds none.

"He's not bleeding. I think the vest stopped it."

Max convulses, struggling for breath. His eyes flutter. He drags a gulp of air into his tortured lungs, shakes his head to clear it, and holds out his hand. Walter pulls him to a sitting position. Max grimaces in pain. He looks down at the ragged pattern on his vest and smiles weakly at Tommy.

"Nice shootin', Tex," he croaks.

Tommy drops to his knees. Tears stream down the big man's face. "I'm sorry, Max. I'm so sorry."

"So am I," Max grunts. "I'm just glad I didn't buy you the bazooka."

Walter helps Max to his feet. He wobbles, unsteady, and moves his arms around to loosen up. He takes a deeper breath but the pain makes him grimace.

"Might have cracked a few ribs."

"Can you continue?" Walter asks.

"No choice," Max shrugs. "But it's okay. It only hurts when I breathe."

Soon they are moving again, searching for the demon's faint trail through the broken corn stalks. Tommy takes the lead, leaving Walter to guard the rear and relegating the injured Max to the safer center. Every step is an eternity of suspense, sweat, and fear.

And pain.

Max covers well, but underneath his shredded body armor, his chest is an angry mass of purple and black bruises that make him wince with each step.

The trail leads out of the corn and ends at a clearing near the center of the cavern. The run-down farm shed they saw from the landing sits in the middle of the wide spot, surrounded by dead grass and dirt. A trash pile smolders to one side of the shed. The three men stand at the edge of the corn and study the scene.

"It must be hiding in the shed," Walter says.

"Or still out in the corn."

Max shakes his head. "No, Walter's right. It's probably in there having a nice cold beer and waiting for us to open the door so it can jump out and eat our faces off."

"I like beer," Tommy says.

Max gives him an amused look. "I'll buy you a case when we get out of here. Now cover me while I check out the shed."

He starts to walk toward the shed, but Tommy grabs his arm and stops him. He turns and sees the giant holding up a Molotov cocktail made from an old whiskey bottle, gasoline, and a strip of cloth.

"Fuck this sneaky shit," Tommy says. "Let's have a barbeque."

He tips the bottle, soaking the rag in gas, then lights it with a shiny Zippo. He heaves the heavy bottle toward the shed. The homemade bomb explodes onto the structure with a *whomp!* and the desiccated wood turns into a raging inferno.

The three train their guns on the burning structure, expecting to see the demon burst from the flames. But the building burns down and nothing comes out, even when the roof collapses in a flurry of smoke and sparks.

"Nobody home," Max says

Tommy huffs and puffs. "They gotta be here somewhere!"

"They are. It's part of the game."

"We've missed something," Walter says.

"No shit," Tommy growls.

Max ignores them and does a three-sixty, studying the landscape again with a more critical eye. Everything looks as normal as an illusionary 1930s farmyard in a magic cavern a hundred feet under the basement of his house can look. Then he sees it; an industrial-sized tin with the jagged top pried open sits half-buried in the pile of trash. It's the kind of container culinary-challenged places like schools and prisons and the chain diners that seem to haunt every interstate off-ramp in America get their vegetables from. There is nothing remarkable about the can itself, but the label is wrong. On it, a cartoon demon in a chef's uniform leers at them.

Max nods to the can, and Tommy and Walter fan out on either side of him, guns pointed at the trash pile. He slings the AK-47 back and draws his .45. He flips on the tactical flashlight slung under the barrel of the pistol as he creeps up on the pile of rubbish. He squats over the trash, holding the gun as far away from himself as possible. The barrel enters the jagged mouth of the tin can. The flashlight shines into the depths. He leans forward and sees the can is...

"Empty." Max sighs and rises, knees creaking.

"They have to fucking be here, don't they?" Tommy rages anew.

"Maybe they got scared and went home," Walter says.

"This *is* their fucking home."

"I don't know," Max says. "It just doesn't seem right. Maybe we should follow the trail out the other way."

"It came this way. I was right behind it."

"Maybe they just don't want to play anymore."

Frustrated, Max shakes his head. "No, they've been adding new stuff every month for a while now. And it's starting to piss me off."

He kicks the can.

As it clatters away a foot-tall demon complete with a forked tail, red scales, horns, and jagged claws explodes from a hole underneath and scurries onto his pants leg. Fangs drip acidic venom and it gibbers in a high-pitched wail. It claws its way up his body at lightning speed, heading for his face. Max jerks backward, trying to get away from the diminutive creature, and falls on his back. He drops his pistol and swats at it with his gloved hands but somehow misses.

Tommy and Walter are frozen in place by the sudden attack; they can only watch as the imp scrambles over Max's chest, opens its mouth wide, and sinks its fangs into his throat.

A frustrated whine erupts from its slavering mouth when it realizes it has bitten into the spiked dog collar around Max's neck. He flails blindly, knocking the thing across the trash heap.

Guns roar. Walter and Tommy open up the instant the beast is clear, bullets tearing into the dirt and trash. Max grabs his pistol from the dirt and adds to the barrage. The demon darts left and right between the shots and somehow escapes unscathed into the corn. The men shoot until their guns are empty, then stand amidst the lingering smoke, staring into the stalks. An eerie silence descends on the field.

"Goddammit!" Max screams in frustration.

While Tommy reloads and keeps watch, Walter squats next to Max and examines his neck. He finds one of the creature's fangs stuck in the collar. The leather is eaten away by the caustic venom, and Max's neck has a raw red spot underneath where the poison dripped down. Max rips the collar off, burning his fingers in the process.

"How the hell did we miss it?" Max asks. He stands up and drops the smoking collar to the ground.

Walter shrugs. "I didn't know they could be that small."

"And fast," says Tommy. "It was like the Road Runner."

Max paces in a circle, rubbing his neck and burning off the adrenaline still coursing through his veins. Then he senses something and stares at the field. He holds up his hand for silence. "Shut up a second."

Walter and Tommy freeze, then crane their heads like Max, trying to hear what he is listening for.

There is nothing at first, not much more than silence as they strain to see through the empty corn, but then a rustling sound begins. It builds with each passing second. A hot wind comes from somewhere, the cornstalks swaying slowly at first then with more intensity as the air swirls faster. Shapes begin moving in the whipping corn, unnatural figures large and small, leaping and cavorting in a mad dance. Cackling demonic laughter echoes from all sides. A flash of heat lightning cracks overhead and thunder rumbles through the air.

Max backs toward the landing. His hands shake as he tries to hold his machine gun steady. He doesn't want to run. He is not a quitter. He wants to win. He wants to kill something. He also wants to follow the rules of this twisted game, afraid of what might happen if he breaks them. And running away might break them. So he grabs the AK's stock tighter, wills the tremors in his hands to cease, and forces his feet to stop retreating. Max is many things, and far from perfect, but he is not a quitter.

Until an inhuman wail joins the rustling of the corn, a foghorn bellowing from the depths of Hell. The sound rises above the monstrous giggles, rips through air and eardrums, and finally pierces the men's souls. Then it drops to a low rumbling growl that impossibly calls out a single name:

"*Maaaaaaaxxxxxxxxxxxxx...*"

Max gives the others a horrified look. "I say we call this one a draw and get the fuck out of here," he says, quitting without even a hint of shame.

"Good idea," Tommy says.

They walk slowly at first, guns whipping in all directions, fire discipline demanding they cover all angles in a calculated retreat. As the wind whips the corn faster and the laughter grows louder and the shapes get closer they break into a jog. And when the hell horn thunders Max's name again they graduate to a full running retreat. They shoot as they run, firing random bursts in all directions to try and keep the monsters at bay. The corn grabs at them as they race for the landing, slowing them down as they fight to pull free of the groping stalks. Behind them, they hear the nightmare symphony closing in.

They dash into the clear at the edge of the field and the landing looms before them. The three men run for the stairs. Walter stumbles in a rut and Max slows to grab his arm and pull him along.

As he drags the man toward safety, Max glances ahead and sees Tommy has reached the steps and grabs for the iron railing to pull himself up. He also sees the railing is no longer plain wrought iron like when they entered the cavern. It is now covered with ornate carvings of snakes and animals. A voice screams in the back of his mind, telling him that the railing is *wrong*, then the warning erupts from his mouth.

"Tommy, no!!!!"

The warning is too late.

Tommy grabs the rail.

The railing comes alive under his grip, slithering and expanding as it turns into a demonic twenty-foot-long snake with a diamond-shaped head, smoldering red eyes, and glistening fangs. The thick serpent whips around Tommy's body with frightening speed. He tries to shoot but his right arm and the shotgun are pinned under the looping body. He gives up on the gun and grabs a knife with his free left hand and stabs at the shiny scales. Man and monster fall back off of the stairs and thrash on the ground in a deadly embrace.

Max and Walter rush over.

"Shoot it!" Tommy bellows as the coils constrict.

"We might hit you!" Max yells back.

"Don't care!"

As Max raises his AK-47 to shoot, the creature's tail whips out and slams him aside. The gun flies from his hands as he hits the ground and rolls to a painful stop. He looks back, past a frozen Walter, to the entwined bodies, to Tommy's knife hand stabbing slower and slower as his life is squeezed out.

After one last weak jab the knife clatters to the ground.

The snake senses victory. Venom drips from its fangs and sizzles on the stone floor. It almost seems to smile as it raises its head to strike.

Tommy sneers back, spitting at the grinning face. "Fuck... you..." he gasps with his last breath.

Just before the serpent strikes, a body leaps through the air and grabs it around the neck. Walter locks his arms just below the gaping maw and heaves with all his might, fear and adrenaline giving him the strength to pull the fangs away from his cohort. The hellish viper hisses in frustration and flops around. A half-conscious Tommy flips free.

The demon twists in Walter's grasp and he finds himself staring into its glowing red eyes. The snake's mouth opens wide, its dripping fangs inches away from his pale and fragile skin.

"Oh my," Walter says.

"Duck!" Max yells from behind.

Walter will never be sure if he obeyed the command because of his fanatical training, his deep respect for his leader, or if his knees just gave out from fear at the perfect moment. But why he slips to the floor and exposes the snake's neck is irrelevant.

What *is* relevant is that Max has a clear shot at the serpentine demon and he takes full advantage of the opportunity, swinging his machete in both hands with all the strength his battered body can muster. Like a gimpy Kirk Gibson blasting his game-winning home run in the World Series, Max slices the snake's head off its body in a fountain of green gore.

He spins with the force of his swing and corkscrews to the ground.

The serpent's head splats down next to him.

The decapitated body whips and lashes in the dirt.

And the crowd roars.

The snake's corpse bloats and shrinks, stretches and compresses, thumps and thrashes in a Kaiju-sized seizure. The skin turns liquid and flows in waves from one part of the body to another and back again, changing colors with each pulse. After a sickening minute of transformation, the carcass shimmers and reforms into a young woman. She has a lean, muscular body barely covered by shredded tights. Her face is obscured by strands of long brown hair.

Walter gasps when he sees the female form and scrambles to her on his hands and knees. "Elizabeth...?"

Max limps over. "Is it her?"

Walter brushes the woman's hair back and stares at her slumbering face. She is pretty, with high cheekbones and full lips. A dark bruise purples the skin above her right temple. He slumps back on his heels and moans.

"No."

Max puts a hand on his friend's shoulder. "I'm sorry, Walter. I really am. But at least we won."

"You won," Walter sobs. "I survived." He shrugs Max's hand off and stumbles for the landing. He passes Tommy, who struggles for breath as he holds out a meaty hand for a shake.

"You—saved me, buddy. I—"

Walter pushes the hand aside and disappears up the stairs.

Max looks around the cavern and watches the blue mist form again. It covers the entire arena, blotting out the nightmare and sending it back to the hell of Walter's mind. After a minute the mist fades and everything is gone; the corn, the shed, the demons. Until the next full moon, the cave is just a cave.

Max's brain reels as it tries to wrap itself around the manifestation.

It hurts.

"Come on. Let's get her out of here."

Tommy grimaces as he grabs the woman and throws her over his shoulder. Max follows them up the steps to the landing.

"We kicked some ass tonight," Tommy says.

Max smiles. His mind is beaten. His body is battered. But his spirit, for the first time in many moons, soars.

"We sure did. I just wish it didn't kick back so hard."

∽

Max lounges behind the wheel of his car in the parking lot of a run-down city park, listening to a classic rock song crackling out of the broken speakers. He stares at the weed-covered playground, the cracked basketball court, and the empty pool. He sits until the sun goes down and the few streetlights still working in the neighborhood flicker on and throw pools of orange light on the ground.

He reaches out to grab his can of Diet Coke and winces; his chest still hurts from where Tommy shot his bulletproof vest the night before. If anything, the throbbing in his chest is worse than when it happened. But as he sits here now and considers the alternative—a bloody hole blasted through him—he knows he is a lucky man indeed. There is an added bonus; the pain blots out the aches in the rest of his body.

He takes a drink and tries to forget the pain by thinking about the park. When he first started coming here many years ago it had been full of people at all hours of the day and night. Families took advantage of the open space to spend time together, free from the urban chaos around them. Then the city budget was cut, like all city budgets are at one time or another, and the park fell into ruin. The decay was subtle at first, the grass growing longer and the pool hours shortened, but it was still a happy place for a few more years. Then the homeless moved in, and the drug dealers followed, and soon the families abandoned the once happy place and it was downhill from there.

Now there is just Max. Sitting alone. The king of the park in his rusty chariot, lording over his empty domain. The drug dealers have long since moved on to greener pastures, and the homeless went to California; when you have to live in a cardboard box in the winter it's a hell of a lot nicer to be someplace warm.

Max doesn't mind his solitary vigil. Decay and all, the park is his happy place. He loved it from the first time he discovered it, a wonderful green world where he could be around people and at the same time be alone. It is the one place from his twisted youth where he remembers having fun. And as he sits there, his thoughts drift to the past.

THEN

Maxine was cleaning the living room of the new house when she heard the doorbell. With a duster in hand, she opened the front door and saw Uncle Edward standing on the porch. Even during the day, the man was dressed to the nines, looking as if he were headed to a fancy luncheon at an exclusive private club instead of visiting the help.

"Good day, Maxine. I hope I am not disturbing you," Edward said in his basso voice.

"Not at all, just cleaning up a bit. Please come in."

"Thank you."

Edward stepped inside, ducking as he entered. "Are you here alone? I had hoped to speak to Joshua."

"He's out cleaning up the garage. It's a real mess."

"And young Max?"

"Running around somewhere. You know kids."

"Yes, I do. Though I have to admit I find it harder to keep up with them as I age."Edward was charming enough, Maxine had decided. It was hard to tell how old he was, though she guessed he was in his forties, with twinkling eyes and a quick smile. And even though he spoke with an odd accent and used strange words she found his rumbling tone soothing. She did have many unanswered questions about the man, but for the life of her, she couldn't understand why Max didn't like him.

"Anyway, I'm glad you came by," she said. "I wanted to thank you."

"For?" Edward's eyebrows rose questioningly.

"For the house. It's perfect for us. And for giving Joshua a job. He really needed it. *We* needed it."

"Nonsense. I recently realized I was getting older and a caretaker would make things much easier for me. Having family I can trust to do the job is best for everyone. And this guest house was just sitting here empty since the last tenants... moved away. I'd much rather have you here than someone I am not acquainted with."

"Well, thank you anyway. And do you mind if I ask you a question?"

"Of course."

"I was just wondering why we had never heard of you before. It just seems odd that Joshua has an uncle we didn't know anything about."

Edward's face darkened for an instant and his smile vanished. "It's because I've spent most of my life on the run, hiding from my treacherous enemies."

Maxine stared at him for a long moment, trying to think of something to say.

A booming laugh broke from Edward's mouth and he touched her on the shoulder. "I am sorry, my dear. The look on your face—I was kidding, of course. Rest assured, the only enemies I have left alive work for the Infernal Revenue Service. And they know *exactly* where I live."

She let out a nervous laugh of her own. "You were so serious..."

"I am a bit of a prankster, you see. And I do love playing games."

"I'll try to remember that."

"But to answer your question, were you aware Joshua was orphaned at a young age and was placed in a home?"

"Yes. He told me."

"Well, it appears the record-keeping and management at the facility were spotty at best, and somehow they never bothered to search for additional family. That, combined with the gypsy-like years I spent traveling the globe on one pursuit or another, led to an unfortunate break in the family tree. If it hadn't been for my recent interest in my bloodline I might not have known he existed either."

She nodded. "Well, lucky for us, you found out."

"Lucky indeed," Edward said.

The back door opened and Joshua walked in, scowling. "Maxine, how many times have I told you to—Oh, Uncle Edward. I, I was going to come up to the main house tomorrow morning like you asked, but—"

"It's fine. Nothing to worry about. I was out and about today and decided to drop by and see how you were settling in. It appears your fine wife is making short work of the dust. You are fortunate to have her."

The scowl on Joshua's face said he thought he was anything but fortunate to be saddled with Maxine, but he quickly replaced it with a satisfied smile and put his arm around her. "She's quite a woman, that's for sure."

Edward turned back toward the door. "I know I didn't ask you to officially start until tomorrow, but if you are free, I could use a hand procuring some items in town."

"Of course. There's nothing in the garage that can't wait."

"Excellent," Edward said, and led the way to the car.

☙

In spite of the salary promised to Joshua by Edward, Maxine had quickly found a cleaning job at a local hotel. She'd been down this road with her husband too many times before to let her guard down now. Even if by some miracle he managed to keep the job, he usually drank most of the money away. So she worked and hid half her money like always, ready for him to screw up again.

Now, months after they had arrived, she was cautiously optimistic. Working for Edward had brought about a change in Joshua. He still drank, but he only got drunk on weekends when he didn't have to work. Throughout the week he stayed on the wagon, even if the wheels wobbled a bit and the axles squeaked. It was as if he had some desperate need to impress his uncle. Or, she laughed to herself one night, it was more likely he was afraid of the admittedly imposing man. But they hadn't fought in weeks, and Joshua was at least tolerating Max, so things could be a lot worse.

She did worry about her son, though. With summer vacation coming up he wouldn't have much to do while she was at work. He had his books, of course; the boy read at a level years above his age and wore his library card thin from constant use. But she didn't want him to become a bookworm. And if it wasn't the books it was the television; he was obsessed with watching kung fu movies and basketball games. While she was glad he showed an interest in a sport—any sport—Maxine decided her son needed fresh air and sunshine before his mind turned to mush.

So one Friday night, with her minimum-wage paycheck burning a hole in her imitation leather purse, she stopped in the sporting goods section of the local K-Mart and bought her son a present. It was more money than she usually felt comfortable spending, but for once she didn't care.

Max was in his bedroom when his mom came home. He spent most of his time there, the door shut, reading. He knew it was her and not his father by the sounds she made. Her movements were soft and tentative, as if she were a guest in her own home. His father, on the other hand, stormed through the house when he came home, his crashing boots sonically claiming the place as his domain.

When he heard her knock, Max put a bookmark in his well-read copy of *The Swiss Family Robinson* and said, "Come in."

Maxine walked in, trying to hide something behind her back. He pretended not to see it.

"Hi, sweetie. How was your day?"

"Okay, I guess. I got some new books at the library."

"Did you meet anyone new while you were there?"

"No kids. Just the librarian. She's nice, I guess."

Maxine sighed. Max took forever to make friends. Then she put it all out of her mind; she couldn't keep her secret any longer. "I got you something today," she said softly. She sat on the side of his bed and handed him a sack.

Max was wary. He didn't like presents. Accepting a present made him feel like he owed the giver something, and he liked to be his own man, even at seven years old. And besides, to him, it seemed like no one ever got anything they wanted anyway.

But this was his mother. And the expectant look on her face told him liking the gift would make her happy. So he grabbed the K-mart bag (wrapping paper was too expensive and it just ended up in the trash anyway) and opened up a new world.

The basketball was far too large for his tiny fingers, but he grabbed it with both hands and felt the finely pebbled skin digging into his flesh. The rubbery smell washed into his nose. He forgot his mother for a second. He forgot everything but the ball, instantly imagining himself dribbling up and down a polished wooden court, faking out player after player and driving to the hoop. His imaginary layup was perfect, gently kissing the backboard and bouncing through the basket for a score. He could even hear the crowd cheering.

Max had loved basketball the first time he played it at school, even though he was too small to get in most of the games unless a teacher intervened. And one time, for reasons neither he nor his mother could ever understand, Joshua had taken them to see the Harlem Globetrotters play at a nearby college gymnasium. It was the closest thing to fun he had ever had in the presence of his dad. The boy was never the same after that. Obsessed with the sport, he went out of his way after school to walk by the playground where he watched pickup games until it was too dark to see. He watched on television whenever the games were aired. Even though he was a child, basketball was pretty much the only thing he had ever been childish about.

"I saw you watching the games on the TV." Maxine sounded almost apologetic. "I thought you might like to play."

Max crushed the ball to his chest and stared up at his mother. He did like it. It was obvious. His eyes had never shined so brightly than at that moment.

"I love it, Mom. Thank you." He was so polite and reserved even when it was all he could do to not bounce up and down on the bed and scream with joy.

"You're welcome." She started to say something else then, something about keeping the ball a secret from his father but knew she didn't have to. "You can go to the park and play tomorrow if you want. Just remember not to talk to strangers."

"I'll remember," he beamed. Then he dropped the ball, threw his hands around her neck, and hugged her fiercely. "I love you, Mom," he said, crying for no reason at all. And for every reason in the world.

"I love you too." She hugged back.

They held each other for a long time. After that, it was time for her to cook dinner. She left Max alone in his room.

It turned out to be the longest night of his life. He lay on the bed, fully dressed, both hands on the basketball, counting the minutes until morning when he could go to the park and play.

And play he did. Through blazing sun, pouring rain, and freezing snow, Max played. He wasn't strong enough to make a basket at first, so he dribbled. The ball felt huge and unforgiving as it bounced off his feet as much as the pavement, but he got better with time. That first basketball was worn to the threads by the end of the first year and Maxine got him another one for Christmas.

The ever-growing pile of deflated balls hidden in his closet became their little secret, a way to bond hidden from his domineering father. Max wore through his tennis shoes nearly as fast as he thrashed the balls, but Maxine gladly scraped up enough money to buy him new ones. She was proud of her boy. Very proud.

He played by himself at first, then finally was good enough to join the pickup games that formed daily in the park. Team ball was a new concept for the reclusive boy, but his dazzling speed and ball-handling ability quickly made up for his lack of height and experience.

Years passed, and Max played. Even as the park decayed, he still came. A fixture, the locals said. A legend in the making. He drew small crowds, hoop fanatics, passing cops, the homeless, and the local high school basketball coach. Even the drug dealers stopped plying their trade to watch him dribble.

The game brought him self-confidence, the respect of his peers, and a popularity he never would have found on his own. And most of all he simply enjoyed playing. It filled him with an unbridled joy that was hard to explain. He couldn't imagine life without the game.

Those years were good for Max. They would have been perfect if it weren't for the times his father had taken him to the mansion, let his uncle play unspeakable games with him, and threatened to beat his mother to death if he ever said a word.

NOW

Bruce Springsteen's gravelly voice pours out of the cracked speakers, pulling Max out of his reverie. He starts the car and puts the warped thoughts of his childhood aside. It all happened too long ago to matter, he thinks grimly. The park is no longer a place to play. It is simply a spot to kill time between the mind-numbing boredom of work and the gothic horrors of home. But that home beckons him now. There is a new guest at the house. The woman they saved will hopefully wake up soon, and as with all the new players in the twisted game, he wants to be there to greet her. Because he can never be sure who will turn out to be a pawn, and who might be a queen.

⁊

Max walks into the living room and sees the TV cabinet is closed and the window blinds are drawn. Walter sits in his chair and stares at the remains of a long-dead fire in the hearth. A leather-bound scrapbook lies open in his lap. He ignores Max and pours whiskey into a tumbler from a nearly empty bottle. He takes a deep drink. He weaves in the chair, obviously a long way down the road to getting wasted.

The woman from the basement sleeps on the couch. She is dressed in a man's sweat suit and draped in a partially kicked-off blanket. A padded cuff is locked on her ankle, and the attached chain snakes to a large metal bracket bolted to the floor. There is enough play in the chain for her to move around, but not enough to leave the room.

It's just a scene from your average suburban house from hell.

"Hey, man. How's she doing?" Max asks.

"She hasn't woken up yet," Walter says, holding his glass up in a toast. "For good or ill."

"It hasn't been that long. She'll be fine."

"Always the optimist."

Max walks over to take a closer look at the woman. The floor creaks as he gets near and she stirs in her sleep. She stretches like a cat, and through the sweats and blanket he can see her body is trim and powerful. He checks the chain, then pulls the blanket up to her chest. When he does, he gets his first clear view of her face and sees something he missed in the adrenaline and pain-filled aftermath of the fight in the basement; she is gorgeous.

"I think I have found her in the book," Walter says from over his shoulder.

Max realizes he has been staring. Embarrassed, he turns around. "Yeah? Who is she?"

Walter holds the scrapbook up to the light and points a finger at a yellowed newspaper clipping pasted on the open page. "The picture isn't of the best quality, but the likeness is clear. Deborah Stevens. The story says she was originally from Madison, Wisconsin. She was in town working with a traveling circus when she—disappeared."

Max takes the book from Walter. He sits in the other chair and examines the article. Under the headline is a grainy black-and-white high school picture of the woman, though she appears older now and the resemblance is not perfect. He reads the story for a minute, then checks the date on the clipping.

"She was gone for a long time. Almost forty years."

"Time is meaningless down there," Walter says.

"I know. You told me before." Max says. "Look, I know it was rough for you in the cave, but you've got to try and move past it."

"I'm sorry."

"It's fine. Just try to see the good side. We got another soul back. Let's just hope she's not bat-shit crazy when she wakes up."

"*If* she wakes up."

Max tires of the man's drunken depression. "Okay then. I think it might be time for you to hit the bed."

"My shift isn't over yet."

"I can handle it from here. I won't sleep tonight anyway."

"Who does?" Walter gets unsteadily to his feet and shuffles out the doorway.

After Walter leaves, Max pours himself a drink and settles deeper into the chair. He sips and reads the article on the woman again, then pulls a laptop out of a drawer and opens it up. He enters her details into a browser's search box and surfs through the few articles he can find. There is a better picture of her online, taken from a circus advertisement, and in it, she is a few years older than in the newspaper photo. The picture confirms she is indeed the woman he has chained to his couch.

He is so engrossed in the computer he doesn't know anything is wrong until he hears the floorboard squeak. Startled, he looks up and sees many things in quick succession: The woman stands beside him. She is awake, but her eyes are glazed over and not fully focused. She has a large vase in her raised hands. She aims it at Max's head.

"No, wait!" He yells.

The woman does not wait; she swings the vase down. It shatters on Max's hastily upraised arm, and the blow drives his arm back into his forehead with a meaty *thump*. He falls sideways out of the chair and tumbles to the floor.

The woman leaps for him, and he scrambles backward. He stays ahead of her for a panicked moment, then he bumps into the couch. She jumps onto him, legs locking around his waist, hands clawing at his face. He grabs her wrists and tries to protect himself from the whirling dervish on top of him. It's all he can do to steer her fingernails away.

"Stop it!" he yells. "I'm here to help!"

The woman keeps pressing downward, trying with all her might to slash Max's face. He thrashes under her, trying to get more leverage, but the nails inch closer.

"Deborah! You have to stop!"

She hesitates at the mention of her name. Confusion replaces the rage twisting her face. Her eyes clear. "Deborah...?"

"Yes! Deborah!"

"Who the hell is Deborah?"

"You are."

"What? No, I'm..." Her face flushes with anger again, and she doubles down on trying to slash his face. Max holds on but her arms slip in his grasp and the fingernails close in again.

"Try to remember," he pleads. "You're Deborah Stevens. You grew up in Madison. You were with the circus when you came to town."

"The circus..."

She stops trying to gouge him. Just the same, he keeps a tight grip on her wrists. Her eyes grow clearer and her face loses the feral look as memories penetrate the fog clouding her mind.

"Yes. The circus."

"I'm Deborah. Deb..." She leans back, body relaxing. The fight floods out of her. She studies the room, takes everything in, then swings her gaze back to him.

He cautiously releases her wrists and holds his open hands up to show he means her no harm. "Are you okay now?"

"I—I don't know. Who the hell are you?"

"Max Brown. Pleased to meet you."

Deb studies his face intently, then looks down and blushes as she realizes her legs are still wrapped around him. She rolls off and scoots a few feet away. She has calmed down, but she still looks around the room like a wild animal caught in a cage. She absent-mindedly fingers the collar around her leg but doesn't seem to realize she is chained up.

"How do you know all this about me?" she asks.

Max sits up and winces as the blood rushes to his bruised head. "Newspaper articles," he says, then gestures at the laptop. "And the Google."

She stares at the computer, confused. "What's the Google?"

"I'll tell you about that later. And a lot of other things too, but we have to take it slow."

"Start by telling me where I am."

"You're in my house. You were here... before. Do you remember anything about that?"

She peers around the room again, studying it, desperately trying to remember. When she focuses on the entryway by the front door her face pales. "N—Not much. Just being tied up, and trying to escape, and that man took me to the basement and—" The words catch in her throat as the horrible memories wash over her.

"It's over now," Max says. "You can relax."

Her voice quivers like a frightened child. "What are you going to do to me?"

"Nothing."

"You're not going to—to—make me go back through the door?"

"I'll never make you do anything you don't want to. I swear."

"Thank you."

"You're welcome," he says, pulling a key out of his pocket and gesturing to the padlock on her leg. "Now, if you promise to stop trying to scratch my eyeballs out, I'll take that thing off your leg."

"I'll stop," she says. "For now." She slides her leg toward him.

He unlocks the cuff and gently takes it off her leg. "Sorry about the chain, but some of the other people are pretty crazy when they... wake up."

"There are other people like me?"

"Yes. Quite a few."

"How am I on the crazy scale?"

"Average. Pretty high on the violence chart, though."

"Sorry about that."

"It comes with the job."

Deb rubs her ankle and stands up. Her eyes flash between Max and the exit. He stands up as well, but steps back, clearing the path to freedom.

"You're free to go if you want. It's unlocked."

Watching him closely, she walks over and reaches for the handle. Her hand hovers over it, then she grabs it and opens the door. Fresh air wafts in as she takes in the barren front yard. She takes a deep breath of freedom. She studies the door panels closely, looks out at the porch railing, and frowns in confusion.

"There were carvings here last night. They covered everything."

"I had them removed. And like I said, you can leave if you want. I won't stop you."

She stares at the grounds for another minute, then closes the door and turns back to Max. "I'm not leaving until you tell me what's going on here."

"I promise I'll tell you everything eventually."

"The hell with that—I want to know *now*."

"There's a lot you won't believe."

She takes a threatening step toward him. "Try me."

He raises his hands in submission. "All right, you asked for it. But please, have a seat. It's going to be a shock."

She does as he asks, but stays on the edge of the couch, ready to bolt if something goes wrong.

Max takes a deep breath, composing his thoughts. "My uncle Edward Braun was a sorcerer who was into black magic. Real magic, not side-show stuff. Honest to God, real-deal sorcery. He used his powers to do some crazy things."

Deb starts when she hears the name. "Edward. That's what they called the man who—who kidnapped me." She begins shaking as more memories boil up inside. She folds her arms over her chest and hugs herself to make it stop.

"That's my great-uncle Ed. Gentleman on the outside, pure devil inside. Among other things, he conjured some sort of extra-dimensional space underneath the house and filled it with demons. That's where he took you that night."

"He made me go through the door. And there was a cave or something, it wasn't very clear. And those things, monsters, demons, whatever. Those things—killed me."

"*Kind of* killed you."

"I don't understand. I tried to fight back, but they ripped me apart. I *felt* it. I had to have died. But then..."

"You're not dead, are you? You're sitting here in my living room clear as day."

Deb looks at the floor and shivers. "I'm not so sure."

"Trust me, you're alive."

She eyes the bottle of whiskey. Max smiles and pours her a large shot. She grabs the glass with shaking hands and downs it in one large gulp. The liquid burns down her throat and steadies her.

"Then what happened? How am I here?"

"It's hard to explain, but it's like a really fucked up magical game of Red Rover. When the full moon shines, the cavern forms and the game is on. That's when Uncle Ed would kidnap people like you and send you into the cave and you'd have to fight with his pet demons. If they kill you, they capture your soul and twist you into one of them, and you join their side and become part of the monster team. And of course, you try to kill the next person he tricked into playing."

"So, the things that attacked me were other people somehow?"

"Yes. Transformed by Ed's magic, or the cave, or some power I don't totally understand."

"And if one of the demons dies somehow, the person comes back?"

"You got it. The demons turn back into people, just like before they 'died.'"

"*Just* like before? You said some people come back crazy."

"Physically, it's like time stopped. Mentally... well, not everyone comes back in one piece. It could be the game screwing with their head, or just the trauma from being kidnapped and abused in the first place. Or both, maybe. The good news is you seem okay," he says with a grin. "So far."

Deb nods but is struggling to understand. "You said it was like time stopped. But this all happened to me last night."

"Um, no. You were asleep a little longer than that. But we can talk about that later. Are you hungry or thirsty or anything?"

"How long was I down there?"

"Look, this is a lot to take in. Even I have a hard time believing it all. Why don't you get a good night's sleep and we can—"

"How long." She stares at him, demanding an answer.

He stares back for a moment, then sighs. "You were gone for thirty-seven years."

"That's impossible."

"I know it's hard to believe. But look here," Max says, and hands her the newspaper. "Hardly anyone reads the paper version these days, but it helps at times like this."

She studies the paper, then tosses it aside. "You could have faked it."

Max shrugs and holds out the laptop.

She takes it and examines it, tentatively at first, then punches the keyboard and wiggles the cursor with the touchpad. Her brow furrows with confusion; the machine is far more advanced than anything she has ever seen.

"What the hell is this?"

"It's a computer, really advanced from what you know. Pretty average for today though."

"I saw one in a magazine once. But it was nothing like this."

"It's a thousand times more powerful than the machines that used to fill up entire buildings. And it's connected to the

Internet, which I won't even try to explain for now, but let's just say if you like dirty movies or funny cat videos you will soon be a very happy person."

"It's incredible..."

Max walks to the entertainment console and opens the cabinet doors to reveal the sleek flat-screen TV. He opens a drawer and digs out a new remote from a bunch of spares and turns the screen on. A newscast pops up, and Deb stares wide-eyed at the graphics and clothes and hairstyles. Max changes the channel to a movie station and giant robots battling huge monsters in high-def glory fill the screen. The blood drains from her face.

"Turn it off, please."

Max does as she asks, and closes the cabinet. "Sorry. I told you it was a lot to process. But look at the bright side," he says, trying to make light of the situation. "At least you missed the Macarena."

Deb doesn't get the joke, or care. Her hands curl into angry fists. "Is Edward still around?"

"No. He's long gone. You don't have to worry about him. Casa de Evil belongs to me now. The house, the cave, and a diary that makes the Satanic Bible look like a Dr. Seuss book. Just a run-of-the-mill inheritance. And from what everyone tells me, I'm a pretty nice guy. Meaning, I'm nothing like Ed." Max's tone is flippant, but when he mentions his uncle, his voice turns dark.

Deb relaxes. The color comes back to her face, but she is still lost in her roiling emotions. "No one could be like him."

"For what it's worth, I'm sorry for what he did to you. I'm sorry for what he took away. But I'm trying to make up for it."

"You go down there, don't you? You save the souls your uncle took. That's how I got back here. You rescued me."

"Yes. Me and my friends."

She digests this as she stares at him, searching for signs of deception or insanity. But all she sees—and feels—is kindness and honesty. Along with a burning intensity to set things right. After another moment's contemplation, Deb stands up.

"I want to see the door."

"Are you sure...?"

"No."

"Good answer," Max says, and leads her toward the basement.

Deb follows Max down the creaky wooden steps into the basement. She stays close behind him and looks ready to run away at any second. They walk past the massive furnace, into the back room, and finally stop in front of the bookcase. She gives him a confused glance.

"Where is it?"

"I keep it covered up," he explains. "To keep anyone from seeing it, or walking in accidentally."

Deb paces around the room, replaying the scene of her capture in her mind. While she does this, Max shoulders the bookcase aside to reveal the door. She stops pacing and studies the ancient wood, eyeing it like a cobra ready to strike. Her voice is an anguished whisper when she speaks.

"He dragged me through. And laughed while they tore me apart."

Max reaches for the handle.

"Don't," she hisses.

He throws it open.

Deb jumps back, expecting a monster to leap out. Instead, she sees nothing but a stone wall on the other side of the door. No tunnel. No demons. No Edward Braun. She steps forward in a daze and touches the stone, refusing to believe it's solid. She turns to Max, bewildered.

"You blocked it off?"

"No. The cavern only forms on the night of the full moon, an hour before midnight. The rest of the time there's nothing there."

She pulls her hand back and sobs quietly. "For God's sake, why did he do all this?"

"His diary says in the beginning it was about research into other dimensions and experiments about demonic entities. Near the end, it was nothing more than a game to him. Entertainment."

"He did that to me for *fun*?"

"He was a world-class asshole. I'm sorry."

Max shuts the door with a *thunk*.

Deb studies him for a long time. His sincerity is evident to her, as is his shame at being connected to the madness and evil brought on by his uncle. But there is one thing she can't figure out about him.

"Why do you stay here?"

He stands tall and grins, eyes shining with mad purpose.

"Somebody has to be the hero."

❦

Max wakes up with a start. It takes him a confused second to figure out where he is. At work. At his desk. Where he has fallen asleep. Again. He has knocked over his overflowing inbox in his sleep and files have spilled to the floor. He checks to see if anyone in the office has noticed, and is relieved to see his co-workers are engrossed in their jobs, oblivious to his nap. He spins his chair to stand up and get some coffee and sees his boss peering down at him over the cubicle wall.

"Late night again last night?" Sam asks.

"Uh, yeah," Max says. "You know. The insomnia."

"You told me about that. Even ran up some big insurance bills trying to figure out what was wrong."

"You made me go to the doctor, remember? I was happy to just stay up all night reading the Bible, but you were worried about me. You are such a good boss, you know that?"

Sam smiles. "World's best. I got the coffee mug to prove it."

"I bought you that for your birthday, didn't I?"

"No. You got me 'world's biggest asshole.'"

Max shrugs. "It's the thought that counts, right?"

"Sure is. Like my thought about switching you to the night shift. That way you could be awake at work and sleep at home."

"Good idea, boss. But there's a flaw in your plan."

"What's that?"

"You'd miss me if I wasn't here all day to keep you company."

"You're right. I don't know how this place could function without you. But all kidding aside, are you doing all right?"

Max stares at his desk, avoiding Sam's gaze. "I'm fine. I just have so much going on I just can't seem to wind down when I need to. And when I do finally fall asleep I have nightmares that would blow your socks off."

"I got a drawer full if you need an extra pair. And plenty of time if you want to tell me about your dreams."

"Thanks," Max says. "One of these days I might just do that."

"I look forward to it," Sam says, squeezing Max's shoulder in a fatherly way. "And for now, unless you want me to write you up for sleeping on the job, you're buying me lunch."

"Is that a threat? Or a bribe?"

"Both," Sam says, then he steers Max toward the cafeteria.

☙

Max pulls the Impala into the driveway after work. As he parks he sees a strange sort of lawn party going on at the side of the house and walks over. But rather than join in, he stands back and watches.

A smiling Tommy and Deb are dressed in sweat suits and have their fists up, circling each other in a martial arts sparring match. Walter sits in a lawn chair with his legs crossed, drinking a large martini. A pile of magazines is next to him, and a *National Geographic* is open on his lap, but his attention is on the combatants.

"Bob and weave, my dear!" Walter coaches Deb. "And watch the left hook. He is rather fast for such a muscle-bound brute."

"He's a brute all right. But I'm pretty fast too, you know."

Tommy feints with his left and Deb dodges—right into a playful right jab.

"Gotcha!" the giant man giggles.

She shakes the blow off and glowers at the man towering over her. "Stop playing around and fight."

"Make me."

"All right."

Deb throws a quick jab and catches him in the nose. Tommy steps back, blinking with more surprise than pain.

Walter claps in delight. "Bravo!"

As she resets, Tommy gives Walter a dirty look, and when he turns back to Deb his face fills with the familiar rage.

Max sees disaster looming and steps forward to intervene. "Tommy! No..."

But he can't get there in time, and can only watch as the man throws a powerful roundhouse right at her head. She sees it coming and ducks under it, and as he spins around she darts forward and kicks the back of his knee. Tommy falls face-first to the ground, his right arm trapped under him, and his left arm flopping out to the side. Deb leaps on his back and twists the muscular limb behind him, pinning him to the ground.

Walter jumps out of his seat and joins Max. The two of them watch as she taps Tommy on the back of his head.

"You give?"

He twists his head around and looks up at her with a wide grin. "Where'd you learn to fight like that?"

"You grow up in a traveling circus, you learn to fight pretty fast. Now say uncle."

"No way."

"I'll dislocate your shoulder if you don't give up."

"When I get up from here—"

"*If* you get up. Now say it!"

"Uncle!" Tommy laughs.

Deb lets go of his arm and pats him on the back before jumping to her feet. As he rolls over, she holds out her hand to help him up. Max tenses—but Tommy just laughs louder and grabs her hand. She pulls him up with a grunt. He stares at her with awe.

"You're okay, you know that? For a girl, I mean."

"You're okay too. For a gorilla."

Everyone laughs as Tommy bends over and makes monkey sounds and chases Deb around the yard.

It's been a long time since Max has heard laughter at the house. Even Walter and Tommy are getting along. And Deb—as he watches her talking with the guys, he gets a strange feeling inside. A good feeling, for once. And though it has to fight past the giant ball of angst lording over the center of his gut, it finally rises to the top and makes him break out in a wide smile.

The smile vanishes when he hears the annoyed voice from the other side of the fence.

"Mr. Brown! You and your friends are being too loud again."

Max looks over and sees his next door neighbor standing on her porch. Old lady Johnson holds a broom across her chest in a threatening manner.

"Sorry, Mrs. J. We'll try to keep it down."

"You better. I'll come over there if I have to." The grumpy woman glances at Tommy, then huffs her way back inside her house and slams the door.

Max nods toward the house. "Let's take it inside, guys. That's one old lady you don't want coming after you."

Tommy helps Walter with the magazines and the two men head inside. Max lags behind to talk to Deb. They casually touch arms as they walk close to each other, but neither of them seems to notice.

"It's good to see you're recovering so fast," he says to her.

She shrugs. "I grew up on the road, so I'm used to new situations. I might even be ready to go out on the town soon."

"Trust me, it's best to take it slow. Forty years of changes could be a real shock to the system."

"I trust you," she says. "And not just about that."

Max warms at the simple truth. "That's good to hear. And thanks, by the way. The guys really like you. And it's nice just to laugh for a while."

"Beats sitting around crying, doesn't it?"

"That's my favorite pastime. And collecting dryer lint."

"You need to get a new hobby."

"You have anything in mind?"

"Lion taming."

"Sounds like it could be dangerous."

"Compared to what goes on in your basement, it'll be a walk in the park."

❦

Max is nine years old. He stands at the faded free-throw line of the basketball court at the park. He holds a worn ball in his small hands and raises it in front of his face, peering over the pebbled curve to the goal so far above him. He hears kids playing on the other side of the grounds, but he tunes them out and focuses his full concentration on his shot. He bends his knees slightly, then takes a deep breath and lets it out slowly just like the book from the library said to do. Then he straightens his legs and at the same time pushes the ball with his right hand and guides it with his left. He flips his fingers gently as the ball flies free and gives it a perfect backward spin. The ball arcs gracefully through the air toward the hoop.

It bounces to the ground five feet short of the goal.

He is just too small, his muscles too weak, to get the ball to the basket. But he doesn't curse at his failure like other kids might do. He doesn't blame the ball. Or the cracked pavement. Or the crooked hoop. He doesn't even blame himself. He just quietly accepts his limited muscle strength and practices his shooting motion a few more times without the ball before he goes to find it.

He sees the ball resting against the outside wall of the park bathroom, half-hidden in overgrown weeds. Max trots over to it. When he bends over to pick it up he hears a gravelly voice speaking to him.

"Why are you playing alone, Max?" the voice asks.

Max looks around but doesn't see anyone there. He is sure he is alone, but then, someone just talked to him, didn't they? With childlike acceptance of an impossible situation, he answers the question.

"The other kids won't play with me."

"Why not?"

He tracks the voice this time, following it to the shadowy entrance of the men's room. He can almost make out a figure there, what looks like a man standing at the edge of the light. It looks like it's part of the shadows.

"I don't know. They just won't."

"I'll play with you if you want."

Max steps closer. It would be nice to have someone to talk to, and he hopes the man will want to play ball with him.

"I don't know. Mom says I'm not supposed to play with strangers."

"I'm not a stranger."

The man takes a step into the light, but stays within the shadowy doorway. Max sees it is his uncle Ed. The strange old man looks amused like he usually does, and he wears a long, black, misshapen cape.

"Uncle Ed...?"

"That's right. You can play with me. I'm family."

"All right. Come on out."

Max bounces the ball to Uncle Ed. He catches it with one hand.

"No. Let's play in here. I've got a new game I want to show you."

Max ponders this, suspicious for some reason he cannot identify, but he pushes the negative feelings aside and walks toward the dark entrance.

Ed's perfect smile widens as Max approaches. When the boy gets close, he turns and disappears into the darkness. Max follows. He walks into the bathroom and finds it empty except for the ball, which sits on a metal drain in the middle of the filthy floor.

"Uncle Ed?" Max's voice echoes off the industrial tiled walls. He turns around, searching for his uncle, but sees the room is empty. He stops turning and steps toward the ball.

Suddenly Ed is there, looming behind the boy. He puts his hands on the child's shoulders. "Hello, Max. Are you ready to play?"

Uncle Ed's cape rustles and a dozen pairs of hands erupt from it, all clawing at Max. He struggles but is caught from head to toe in a hellish grip.

"Mom!" Max screams to no avail. "Let me go!"

A clawed hand covers his mouth and roughly quiets him. He twists his head and looks up to see Uncle Ed towering above him, his lips curled into a jagged leer. A forked tongue slithers between his fangs.

"You can't escape me," Ed hisses. "It's my game, and I make the rules..."

Max tosses and turns in bed. It's two in the morning. He is trapped in the nightmare. Trapped in the park. Then he wakes with a start and jerks upright on the mattress. Cold sweat plasters his hair to his head. He scans the shadowy room, scanning for threats, but sees nothing other than Fleabag snoozing peacefully by his feet. He reflexively reaches for an old-fashioned rotary dial telephone on the nightstand, then stops his hand halfway there. He turns from the phone, pulls on a shirt and pants, and heads downstairs.

There's a light on in the kitchen. He walks in and finds Deb and Walter sitting at the table, drinking shots from a fifth of whiskey. Deb looks slightly tipsy, but Walter is well on his way to being smashed. Again.

"Hey," Max says.

"Hey Max," Walter says.

"Howdy," Deb adds.

Max points to the bottle. "That any good?"

"Nope," she replies. "Ulcers guaranteed or your money back."

"Just what I need." Max grabs a glass and pours. He takes a deep drink and winces as the alcohol burns a path to his stomach.

"What are you doing up so late?"

"I'm the designated insomniac," he says as a knot forms in his gut. It's not from the booze. "And I had another nightmare."

"The park again?" Walter asks.

Max nods his acknowledgment as he sits down at the table. Walter shivers. The two men look embarrassed, as if sharing a dirty secret.

Deb eyes them both, wanting in on the tale. "What happens in the park?"

"Nothing," Max lies.

"I bet."

He changes the subject. "What are you guys talking about? Politics? Religion?"

"I was trying to explain more about the game to Deborah, but I'm afraid I'm not doing a very good job," Walter says.

"It's a complicated mess, that's for sure. And you're drunk."

"Touché."

"It sounds like you just go down and fight it out," she says. "Like wrestling or boxing."

"That's how it used to be," Max replies. "We'd go into the cavern and belt it out with a B-movie demon and whoever was still standing at the end of the round got the other's soul. We only lost by stupid mistakes. But they got faster and stronger, so we went to knives, and then guns, and now there's an arms race going on. They're adapting to the way we fight, countering our tactics, changing their shapes and sizes, and coming up with traps and weapons you can't even imagine until it's too late. The worst part is, they get into our minds and use our nightmares against us. And it's working—in the last four months, we've lost three people and only saved you. It seems like the hurrier I go, the behinder I get."

As Deb absorbs the information, she subconsciously rubs a finger in a deep groove in the table. It looks like it was cut there by a knife many years ago. As she touches it the true horror of the house washes over her and she starts to tremble. She wraps her arms tightly around her chest and fights the tremors.

"Are you okay?" he asks, his voice filled with concern.

She locks eyes with him, and the calming energy flowing through his gaze helps stop her shaking. Suddenly she sees past his jokes, past his bravado, past the nice guy persona, and sees the real Max—a stubborn, hard-working man doing everything in his power to right a wrong caused by his family, heedless of the cost to himself. And the cost is high, though she wonders if he realizes it.

"I'm fine, thanks. Or getting there, at least."

"Good."

She looks away. "Walter said Ed left a magic spell book behind," Deb asks. "Did you ever think of using it? Maybe you could put everything back the way it was."

Max scowls at Walter. "The book is supposed to be a secret, remember?"

"She asked me. Was I supposed to ?"

"Well, yeah."

"So there's a secret book that's not a secret," she says. "Whatever. Did you try to use it or not?" She is nothing if not direct.

"In case you get any funny ideas, it's locked up. In my safe. And it's written in Greek, Latin, and Sanskrit."

Deb grins. "It's a good thing I can pick locks, then. And I got straight A's in Latin. Caveat emptor, baby."

Max jerks in alarm. "What?"

"Kidding. Though I do speak some French. Now stop changing the subject and answer my question."

He holds up his hands in submission. "All right, all right. I tried to use the book once, a long time ago."

"Tried?"

"I had a couple of passages translated when I first found it. A professor at the community college did it for fifty bucks."

"What happened?"

"The first spell was supposed to summon a wind elemental—whatever that is. I thought it was all a joke, so I just set everything up and read the passage. It blew all the windows out of the house. And every house in the neighborhood. The fire department came, and the cops. Old lady Johnson next door was *not* happy. But I don't think she's ever been happy."

"How did you explain it?"

"I didn't have to. The weather guy from Channel Four said it was a localized low-pressure cell that formed a mini tornado or something like that. Everyone bought it, even the insurance company. Hell, *I* believed it until the science lab at the college blew up the next day."

"Jesus."

"Yeah. The second passage was for creating fire. The professor must have made a copy without telling me and tried it on his lunch break. The poor guy never knew what hit him. And those were simple spells. Imagine what might happen if I tried to do something as complicated as shutting down the cavern and turning all the demons back into people. I might accidentally open the gate to Hell. Magic isn't as easy as reading a recipe out of a book, and it's not worth taking the chance."

"It's too bad."

'Too bad indeed," adds Walter. "Though if you would allow me, I would attempt—"

"No," Max cuts him off. "We've talked about that. There are no shortcuts in life. None without a price, anyway.

"That's rather profound for you."

"I read it in a fortune cookie."

"So, you fight back the old-fashioned way," Deb says. "With guns and guts."

"I'm working on getting some grenades, too."

"Why don't you just call the police?"

"You think they'd listen? You were down there and *know* it's real, and you're still looking at me like you think I'm crazy. And even if they did believe me, then what? As soon as word got out the government would take over and start screwing with everything to try and figure out how to turn the cave and the demons into weapons of mass destruction. No, I think I'm just going to keep it in the family."

"I can't argue with that. So, what happens to the people you save?"

"Most of the sane ones leave and try to get on with what's left of their lives. I don't blame them. But a few stay behind and help me fight, like Tommy and Walter. I try to help the others as much as I can. Sometimes they can go back to their old identities with a cover story, but other times I have to fake everything and start them over in a new life. Most of them adjust pretty well. Some never do. There's been a few suicides. And one woman is wasting away in a mental home babbling about demons. I try to visit her, but it only seems to make things worse."

"Maybe you remind her of Edward," Walter says.

"Maybe. I don't know. I just wish I could do something for her."

"You do more than anyone could ask."

Max doesn't believe it. Like when he played basketball, he accepts nothing short of a perfect game, of hitting every shot. "Anyway, the whole thing's gotta fry your brain to a certain extent. The transformation is pretty traumatic."

"You're telling me," Deb whispers, a haunted expression creeping onto her face. "Is there a pattern to who comes back crazy and who comes back okay? Like, the longer you're down there, the more unstable you are when you come back?"

"You worried?" Max jokes.

"Yes," Deb replies. She is not joking.

"Relax. You'll be fine. The only pattern seems to be the faster you wake up, the better off you are in the long run. The stronger people don't seem to need as long to recover. You slept about eighteen hours."

"Is that long?"

"Short, actually. The average is two or three days. And there was one guy who never woke up at all. It's not a perfect science."

Walter raises his glass to her. "Six hours," he says.

"Don't get cocky," Max says. "Tommy woke up as soon as he transformed. He walked out of the cave on his own. Which was a good thing, because there was no way I could have carried him up."

"No offense," Deb says carefully. "But that kind of blows your theory. He doesn't seem like he's got all his marbles."

"No offense taken. At least by me. But you're right. He's obviously got some issues. I just don't know if they came from the game, or if he was like that before he was taken. He doesn't remember much of anything before, but I found some stuff on him in the papers like we did with you. He was a decorated soldier in Vietnam, a real badass. Saved his whole platoon one night when their firebase got overran. Hand-to-hand combat, a real mess. He saved a lot of people. Got a nasty head wound out of it, so maybe that's what messed him up—or protected him. I just know he's pretty damn handy to have around when the shit starts flying. In between, well... he's a handful."

"You could have been a politician," Walter says.

"I'd rather fight demons, thanks. As for Tommy, all I know is he sleeps like a baby at night. Life was a big violent game to him in the first place, so maybe this is all just part of the program."

"To Tommy." Deb makes a toast. Max joins her. Walter hesitates, then clinks his glass to be polite.

Max changes the subject. "So how do you like the future so far?"

"I'm still catching up. The Internet helps, but there's so much information I get lost pretty quick." She glances at Walter. "How about you? You were down there a lot longer than me. Was it hard to adjust?

"Um, Deb—"

Walter waves Max off. "It's okay. I don't mind talking about it. It may help her. So, in that respect, you should know it's been... very hard for me."

"I'm sorry. Is it the technology, or what?"

Walter frowns. "You may have heard I hate the television, but I don't dislike the machine. I was used to seeing movies in theatres and listening to the radio before my capture. And though I do have a hard time accepting a box in the living room that shows hundreds of full-color channels, that's not what bothers me the most. It's what it represents. It reminds me of all the years I lost when I was down there. It reminds me that I lost *her*."

"Who was she?"

"My love. My life. My fiancée Elizabeth. I lost her to Edward's nightmare game, and though I was never much of a fighting man I have done everything in my power to become one so I may somehow win her back."

Tears flow down his face. Deb and Max can't help but fight some back too.

"Walter and Elizabeth are unique among Uncle Ed's victims," Max says. It's the only time I know of that he took two people."

"Both in the same month?"

"No," Walter croaks. "That would have been a relief in a way. I wouldn't have had to watch her demise."

She puts a hand on his arm. "You can stop if you want. It's okay."

"I don't mind telling the story again. It reminds me of her. And why I am still here."

"What was she like?" Deb asks.

"She was... the most wonderful woman you could imagine. Sweet, gentle, far too good for me, but for some reason I caught her eye. To this day I don't know why. You wouldn't know it from the wretch before you, but at one time I was the luckiest man in the world. An important man. I read Greek, you know. And Latin. I was a university professor before all this. The head of my department and a renowned researcher in a dozen fields. I was *somebody*."

"You still are," Max says.

"So you say."

"He's right, Walter. You're as important as you ever were. Now tell me more. Did you know Edward before he trapped you?"

"No. We were invited to one of his parties by a friend. I didn't want to go, of course. I was never one for social gatherings. But Elizabeth sparkled in a crowd. So I went for her sake."

"How did he get you into the basement? Did he drug you?"

Walter snorts. "The worst drug of all. Hubris."

"Is that like heroin or something?"

"No, my dear. It's the Greek word for pride. I was too proud to admit we were in danger. And the game can humble the strongest man." He gathers his strength to continue. "It was 1946. And we were in this very house..."

THEN

An Andrews Sisters record spun on the player and their harmonious voices floated through the cavernous rooms of the mansion. A few people danced; tight dresses hugged the women's thighs as they twisted, starched collars scratched the men's necks. Sweat poured from both. Couples kissed in darkened corners, groping at each other, oblivious to those passing by. Or those watching.

The party was going well by all accounts, but the real action was in the parlor. Though the door was already shut, the bulk of the revelers stole glances through cracks in the curtains. What they saw appeared normal from the outside; Thirteen people sat around an enormous mahogany table in the center of the room. Twelve of them would be forgotten seconds after they were seen on the street, but the thirteenth, the man sitting at the head of the table, would be remembered until the day they died.

Edward Braun swept his electric gaze over the people assembled before him. They held hands with each other, forming an uninterrupted circuit. A girl barely out of her teens sat at the foot of the table. Shy and smiling, she giggled nervously as Edward's eyes settled on her. Walter sat next to the girl, and on the other side of him was a pretty, dark-featured woman who fairly glowed from deep inside.

Elizabeth.

Edward smiled at the assemblage, then muttered something in a strange tongue and snapped his fingers. A candle in an ornate silver holder in front of him burst magically into flame. The twelve muttered in astonishment, but Edward's booming voice cut them off.

"Begin."

The word echoed around the room, and the glass bells of the chandelier rang sympathetically for a moment. The group focused on the weak blue fire and began to chant as instructed. Whispering at first, then growing louder with each repetition, the group of twelve partygoers mouthed a bizarre-sounding word.

"Malacoda... Malacoda... Malacoda..."

A slight wind sprang from somewhere, in defiance of the tightly shut windows. Hairs ruffled and the chandelier tinkled as it swung slightly. The candle flame flickered. The chanting grew louder.

The wind gusted and blew stray papers around the room in a miniature tornado. Edward slowly rose out of his seat to tower over the table. The twelve chanted on. The curtains fluttered madly, giving then taking away the views of the audience outside the room. The candle flame glowed brightly in the maelstrom.

The chanting grew to a shout. As voices strained, Edward traced a symbol in the air in front of his face, drew himself up to his full height, and shouted another command.

"Stop!"

Instantly the chanting ceased. The wind died down. The curtains shuffled back into place. The chandelier settled. And everyone followed Edward's gaze to the girl sitting at the foot of the table.

She resembled a rag doll now more than a human being with her head lolling to one side, eyes showing nothing but white, and a line of spittle dripping down her chin and soaking her dress.

Her jaw opened and closed a few times as if testing the movement, then a masculine, distorted voice sounded that had no natural place in her mouth.

"Cold…"

The partygoers flinched around her. Walter shivered as he held her left hand, and looked ready to bolt. Sensing this, Edward commanded him without looking away from the girl.

"Sit still. And do *not* break the chain."

Walter kept his grip on the girl's hand as ordered, but he slid sideways in his chair, getting as far away from the girl as possible. His other hand grasped Elizabeth's tightly. Her fingers turned white from the pressure.

"Walter," she whispered, catching his eye and directing it to her hand. Seeing what he was doing, he relaxed his grip but still held tight. Elizabeth forced a thin smile and they turned their attention back to the girl.

The disembodied voice croaked again. "So cold…"

"Can you hear me, demon?" Edward leaned further over the table as he spoke. The flickering candle cast dancing shadows on his face.

"So cold in this place."

"Can you hear me?" Edward was more forceful now.

The girl rolled her head around, then she spoke again. The voice sounded like it was in pain. "Cannot see you. Feel… the wind. Can you make it stop?"

"I have a question for you."

"Release me, Edward Braun."

"Answer my question first."

"Please. So cold…" it all but whimpered.

Walter shifted in his seat again. Where moments before he'd been afraid of the thing sitting next to him, he was now sympathetic. It sounded so… scared. He spoke to Edward. "This is silly. If you have really captured something, you should let it go."

Edward glanced away from the girl, and he glared at Walter. "Silence! It will answer the question or freeze on this plane forever."

Chastised, Walter stared down at the table.

Edward looked back at the girl. "I am in command here, demon. I and no other. You will do as I say or suffer."

A sigh wheezed out of the girl's mouth. "Ask your question, Edward Braun."

Edward beamed in triumph. "What is the hidden object I seek?"

"You summoned me for a *game*?" the voice hissed angrily.

"I will summon you for anything I desire. What is the object I seek? Tell me or freeze."

The girl slumped back in submission. "Very well. It is a pyramid. You seek a pyramid."

A collective gasp issued around the table.

Edward beamed in satisfaction. He wrote another symbol in the air. "I release you, demon, and charge you to do us no harm." With a snap of his fingers, another burst of wind snuffed the candle out. The curtains billowed and the windows rattled.

The girl's eyelids fluttered. She blinked at the group as if waking from a dream and asked a question in her own voice. "Well? When are we going to start?"

Walter and Elizabeth stood in a corner of the kitchen, away from the throng of people feasting on refreshments. Walter's stoic demeanor had returned once the irrational fear he felt during the séance had vanished, but Elizabeth bubbled with excitement.

"Can you imagine? How could he know we drew a pyramid? We sealed the envelope in the other room. It defies all logic."

Walter snorted at the thought. "He could have seen the image somehow. A mirror on the wall, perhaps. Or an accomplice."

"And how would you explain her voice?"

"I do believe I saw her smoking a cigar earlier."

"Walter..." Elizabeth gave him an admonishing look.

"All right. I can't explain it. I just don't believe it, that's all."

"And why not?"

"All of this magical hocus-pocus is just too far-fetched for me. It flies in the face of science."

"That wasn't science breaking my hand in there."

He blushed. "It was a rather convincing performance. I just don't know why you insist on believing it must be supernatural."

"Admit it. You were scared." She tickled his stomach.

Annoyed, he grabbed her hands and held them back. "Yes, dammit. I was afraid."

"Then you do believe it."

"Can we not talk about it anymore? I came to a party, not a séance." Walter growled.

"You knew whose house it was before you came, and what they say about him."

"Forget it."

Elizabeth pouted. "You're no fun."

Walter pulled her close and nuzzled her ear. "I'm lots of fun, and I'll prove it if we can go someplace more private."

"So you're doing magic now as well?"

"What do you mean?"

She held up her hand and wiggled her ring finger. "You're going to make a ring appear on my finger? Even Mr. Braun might have trouble with that."

He moaned with frustration. "Elizabeth..."

"You know the conditions. If you want me, you have to marry me."

"But I love you."

"Prove it."

"You—you know I have to save up until I can afford to take care of you properly," he stammered.

She kissed him on the end of his nose. "I know, silly. I was just teasing. I know how much you love me. And I love you right back."

Walter blushed, relieved and flustered at the same time. "I wish you wouldn't taunt me. It makes me feel—"

"Shhh. Here he comes," Elizabeth said, cutting him off when she saw Edward enter the room. "We can't have our host thinking you consider him a fraud."

The crowd parted before their host. His dominating physical presence and magnetic personality drew attention from everyone. He poured brandy from a decanter and sniffed the amber fluid in his glass, smiling at the delicate aroma before taking a deep drink.

Elizabeth watched with morbid curiosity from across the room. "I want to talk to him."

Walter groaned inwardly at the thought. "I don't like it. There's something dangerous about him."

"All the more reason."

Elizabeth dragged him by the hand across the room and they stopped in front of Edward.

"Mister Braun?"

Edward gave her a curious look. "Yes, my dear? Elizabeth, wasn't it?"

She flushed at his recognition. "Yes. And Walter. My fiancée. We were in the séance."

"I remember. Your fiancée wanted me to stop, if I recall."

Walter stepped forward. "I was taken in by your rather persuasive show."

Edward snorted. "It was not a show. You heard the fiend speak."

"It... sounded like it was in pain," Elizabeth said.

"It was. By design. Such creatures must be kept weak and distracted, else they will wreak havoc on our world."

Elizabeth shivered, excited. "What was it exactly? A ghost?"

"A minor demon. Nothing to be afraid of if you know what you are up against. I simply teased it with the promise of an untainted soul to get it close, then used the psychic power of the group to trap it."

"My God… that's amazing," Elizabeth gushed.

His chest puffed at the attention. "Nothing but child's play."

"I'll say," Walter said.

"A skeptic in every crowd," Edward said with a smirk. "Could you do better?"

"No!" Elizabeth said. "Of course, he couldn't. Walter just doesn't believe in magic, that's all."

Edward glanced up at a clock on a shelf and noted the time: ten minutes to midnight. "Perhaps another demonstration would convince you?"

"It's late," Walter said. "And we have work to do in the morning."

Edward bored in. "Unless you are afraid?"

Walter bristled. "I am not afraid. Let's see your charade."

"As you wish. Follow me."

He turned and walked out and disappeared down the hallway. Elizabeth and Walter exchanged glances, then gathered their nerves and followed.

They found Edward waiting for them at the door to the basement. He opened it but paused before passing through. "We may be gone for some time. Is there anyone here you should tell?"

"No," Elizabeth answered. "We came alone."

Edward smiled wide. "Perfect."

An electric light flashed on and dimly lit the cellar stairs. Edward led the way down the cobwebbed steps, with Walter and Elizabeth walking behind. The two lovers held hands tightly.

Edward ducked to miss an overhead pipe at the landing, and the other two passed under easily. He took a candelabra off a shelf near the stairs and lit the candles, then walked around the furnace and into the back cellar chamber. He glanced back at his charges.

"Coming?" he asked.

Walter and Elizabeth followed in silence.

Edward stopped beside an antique desk and set the candles down. The flickering light revealed a large, leather-bound book and a fountain pen sitting next to it on the writing surface. He pulled out a high-backed wooden chair and settled into it. His eyes glittered as he regarded his guests.

"Well?" Walter asked impatiently.

"Your proof is in there," Edward said, pointing to the wall opposite the desk where the ancient door beckoned from the shadows.

Elizabeth shot a glance at the opening, her earlier bravado gone. "What's in there?" she asked.

"You'll have to discover that for yourself, my dear. If you truly aren't afraid."

"We're not afraid of your tricks."

Edward leaned forward in his chair. "There are no parlor tricks here, no childish games. We've left the natural world far behind. All there is left is inescapable proof of worlds beyond your knowing. If you can but summon the will to open the door, you will see the truth spread before you."

He opened the book to a blank page, took a gold watch out of a breast pocket, and filled the fountain pen with ink. His preparations complete, he stared expectantly at the two.

Elizabeth grabbed Walter's arm tightly. "I'm scared. Let's go back upstairs."

Walter was frightened as well. But stoked well enough, the flames of macho pride could burn through any amount of fear.

"Don't you see?" he asked her. "That's what he wants us to do. We run away and his legend grows."

"But—"

Walter grabbed her hand and pulled her toward the portal. "Come on. It's probably just a stuffed tiger or something equally ridiculous."

He reached out and pulled the handle, too angry to notice the slimy feel of the metal. The door swung silently open. A rush of warm air moaned out of the exposed opening, pushing their hair back and fluttering their clothes. The couple caught their breath at the earthly smell. The candles flickered on the desk. A dim yellow glow came from inside, artificially lighting the cellar room.

"I'll be waiting." Edward gloated.

Walter stepped forward, walking into the unknown. Elizabeth followed, their hands forming a fragile chain. Before they passed beyond the frame they saw one last glimpse of Edward sitting at the desk. The man calmly took notes, his pen scratching the paper in the near silence of the cellar. The door *thumped* shut behind them and cut off the view.

Walter paused on the stone landing and was startled when Elizabeth bumped into him from behind. He put his arm around her and together they studied the vast cavern stretching into the distance.

"How did he make all this?" she asked.

"I don't think he did," Walter said. "He must have found this cavern, then built the house over it. Or discovered it afterward."

"It doesn't matter. I've seen enough. I want to go back."

"If we go back too soon, he'll say we were scared."

"I *am* scared."

"Nonsense. It's just a cavern. Or possibly an old mine. We may as well explore the place since we're here. And if I don't get a sample of that luciferin mold, the biology department will never forgive me."

Walter led her toward the rough steps. As they stood at the top, a blue mist formed and covered the floor.

"This is incredible. It must be some sort of water vapor..." Leaving Elizabeth behind, he went down the steps and walked into the mist. It swirled around his waist, and he swished his hands around as if he were in a pool of water. He waved for Elizabeth to join him.

"You have to feel this. It's like liquid silk."

"Please, Walter."

"Really, my dear. Come try it."

Elizabeth reluctantly followed him into the mist. She hurried over to him and grabbed onto him. He swished a handful of mist toward her.

"Can you feel it?"

"Yes. And it's not right. I don't like it. Please, can we go now? I don't care if Mr. Braun makes fun of us. I want to go home."

Walter glanced down and saw her eyes were wide with fear. "I'm sorry, Elizabeth. You're right. We should go now. But I have a lot to talk to Edward Braun about before we take our leave."

He headed for the steps with Elizabeth right behind. The mist thickened and completely covered them both. Walter reached out to find her hand but grabbed nothing but vapor.

"Where are you?" she yelled. Her voice sounded muffled and distant.

"I'm here, Elizabeth!" he yelled into the blue. He stumbled back through the mist to find her. It was so thick he could barely see his hand in front of his face. Finally, the mist began to fade, and he saw a figure standing ahead of him. He rushed over to it.

"There you are, my dear. I lost you in the—"

The mist evaporated just as Walter reached the figure. To his horror, he saw it was not Elizabeth at all. It was a red-skinned, leering demon straight out of a nightmare. The vile thing hissed angrily and raised its hand to strike. Walter fell backward and the claw slashed through his coat, ripping a bloody tear in his chest. As he scuttled backward toward the steps, he heard an agonizing screech.

"Walter!"

Both Walter and the demon looked over and saw Elizabeth staring at them in horror. The monster made a noise that sounded like a laugh, then bounded toward her. Walter scrambled after it—though as fast as he ran, it seemed as if he was moving in slow motion.

The demon danced around Elizabeth and cackled louder, then it stopped behind her and leered at Walter. She sank to her knees and held a hand out toward her fiancé. They locked eyes.

And the creature struck.

Walter staggered into the basement. The door swung shut behind him. His mouth was frozen around a silent howl. His hair had turned white. His suit coat was ripped and bloody. He grabbed Edward by the lapels and pulled the man close, all rational thought drained from his mind. It was all he could do to talk instead of scream.

"She—you've got to help her! Please. Elizabeth—"

Edward peered down at the trembling man. "My dear boy. You're bleeding."

"Please. Help me save her."

"You want my help?"

"I'll do anything..."

Edward pried Walter's hands from his coat and casually shoved him backward, then pocketed the watch and closed the book. "We may get to test your offer, so I hope you're sincere."

"Anything. I swear it."

Edward regarded the shattered man as if he were little more than a bug. "If you want to get your fiancée back, I suggest you see me on the next full moon. Nothing can be done until then."

A desperate wail tore itself from Walter's soul. "A month? We can't wait a month! We've got to go back down there and help her *now!*"

"Back down where?" Edward said.

Walter scrambled to the door. He grabbed the handle and threw it open. "Back to the—" His mind reeled when he saw the rock wall on the other side. "But there was a cave. And a monster. You have to believe me."

"Are you saying that you finally believe in magic?"

"Yes. I believe. You were right and I was wrong. Now you have to help me break through the wall and—"

"And do what? Sacrifice yourself on the altar of stupidity?" Edward interrupted. "No, you've done quite enough of that for one night."

"But—"

Edward grabbed Walter by the coat and slammed him against the desk. His eyes blazed and his voice was a feral growl. "Listen to me. The party is over. You will leave now. You will come back and see me on the next full moon. You will come alone. Do you understand?"

Walter reeled before the hypnotic power flowing from Edward in tangible waves. When he spoke again, his words came out slow. Deliberate. Beaten.

"I... understand."

Edward released his grip and Walter fell to the dirty floor.

As he walked for the stairway, Edward called across his shoulder to the broken man. "And do try to keep all this a secret, would you? I don't know what I'd be forced to do if you told anyone about our little adventure."

NOW

"I don't know how I made it through the month," Walter says. "I couldn't sleep, I couldn't work, so I took leave from the university and just sat in my room and watched the sun go up and down until the next full moon."

"Did you tell anyone?"

"I wanted to. But every time I tried the words wouldn't come."

"He hypnotized you."

"No," Walter says. "Yes. But more than that, I couldn't take the chance of angering him and losing the chance to save Elizabeth."

"So, you went back."

"Like a good dog. Edward met me at the front door and invited me in as if I was there for tea, the sanctimonious bastard. We went to the basement, and I went into the cavern again. But the second time I didn't return. I—I failed her."

"You didn't fail anyone. There was no way you could fight against them."

"If I hadn't been so arrogant..." Walter cries.

Max puts a hand on his heaving shoulders. "We'll get her back."

Walter stands up, coldly slipping out from under Max's grip. He slams back a final shot of whiskey and his voice quivers when he speaks. "I used to believe that."

Max watches the tortured man stagger toward the living room. He refills the remaining two glasses, then makes a toast. "Here's to love. Makes you do the damnedest things."

"Fuck love," Deb says. "Here's to hating Uncle Ed."

As he clinks her glass, a warm feeling rushes through Max as he realizes how attractive she is. He knew she was pretty, of course. That was obvious the first time he got a good look at her in the living room. But in his mind there had always been a gulf between beauty and attractiveness. Deb, he has suddenly noticed, has a rare combination of looks, personality, and shared experience that effortlessly bridges the gulf and makes her hotter than hell. But what really turns him on is that she'd obviously love to chop Uncle Ed's head off with a dull butter knife, dump gasoline on his corpse, and laugh as she lit the funeral pyre. And if she could figure out how to use the magic book to keep him alive during the process so he could feel every last second of agony, she'd do that too.

No doubt about it, she's his kind of girl.

Of course, there's no way he's going to say anything. First, because he is a gentleman who understands he occupies a unique position of savior and benefactor to her, and he would never take advantage of that. And second, he knows if he tried anything and she didn't feel the same way, she might break his arm off and beat him to death with it. So he files the attraction away in a mental box labeled "If we're still alive in a month or two and she makes the first move maybe we can go see a movie together or something" and pounds his shot.

He glances up at the clock. Three-thirty AM. An early night for him.

"I think I'm going to try and hit the rack again."

"Me too," Deb says. "It's been a long day. And this shit you call whiskey is kicking my ass up one side and down the other."

"I'll pick up something better when I go shopping tomorrow. Thank God it's Saturday and I can sleep in."

"Can I go with you? It'd be nice to get out of the house."

"If you think you're ready. Might be good to see how the world's changed in person since you were here last."

"That, and I need some new underwear. I appreciate the spare clothes you gave me, but I get the feeling the last woman you bought anything for was your mother."

He barely stops his mouth from dropping open. But he can't stop himself from blushing. Deb will never know how close to the mark she is. Until he tells her, of course. That will be later, if at all. For now, all he can do is mumble an embarrassed "good night."

❧

Max comes down the stairs the next day and finds the front door standing open. He sees Deb standing on the front porch, lost in memory as she literally looks across the half-dead lawn and figuratively across the missing years. He knows the feeling; he spends a lot of time thinking about the past himself.

"Good morning," he says.

His voice brings her back to the present. She pauses to wipe her eyes before she turns around. "Hi."

"You get any sleep?"

"About as much as you did, I bet."

Max joins her on the porch. "You okay?"

"Yeah. Just a little worried about what I'm going to find out there."

"Everything is pretty much the same, except the music is a lot worse."

"That I can deal with."

"Only because you missed boy bands," he says as he walks down the steps into the golden afternoon sun. He opens the car door and looks behind to see she is frozen on the top step. He calls out to her. "You can do this."

"I know," Deb says, then steels herself and walks down the stairs. She joins him by the car and raises an eyebrow as she examines the dilapidated car. "This thing was old before I got kidnapped."

"It's paid for," he says. "And it's still got a great cassette player."

"People still listen to those?"

"Some people," Max says defensively.

She smiles at his discomfort. "I figured this far into the future everyone would have a flying car."

"Oh, I keep that in the garage. I just didn't want to overwhelm you."

"Thanks," she says, and pats the Impala's roof. "Old Rusty it is then." Deb slides into the passenger seat and he closes the door behind her.

Max drives slowly down the road. He steers with one hand, and nervously drums his fingers on the seat with the other. He keeps shooting concerned looks at Deb. She finally shoots one back.

"Stop it," she says.

"Stop what?"

"Stop acting like I'm going to freak out. I'm fine."

"Sorry. I'm just worried. A lot of people don't react well to the changes."

"I'm not a lot of people. I think you should know by now I'm— what the hell is that thing?"

He follows her bewildered gaze and sees an odd-looking, angular vehicle coming in the opposite direction. "It's a truck. A lot of people drive them."

"You're an asshole."

Max smiles and keeps driving.

Deb stands next to Max inside the main entrance to the Galleria. Her face is a mask as she takes everything in. The glitzy décor, the new fashions, the hundreds of people staring at their phone screens instead of where they are walking.

"What are they all looking at?" She asks, confused.

"Those are smartphones."

"If they were smart, they'd watch where they were going."

"The people aren't smart, the phones are. They're little computers, connected to the Internet. People use them to send each other text messages, watch videos, listen to music, play games, all kinds of stuff."

"Does anyone even talk to each other anymore?"

"Yeah. On social media."

She shakes her head. "I don't even want to know."

Max stares at the racy window displays at Victoria's Secret, wondering if this is the type of clothes Deb has in mind. He is embarrassed when he realizes he's gawking, but no one else seems to care.

"You said you wanted underwear, so I guess we start here," he says to her over his shoulder.

When she doesn't answer, he turns around to see what's wrong. What's wrong is, she is not there. He fights down a brief surge of panic and searches the crowd. He spots her a few seconds later, on the other side of the courtyard, walking into a sporting goods store.

By the time he gets into the store, she has a pile of shirts and pants over one arm and is heading for the hiking boots. He follows her from department to department and is soon buried in clothes and shoes and gear. Deb smiles as she shops, delighting in the new fabrics and styles. Max smiles too. It feels good to see her happy, and he is relieved at how well she is adjusting.

Even if his credit card is taking a beating.

❧

Max and Deb sit on the hood of his car in the park, watching the sun sink over the basketball court. They are relaxed and comfortable, two average people sharing a pleasant afternoon. A Pizza King box sits open between them, and the pie inside is half gone. The back seat of the car is full of shopping bags. The park is nearly empty, with only a few people playing with their dogs on the far side.

"Is this the park from your nightmares?" She asks.

"Yeah. I spent a lot of time here when I was a kid."

"Doesn't look scary."

"It's different in the daylight."

She nods to the horizon. "Sun's going down."

"Thanks for reminding me," he says. "We better get the machine guns out of the trunk."

"Do you really have guns with you?"

"No. Well, yes, but not a machine gun. They draw too much attention."

"And you don't like attention."

"Nope."

He grabs the pizza box and holds it up so she can get another serving. Deb grabs a piece and inhales it. "This really is good," she says. "Thanks. And thanks for all the clothes and stuff too."

Max wipes his hands on a napkin and shrugs. "It's a fair trade. A couple of new outfits in exchange for you washing the dishes for the next ten years."

"And when did I agree to that?"

"Somewhere between the three-hundred-dollar yoga pants and the fitness tracker, I think."

She holds up her arm and grins at the device wrapped around her wrist. "It knows how far I walk!"

"And how much you eat. So lay off the pizza or it'll shock you."

"Really…?"

"No, not really. Eat all you want. You just have to work it off."

"Maybe I'll take a run later."

"I've got something better in mind," he says, and slides off the hood and walks to the trunk.

Max dribbles the basketball between his legs, keeping it just out of Deb's reach. She almost steals it, so he turns to the side and holds the ball in one hand, away from the basket, with his body blocking her from grabbing it.

"What are you going to do now, hotshot?" she asks.

"Skyhook," he says, jumping into the air and flipping the ball above his head toward the goal. It arcs high over her outstretched hands and swishes through the net. "The signature move of Kareem Abdul-Jabbar."

She puts her hands on her hips and shakes her head. "That's the guy from the Airplane movie, right?"

"Yeah. And Game of Death, with Bruce Lee. He's also a writer and social activist."

"You're a total dork, you know that? And you're a liar. You told me you sucked at basketball."

"So I stretched the truth a little. I'm way out of practice. And nowhere near as good as I used to be." A sad look flickers over his face as he retrieves the ball, but he banishes it with a thin smile. "Anyway, that was a long time ago."

"Were you really that good?"

He sits down on a bench and takes a drink of Diet Coke before answering. "They said I was. But I had a great team. And a really great coach."

"Why'd you quit?" She asks, sitting down next to him.

"Life." He spins the ball on an upraised finger. "Part of which was inheriting a demon-infested mansion. The rest is history."

They sit for a while, each lost in thought as bugs flit around the lights above them and crickets chirp in the grass.

Deb pulls her feet up off the ground and hugs her legs defensively. "I lied too," she says. "The other night, when I said I didn't remember what happened to me. I remember everything."

"That's okay. It's personal. You don't have to talk about it."

"But you want to know, right?"

"Yes." He almost sounds ashamed. "I want to know. I mean, part of it is I might get some information out of it, something that can help me beat the game."

"What's the other part?"

Max hesitates. He's used to dangerous situations, strapping on guns and knives and body armor and heading into combat against vicious monsters that want to gleefully rip his throat out. But the situation he finds himself in now is a hundred times scarier. When he realizes he can't shoot his way out of it, he gathers his considerable courage and says what's on his mind.

"I just want to know more about you."

Deb blushes. "Really."

"Yes. I think you're—interesting."

"Just, 'interesting?'"

"Yes, I mean no, I mean, that's a stupid word," he fumbles. "I think you're—oh, never mind. I shouldn't have said anything in the first place."

"Why not?"

"You've been through a lot, and we barely know each other. I shouldn't be moving this fast."

"I was dead for almost forty years, remember? Now that I've got another chance, I'm not going to waste a second of it. So if you don't move fast, I will."

"Really?"

"Watch me. Because for the record, I think you're kind of interesting too."

"Good to hear. I didn't want you feeling weird or unsafe around me."

"Strange as it sounds, I've never felt this safe in my life."

Deb scoots closer. Their arms touch. Electricity flows between them. They smile in relief that their secret attraction is out in the open and they no longer have to tiptoe around the obvious. But something still bothers Max.

"You, um, didn't leave anybody behind, did you? I know the past was just like last week to you."

"No," she says. "There was nobody back then. Nothing serious, anyway."

"Nice to know. Well, not nice, but you know what I mean. I hope."

"I know what you mean. How about you? Any special women in your life?"

Max's gut clenches. Of course there is. But not in the way Deb is asking about. "No. Not anymore. And I don't have a lot of time for dating these days, with my work-death balance being so out of whack."

"Not sorry to hear that. Now tell me, do you hit on everyone you rescue?"

"Just the hot brunettes. The hot *female* brunettes, I mean. Not the guys. Not that there's anything wrong with that. I just like women."

"You talk a lot when you're nervous."

"Talk, shoot things with a bazooka, whatever works."

"Just relax. You don't have to be nervous around me."

"Okay, but you should know I'm usually the one who calms people down."

"Then enjoy your night off," Deb says, and grabs his hand.

Max does as he is told. He shuts up and just sits there quietly, enjoying the night and the thrill of her touch. It is a simple, innocent thing, holding hands, but in the pressure cooker world he lives in, the gesture screams volumes. He lifts her hand, studying their entwined fingers. Then his eyes drift to the fitness tracker.

"Your heart rate is up," he says.

"Basketball's a pretty good workout."

"So is shopping."

They share a laugh. Deb stands up and stretches. Max can't help but stare at her body as she does. She catches the look and smiles.

"You still want to know what happened to me?"

"If you still want to tell me."

"I do," she says. "You knew I was with the circus, right?"

"Yeah, you were the bearded lady or something?"

"I was a trapeze artist, you asshole. And a knife thrower. So you might want to watch the smart comments."

"Sorry. Please continue."

Deb takes a deep breath, then begins her tale. "We'd been in town for a week..."

THEN

The trapeze cables creaked as Deb swung across the big top underneath the glaring lights. The bar felt solid—*felt good*—tucked in the crook of her knees. She loved the sense of freedom flying through the air gave her, cheering crowds be damned. It was moments like this that kept her going, the simple thrill of flight, her body hanging casually upside down from the bar while the passing air blew her hair back from her inverted face, briefly keeping the oppressive Midwestern humidity at bay.

The bar was the only thing separating her from a fifty-foot fall to the safety net, but she knew there was nothing safe about it. If she did slip, or miss the next bar and fell, she could just as likely land with her neck through the holes in the net. That would be the end of her career with the Flying Fellini's. Not to mention, her life.

But she didn't slip.

She didn't miss.

She never did.

Near the end of the arc she curled forward and opened her legs, flipping through the air in a twisting somersault that ended with her open hands slapping the second bar dead center. She grabbed it and swung for the far platform, right side up this time and wearing a giant grin. She landed and let the applause wash over her. Then she stepped aside and let another member of the troupe take the trapeze for his routine while she slid down a rope to the ground.

As she walked past the bleachers toward the dressing rooms something pulled her gaze into the crowd. She saw a large man staring at her from where he sat by himself near the top of the bleachers. He wore a suit far too formal for the circus. She realized she could give him a top hat and he could step in for the Ringmaster—and she knew somehow he would do a better job. The man nodded at her and smiled, and a chill ran down her back. Her view of him was cut off as she walked under the seats.

In the dressing room, Deb quickly unwrapped the tape from around her hands and shook them to get the blood flowing. She heard someone come into the tent behind her and turned to see two carnies standing there, hard men she knew well from their years of travel together.

The first, a thick-set, grubby man named Teddy, gnawed on a cigar. Teddy knew he was overweight. How could he *not* know, with his wife constantly nagging him about cutting down on the desserts after every giant fried meal she served, or laying off the beers that helped him drown out her incessant droning so he could get some sleep at night? He was, however, unaware of the thin sheen of dirt and grime blanketing his skin and coveralls and what was left of his hair. Bathing regularly simply wasn't something he or those around him did, so being dirty was just his base state of being.

Jeff, the thinner man next to Teddy, shared the grooming habits as his partner. And though he also partook of the same dinners and desserts and beers, his metabolism, fueled in no small part by the pep pills he washed down regularly with gulps of lukewarm rye whiskey from the ever-present flask kept in his pants pocket, chewed up the extra calories and contributed to his deep storehouse of nervous energy. That energy was spent less on work than avoiding it, and more often than not, got both men into questionable situations.

Like the one tonight.

"What are you guys doing in here?" Deb asked.

"We, uh, need to talk to you about something," Teddy said. As he talked, Jeff walked around the edge of the tent on her right.

Something in his movements made her keep an eye on him even as she talked to Teddy. "Yeah? Well, make it fast. I have to get ready for the finale."

"See, there's this guy in the audience tonight," Teddy said. "He told us he wanted to talk to you about something."

"About what?" Her mind flashed back to the man she saw in the bleachers.

"He wants you to come up to his house after the show. Says he's got a big old mansion on the edge of town."

"Good for him. But I'm not going. He can go find a hooker somewhere, or if he's desperate enough I'm sure Jeff will blow him."

"Fuck you," Jeff said.

Deb cracked her knuckles and smiled at the thin man. "You already tried that, remember?"

Jeff's face flushed red, and he reflexively moved a hand toward his crotch. Teddy stepped closer and she turned her attention back to him.

"I told him you'd say that. Well, not the part about Jeff, but I knew you'd say no."

"So why the hell are you bothering me?"

"Because he said he'd give us a lot of money to get you out there. One way or the other."

She stared at Teddy, finally realizing she was in danger. The carnies blocked the path to the exit, and they had both worked their way into grabbing distance. As she opened her mouth to scream for help, Jeff tackled her from the side, wrapping his wiry arms around her torso. Her scream died. She instantly started beating on Jeff's back and head to get him to let go, and as she did, she saw Teddy move. The fat man pulled a wooden club from behind his back and bounced it off the side of her head.

Deb's vision swam, then everything went black.

A rough bump brought Deb back to groggy consciousness. She could feel movement and road noise and realized she was in a moving vehicle. She opened her eyes but could see nothing but blackness. Fighting panic, she blinked until her vision returned, but everything was still fuzzy. A passing streetlight shined in through a window and she saw she was in the back of an old panel van. She looked to the front where she saw Teddy driving the van and Jeff riding shotgun. The traitorous carnies ignored her.

She tried to move and found her hands were tied behind her back, and her feet were tied together also. The ropes were too tight for her to slip free. As quietly as she could she struggled to sit up. Pain lanced through her head as she got halfway to a sitting position. A wave of nausea washed over her, and she waited for the pain to pass before rising the rest of the way. She stared out over Teddy and Jeff's shoulders, through the cracked windshield, trying to figure out where they were going.

Irregular streetlights and the silvery glow pouring from the fat full moon helped show the way, but the night seemed darker than usual, if such a thing were possible. Deb blamed it on the blow to her head. She saw they were driving through a town, and the gaps between houses grew larger the further they went. After a few miles, the last house went by on the left and disappeared behind them. She lay back down and started working on loosening the ropes around her feet as she listened to the two babble.

"You sure this is the right way?" Teddy growled.

"I followed the directions just like the guy told me," Jeff replied.

"Doesn't seem like there's much out here."

"He said it was just out of town. Said we couldn't miss it. So relax."

"Sure, relax. With her back there." Teddy jerked his chin toward the cargo area and Deb froze. But neither of the men looked back. She went back to work on the knots.

Jeff smiled wickedly. "The only thing back there is easy money, Teddy. Easy money."

"I've heard that before."

They kept driving, and from the floor she saw dark trees passing on either side of the road. Then the van slowed down, made a sharp turn, and stopped. Teddy rolled down his window. She lifted herself as high as she could and saw a stone gate out of the side window, and through the windshield a three-story Victorian mansion looming on a small rise.

"Braun Manor?" Teddy read off a shining brass plaque on the gate post.

"Yeah, that was the name. This is it."

"Sounds uppity," Teddy grunted.

"Uppity means money, shithead. Pull up and let's get this over with."

Deb felt the van steer up a long curving driveway. It stopped by the front steps with a squeal of brakes. Both men got out and stood by the vehicle. She saw them gaping at the house. She sat up between the seats and looked at the broad porch and the wooden front door through the window. It was hard to make out from her angle, but it seemed like everything was covered with strange swirling symbols carved into the wood. Her stomach churned again as she studied the images, and saw the carnies step back away from them as well.

"What the hell...?" Teddy said.

"You tell me, buddy. Must be some rich guy thing."

"You go ring the bell. I'm staying here."

Jeff studied the serpentine coils around the doorbell. "Whatever, you big—"

The front door opened and a thin man stepped onto the porch with a cigarette dangling from his lips. He was in his thirties but appeared older thanks to thinning hair, skin ravaged by smoke and drink, and an overbearing sense of nervousness. He took a last drag on his smoke and tossed the butt to the ground as he came down the steps.

"Are you Joshua? Mr. Braun said to talk to you," Teddy asked.

"I am. And you're late," Joshua snapped in reply.

"It wasn't easy. She put up a hell of a fight," Teddy growled.

"Yeah, then we had to sneak her out of the camp. They'll be looking for her, you know," said Jeff.

"You ain't being paid for excuses," Joshua said. He scanned the road to make sure there were no other cars around, then nodded at the back of the van. "Let's get her inside."

Teddy walked to the back of the van. Deb quickly lay back down and closed her eyes to slits. The cargo doors opened and she saw Teddy and Jeff reaching for her.

"Grab hold," Teddy grunted, and they pulled her out of the van.

The man led them up the steps and held the front door wide as they awkwardly carried her onto the porch. Both men pulled their arms in as far as they could, afraid to touch the sculpted wood.

Joshua jerked his head toward the entry. "Stop wasting time."

Deb got a closer look at the carvings as she was carried past and gritted her teeth against the wave of nausea sweeping over her.

The carnies carried her over the threshold and stopped in the large entryway. The house was full of ornate, dark wood fixtures and expensive antique furniture. To their relief, the carvings stopped at the entrance.

Joshua followed them in. He shut the door behind him, locked it, and pocketed the key. He pointed to the middle of the floor. "Put her there."

They dumped Deb roughly on the floor. As she fell, the rope around her ankles fell free. The men didn't notice. Joshua leaned over and examined her face, flushing with anger when he saw the bruise on her temple.

"She wasn't supposed to be hurt."

"How the hell did you expect us to get her here? She fought like a wildcat and we had to knock her out," Jeff said.

Teddy leaned over and slapped her face. "She'll come around, you'll see. Now how about our money—"

Deb's eyes snapped open. She took a quick glance around to get her bearings, then exploded into action. She pulled both her feet back toward her chest, one knee cracking Teddy in the mouth as it passed by. As he went sprawling, she kicked back out savagely and pistoned both feet into Joshua's stomach. Air woofed out of his mouth as he fell back against the wall and cracked his head.

She pulled her legs back again, flipping them back over her head and letting the momentum pull her into a somersault. As she rolled over, she pushed off the floor with her bound hands, then whipped them down around her feet in a quick motion. In an instant she was standing up with her tied hands in front of her, glaring at the stunned men.

Teddy got his wits about him first. "Get her!" he yelled through his bloody mouth, and Jeff leaped forward to grab her. This time she was ready for him; she took a quick step to the side, easily dodging him, and used her bound fists like a club to hit him on the side of his head as he passed. Jeff stumbled from the blow and fell to his knees.

She jumped for the door. She grabbed the handle in her hands and found it was locked. Without hesitating she leaped over the still-recovering Joshua and ran down the hallway, deeper into the house.

Deb dashed into the kitchen, ran around the large wooden table in the middle, and ran for the drawers by the sink. She fumbled the top one open and saw it was full of silverware. She quickly slammed it shut and clawed at the next drawer down. Her face lit up when she saw a set of carving knives in a holder.

She pulled one out, put the handle in her mouth, and began sawing at the rope around her wrists. Just as the last tendrils were cut, Jeff ran in.

"You're gonna get it now, bitch!" he yelled.

Deb threw as she turned, and the knife flipped through the air and slammed into the wall an inch away from his startled face. He dove under the table as she threw the next knife, and it dug a deep furrow in the surface where his face had slipped by an instant before.

She grabbed the last knife in the drawer as Teddy stumbled into the room. He froze in the doorway, surprised to see his partner on the floor and Deb's hands untied, and in that moment she whipped her arm forward and let the knife fly. The blade plunged into Teddy's shoulder. Blood spurted as he fell back into Joshua's arms.

Jeff tried to grab her legs from under the table. She jumped out of his grasp and landed on the tabletop, then bounded out of the service entrance as he got to his feet.

Deb ran down a dark hallway toward the rear of the house. She glanced back as the kitchen door crashed open behind her and saw Jeff and Joshua giving chase, with Teddy limping behind. Light spilled into the hallway ahead from a partially open door, and she sprinted for it. Another man stepped out and filled the hall. She crashed into him in headlong flight. He shrugged off the impact, but she bounced back and fell to the floor.

Staggered, Deb stared up at him. It was the man she had seen at the circus. The light behind him shrouded his face in shadow, but his eyes seemed to glow from within. She reached up to him from where she lay on the carpet.

"Help me," she pleaded.

The man reached down. But rather than grabbing her hand, he backhanded her across the face. The blow knocked her back to the floor. She fought to stay conscious as she heard Joshua and the carnies' footsteps come up the hall.

"I'm sorry, Edward. She got away from us. She's got a lot of fight in her," Joshua said.

"That's why I picked her, of course," Edward replied in a rumbling voice. He turned to the two carnies. Jeff was holding up his wounded partner. Teddy was pale, gritting his teeth in pain.

Jeff nodded toward Deb. "I don't know what you're gonna do with her, but I hope it hurts."

Edward smiled. "How easy you betray one of your own."

"It's a tough world, mister. Kill or be killed."

"Indeed."

Edward stepped forward and towered over them. He glanced at the wounded Teddy, then tapped the protruding knife handle. Teddy groaned.

"She is a fiery one, isn't she?" Edward said. "Or were you just sloppy?"

Offended, Jeff glared at Edward. "We done our part, now pay up. And maybe give us a little extra for my friend here. Gonna cost a lot of money to stitch that up."

"I don't think he has to worry about such a little scratch."

"Why the hell not?"

With a hand blurred by speed, Edward grabbed the knife, pulled it out of Teddy's shoulder, and slashed the blade across the fat man's throat. His neck was cut to the spine and a fountain of blood gushed out as he collapsed.

"Because he's dead, of course," Edward said. He smiled again, but this time there was no mirth in the expression, only pure malice. "Just like you."

Edward jammed the knife into Jeff's gut and pulled upward in a ripping motion. The knife bit deep and caught on the man's rib cage. His feet rose from the floor as Edward lifted him by knifepoint. Blood poured from his mouth as he wheezed his last breath.

When Jeff stopped jerking, Edward dropped his corpse to the floor. He turned to Joshua. "Take her downstairs for me, will you? Then come back up here and clean up this mess."

"Yes, Edward." Joshua cowered and reached for Deb. She tried to back away but was still woozy from Edward's blow. Through the haze, she noted Joshua was surprisingly strong for such a small man. He threw her over his shoulder and headed for the basement.

Edward stared blankly at the corpses, then followed them down the steps.

Deb moaned softly as Joshua dumped her on the concrete floor, fighting to clear her head. She looked around and saw the cavernous cellar was filled with dusty furniture and battered trunks, all lorded over by a massive furnace belching heat from its gut.

Joshua glanced up as Edward walked down the squeaky wooden stairs. "Do you need anything else down here?"

"No," Edward replied. "Lock the door behind you like always. And do not come back until I call."

Joshua paled, nodded, and scurried up the stairs.

Edward dug a gold watch out of a coat pocket and flipped it open. He noted the time, then snapped the cover shut. He saw she had sat up and was staring at him with terrified eyes.

"And now for you, my dear."

Deb scuttled away from him as he walked toward her. "Please. Let me go," she pleaded.

"We're far beyond that now."

She backed up further, stopping when she bumped into an old wooden shipping crate. She looked deeper into the basement for a place to run and saw something that chilled her to the bone.

The door.

It was set in the far concrete wall. Made of ancient, rotting wood splotched with mold and slime, she instinctively knew that somehow, as insane as it seemed, it was older than the wall surrounding it. It was an alien presence in the cellar, yet it was there, nonetheless. She knew deep in her soul whatever lurked behind it was worse than the man before her.

Far worse.

The door swung open at a gesture from Edward's hand. A yellow glow leaked from the opening just ahead of a fetid gust of stale air.

She gagged at the smell.

He motioned toward the opening. "Come now. We don't have much time."

"W—Why are you doing this?" she stammered.

"For reasons you couldn't possibly understand," Edward said, then grabbed her by the arm and dragged her through the portal.

NOW

Deb shivers on the park bench as the memory overwhelms her.

Max leans closer and hugs her tight. "It's okay," he says softly.

"No, it's not okay." She hisses. "None of this is okay. He dragged me into the cave and threw me to his pet demons and fucking took notes while they tore me apart."

Deb shakes as rage and fear overwhelm her. He holds her until the trembling stops.

"Sorry," she says, embarrassed. "It's just all so raw."

"You have nothing to be sorry about. None of this was your fault."

"I know, but it feels like it. Survivor's guilt or something."

"The only guilty people are Ed and my dad. Sorry you had to meet them both on the same night."

She is confused for a second, then realizes who he is talking about. "Joshua was your father?"

"Sperm donor is more like it. He and Ed were made for each other, two slime-bags in one mansion."

"So... you were there that night?"

"A few blocks away, yeah. If I would have known, I would have tried to stop them."

"Right. You were what, seven or eight?"

"I was a *mean* seven or eight, thank you. And I watched a lot of kung fu movies."

"It's a nice thought, but I'm glad you weren't around. It was bad enough for an adult. It would have been terrible for a kid to be there."

Her head lies against Max's chest, so she can't see the dark wave of emotion washing over his face when he hears the comment. He grits his teeth, trying to contain decades of rage. After a brief struggle he drives the tsunami back into the vault in his gut and locks it away again.

"Yeah. Lucky me," he whispers. He kisses her on the top of the head.

"So, tell me. With role models like those two, how did you wind up being such a gentleman?"

"I got it from my mom," he says. "She taught me to be a good person, and that there's always something good to look forward to, no matter how bad things seem. Keep that in mind if this ever gets too much for you."

"I will. Thank you." She looks at him and smiles. "I guess you're back on duty, calming people down."

"It's part of the job. And sometimes I don't mind going to work."

The kiss is a quick, soft, natural thing that takes them both by surprise. When it's over they stare into each other's eyes.

"I like your park," Deb says. "Let's come here more often."

"Okay. For now, we should get back to the house. I don't like to leave Tommy and Walter alone this long. You never know what might happen with those two."

"Checkmate," Tommy says.

He sits back from the table and grins at Walter, who leans forward with a shocked expression and examines the board.

"That's impossible..."

"Whatever you say. Wanna play again?"

Before Walter can answer the front door opens and Max and Deb walk in, carrying a mass of shopping bags.

Max is confused when he sees the chessboard. "...And this is not what I expected to see."

Deb drops her bags on the floor and states the obvious: "You're playing chess?"

"Yup. And I just beat the pants off Walter again." Tommy beams.

"It turns out Tommy is—surprisingly good at the game," Walter says.

"God bless America," Max says. "You learn something new every day.

"Indeed. And where have you been?"

Max and Deb share a conspiratorial glance.

"We went to the Mall," she says. "I like shopping a lot, and I like it a lot more when someone else is paying for it."

"I like the cinnamon rolls they got there," Tommy says. "I can eat about twenty of them before I get sick."

"Well, we didn't get any of those, but we did get you guys something," Max says as he digs around in a bag. He pulls out a hardcover book and hands it to Walter.

"The Iliad and the Odyssey," the man says, face lighting up as he flips through the leather-bound pages. "Thank you."

"I figured my Stephen King collection wasn't your kind of thing."

Deb glances over at Tommy. "And you, big guy. It's time for a new shirt."

Tommy gawks at the monster-truck emblazoned T-shirt stretched over his bulging muscles. "What's wrong with this one?"

"Nothing. But this one is better." She pulls a giant red-hued Hawaiian shirt out of a bag and holds it up for all to see.

Tommy's eyes bulge when he sees it. He snatches it out of her hands and pulls it over his vast shoulders. He spins around like a muscle-bound fashion model, showing it off. Even Walter smiles at his child-like enthusiasm.

"Thank you, Max! Thank you, Deb! Now I look just like Magnum!" He picks her up off the floor and spins her around the room. Then he tries to grab Max.

"Oh no, not me. I break easy."

Max runs around the couch with Tommy chasing him. Tommy catches up and wraps him in a bone-crushing hug.

"My ribs…" Max wheezes.

Tommy drops him. "Sorry, I forgot I shot you."

"He shot you?" She asks.

"Your rescue was not without incident," Walter says.

"Nothing around here is," Max says, and they gather around to tell Deb the story of her rescue, with a few slight heroic embellishments. It's just another average Saturday night at Brown Manor.

ဆာ

Max sits at his desk, absorbed in his work. His inbox is nearly empty. His fingers fly across the keyboard. He is well-rested and refreshed, and his face no longer sports the pale, haggard visage his coworkers have come to know so well. But the haunted look still lurks in his eyes. Because even though the last few weeks have been good for him, and he has enjoyed the time he's spent with Deb and Walter and Tommy, he can't escape the siren-like call of the calendar pinned to the wall of his cubicle, a chronicle full of red slashes that mark off the days until the next full moon. He tries not to brood. Even if his imminent doom is a few weeks away, there's nothing he can do about it. So he turns his attention back to the ledger and loses himself in the numbers. And many thoughts of Deb.

Hours later he finishes up and saves his work. He drinks a Diet Coke as he watches the report print, then he gathers the papers and walks to Sam's office. He knocks on the half-open door, but the boss is not in. Max walks in, intending to leave the papers, but stops when he sees the framed photograph hanging behind the desk.

It's a shot of a high school varsity basketball team. The uniforms and hairstyles depict a time more than twenty years gone. A teenaged Max kneels in the center of the front row with a ball tucked under his arm. The coach stands to the side, and even though he has known the man for most of his life, it takes Max a second to recognize Sam with a full head of hair.

He is so lost in memories that he doesn't hear Sam walk up behind him. His boss starts to say something, then sees what Max is staring at. He, too, gets pulled into the swirl of time and memories. Both men hear the echoes of a cheering crowd on a fateful day so many years ago.

THEN

The basketball bounced off the hoop and arced toward the floor. Taller players on the other team jumped for the rebound, but Max slid between them and snatched the ball away. He dribbled it between his legs as he slashed free of the defenders and raced up the court. There was one player between him and the basket. Max drove straight at the boy and head-faked to the right. The defender lunged to cut him off. Max changed direction and blew by him on the left. The boy tripped, and Max dribbled the last twenty feet uncontested and laid the ball into the hoop for an easy score.

The five-thousand-strong hometown fans screamed and clapped for their hero, whipped to a frenzy by the exuberant cheerleading squad.

The visiting team was bigger and stronger than Max's home team by far and favored by every book in the area. Their school was larger, the talent pool deeper, but they didn't have Max Brown.

He wasn't big enough, the papers said. And they were right. He lacked fundamentals, a scout claimed. It was true. His shot was unconventional, boosters complained. Bingo. But Max had heart. Sam knew that from the beginning. A heart that would make a lion jealous. And blazing speed, as he had learned. The coach had first seen the boy playing in the park and was dazzled by his reflexes. At times it seemed he was reading his opponents' minds. On top of his physical skills, the coach was mesmerized by the intensity with which the kid played. The outside world disappeared when Max was on the court and nothing mattered but the game.

It took Sam over a month of visits to get a word out of the child; he rarely talked to anyone and had an almost morbid fear of strangers. It was another month, with permission from Max's mother, before the coach could buy him a Diet Coke after a game. From there the relationship blossomed. But though they spent almost every day together practicing after school, he would never say they were close in those days; Max was emotionally detached from the world and everyone in it. Sam figured some childhood event had shattered the boy's trust in people, and when he talked about his home life on rare occasions, it was always about his mother. It was obvious the shy child had never had a father figure, so he made sure he was available to Max at any time. This arrangement worked both ways. Sam and his wife couldn't have the children they wanted, so they unofficially adopted Max. In return, the boy got his father figure and a stable family. Win, win, some would say.

Max quickly picked up the high school game when he arrived, and by the end of his freshman year, he was a starter. His sophomore season saw him take over the team and drive them to a record finish. The town was elated. Long the whipping post of the division, under Max they were a team to be feared. His junior year was even more incredible. He raised his teammates to a new level of play. For the first time in years the school was in the chase for the state title.

He was voted team captain and took the role seriously. Though he was the best player on the team, Max always made sure the other guys got their shots. He understood the basic lesson Sam taught him—it was a team sport, and even the best player couldn't beat five opponents on his own. By making his team better he made *himself* better.

Sam was proud of how far the boy had come. And he was even prouder that thanks to his star, college scouts filled the bleachers to watch all his kids play. The only thing bothering him was that Max's family never came to the games. When he was questioned about the reason, the young man always said his parents were working. But the upcoming playoff game was important and Sam felt they should be there to support their son. So a week before, he had visited Max's house.

Nobody answered at first. It was an overcast Saturday afternoon, and Sam knew Max would be playing ball at the park. He didn't want the boy to know about his visit; he hoped to surprise him at the game. He rang the doorbell again and waited. After a time he heard shuffling inside, then the door opened a crack. Maxine Brown looked out, her face puffy from sleep.

"Coach Wheeler," she yawned. "Is something wrong?"

He was surprised at how much she had aged since they had first met. "No, Mrs. Brown, nothing's wrong. I just wanted to talk to you. If it's a bad time...?"

"It's okay, I was just taking a nap. I work the night shift on Fridays and it's hard to reset. But anyway, please come in."

She opened the door in invitation and Sam walked inside. He glanced at the sparsely furnished but spotless room and summed up the situation: not a lot of money here, but a lot of pride. He settled on the couch and Maxine sat opposite him in a burnished wicker chair.

"Sorry for the mess," she said.

"I wish my house was this messy. You've got nothing to apologize for."

She accepted the compliment with a thin smile. "It seems like I never have time to catch up."

"Max says you work a lot."

"I work two jobs, and both together are just enough to keep food on the table."

Sam blushed. "I'm sorry. I didn't mean to pry."

"It's all right. You obviously care about Max, or you wouldn't be here. So of course you want to know about his home life."

"Busted."

Maxine's smile faded. "I grew up farm poor in Kentucky, Mr. Wheeler. I didn't finish school, but I learned the value of hard work."

"I grew up on a farm too. It's a tough life. And you can call me Sam."

"Sam it is. Is there anything else you want to know?"

He searches for the right words. "I'm sorry if this sounds blunt, Mrs. Brown, but—"

"You don't have to be so formal."

"Okay. Maxine. I came over to find out why you never come to the games. The other parents—"

"I'm sure the other parents don't work as much as I do."

"Surely you or your husband could find the time between you."

Her smile vanished. "My husband is an unreliable drunk who doesn't have time for anything other than his job, his rich uncle, and his bottle."

Sam was startled by her blunt honesty. "I didn't know."

"It's not the kind of thing you run around telling your neighbors. Although I'm sure most of them know anyway. Our fights can get rather loud."

"Is he abusive?"

"I hold my own. To be frank, after so many years it's pretty much routine."

"I'm sorry to hear that. Is there anything I can do?"

"You're already doing it. You've given Max something to live for."

"He was playing basketball before he met me."

"Yes, but he never had a father."

The comment kicked Sam in the gut. Hard.

"He adores you," Maxine continued. "Though I'm sure he never said anything."

"He doesn't talk a lot."

"He never did." Her face softened when she talked about her son. "He's always too busy reading and playing ball. When he does talk, it's about something you said, or did, or showed him."

"I don't know what to say."

"You don't have to say anything. Just accept my thanks."

"I accept."

"Good."

Sam stood up to leave. "I guess I understand why you never came to see him play before. But this week's different. It's a pretty big game. If there's any chance you could come, any chance at all, I think it would be something you'd treasure."

Maxine stood as well. "I don't think you understand me at all. Max and his games are the only things I *do* treasure."

"But you've never been to one."

"I see them in my head. He tells me every detail when he comes home."

"I'm missing something here, aren't I."

Maxine's face twisted as she decided whether or not to tell him her secret thoughts. "I suppose you deserve the truth. But please know this isn't me asking for help, or some kind of pity."

"All right."

"My life hasn't been the greatest. That's no secret. It never has been. I've always felt like there was a storm following me around. No matter where I go, or what I do, dark clouds follow me. There's just something, I don't know, wrong about things."

"Have you seen a doctor? Depression can make things seem hopeless."

"I have. And the drugs they pumped into me were worse than the problem most of the time. No, I've just accepted I was born under a bad sign. I live with the darkness. But Max is my sunshine. He's been a ray of light since the day he was born. I live for him, through him, and that helps me get by."

"He's a good boy."

"And basketball is his life. You've seen it. The way he lights up when he plays. I remember when I got him his first ball..." She drifted off into a happy memory, then snapped back. "Anyway, the real reason why I don't come to the games is I want to keep our worlds separate. I guess I'm afraid if come around I might bring the storm clouds with me."

"You know that's ridiculous, right?"

"Maybe, but I don't know if I want to take the chance."

"You've got a good son, Maxine. And if you don't mind my saying so, I think you should stop being so hard on yourself and enjoy yourself a little."

Maxine thought it over, then looked at Sam. "It's an important game?"

"The biggest one in years. If we win this one, we go to the state finals. There'll be college scouts all over the place, and I think he has a shot at a full scholarship from a major school."

"Really?"

"He's the star of the team. Hell, I ran out of things to teach him last summer. He's showing me stuff now."

"He never told me he was that good. He just talks about the team and how well they play together."

"Well, he's the most modest hotshot I ever met. If I was half as good of a coach, you'd hear me bragging all over town."

"Somehow I don't think so."

"Anyway," he said, stepping out onto the porch, "I'll let you get back to your nap. But I'll leave some tickets at the will-call window in case you decide to come. And I hope you do. Max is something special."

"I already knew that."

"Yeah, but you should see a lot of other people know it too."

Sam left. Maxine watched him drive away, then closed the door. She sat back down in the chair and wondered what she would say to Joshua.

Later, as the first quarter of the game was almost over, the seats Sam had reserved for Max's parents were empty. He didn't understand; he was sure he had convinced Maxine to come. But he had a game to coach and put it out of his mind. He pulled out his clipboard and drew up a play.

Joshua came home late. Nothing unusual there, but Maxine had told him the game was important, and he had promised to leave Edward's early so they could make it on time. She would have left without him, but he had the car, and the buses didn't run this late. She was inches away from spending precious money on a taxi when she heard the car pull up out front. Maxine stepped onto the porch and knew from the crooked way he parked he'd been drinking. She locked the front door and met him as he stumbled out of the car.

"You're late," she hissed.

"I had to work overtime."

"You did not. You were at the bar again."

He leaned against the car, crossed his arms, and scowled. "A man has a right to have a beer with his friends every now and then."

She stormed forward and stopped right in his face. "It's every night with you."

"It's going to be like that, is it?" Joshua was ready for a fight.

"No. It's not going to be anything. I just want to see Max play."

He shrugged. "Then go."

She held out her hand. "Give me the keys."

He held the keys above her head, just out of her reach. "You gonna go without me?"

"I don't have time to play games. We're late already."

"Say please," he jingled the keys.

"Joshua!"

"Pretty please?" he slurred.

Maxine's face fell. "Pretty please."

He lowered the keys and waved her toward the car. "See what happens when you give me the proper respect?"

She walked to the driver's side and started to get in. Joshua grabbed her arm and pulled her back.

"I'm driving," he said.

"You're drunk. I can smell it all over you."

"It's my car."

"It isn't safe."

"I can drive better drunk than you can sober. Now get in." He pushed her toward the other side of the car.

"Joshua, please."

He slid behind the wheel, started the motor, and leered at her through the windshield. "I'm going to the game. You coming or not?"

Maxine checked her watch. The game started in twenty minutes. There was no other way to get there in time. "God damn you," she said, and got in the car.

The band played. The bleachers rocked. Max was on fire. As the second quarter wound down, he already had an entire game's worth of stats. And more importantly, the visiting team was behind by a dozen points. With ten seconds to go he stole the ball out of a lazy opponent's hands and tossed it to a teammate. The boy streaked toward their basket and scored.

The buzzer blared to end the half, but it was drowned out by the cheers of the home crowd—and many of the visitors. A mass of people surged around Max as he tried to get off the court. Sam put his arm around him and ushered him off the court.

As they neared the locker room, Sam saw the school principal waving to him in the hallway under the bleachers. A state police officer stood behind the administrator. Sensing something wrong, Sam pushed Max ahead.

"I'll be there in a minute," Sam said.

Max leaned back on the bench, head propped against his locker. The sound of the school band filtered through the concrete wall, mixing in with the excited jabbering of the team.

"That was awesome!" one player said.

"You burned him bad!" another teammate cried.

"We're kicking their asses!" yelled a third.

Max absorbed the compliments, but didn't care what the guys thought; he played the game with the same intensity no matter what the circumstances. His motivation was internal. The accolades didn't matter as long as they won. He took a deep drink of water and wondered what was keeping Sam.

Sam walked up to the principal and stopped. "What's going on, Bob?"

The principal nodded to the policeman. "Coach, this is Trooper Williams. There's been an accident."

Sam's first horrified thought was for his wife. "Cindy...?"

The principal shook his head. "She's fine. It's Max Brown's parents. They went off the highway and took out a tree."

"Are they all right?"

The trooper stepped forward. "His dad's a little shaken up, but he's fine. He was driving drunk. His mother got the worst of it. She's in a coma, but stable for now."

Sam winced as if from a physical blow. Searing, selfish guilt burned through him; they wouldn't have been on the road if he hadn't asked them to come to the game. The adrenaline rush from the game flooded out of him. "I'll go get Max."

"I'll be out front to give him a ride," The policeman headed for the exit.

Sam nodded. "Thanks." He turned for the locker room, but the principal grabbed his arm and stopped him.

"Hold on a second, Sam."

"What?"

The principal looked around, making sure no one was listening. "You heard the man. Mrs. Brown is stable. I'm sure the doctors will pull her through."

Sam was confused. "That's good. I'll be sure to tell Max."

"That's what I wanted to talk to you about."

"I'm not following you, Bob."

"Look, I know this might sound funny, but it's not going to make a difference if he gets to the hospital now, or in an hour."

"You want me to not tell him?"

"Just put it off until the end of the game, that's all," the principal pleaded. "Listen to the crowd. There are college scouts all over the place, and more reporters than I've ever seen. This is the best thing that's happened to the school in years. If we win this one and go to the finals we'll be on top of the world. Max could get a scholarship to any school he wants. I'm just thinking about him."

Anger pounded through Sam's veins. He realized his hands were clenched into fists, and he relaxed them. "I'm going to forget I ever heard that," he snarled and shoved the principal out of his way.

ↄ

Max stood outside the intensive care ward, staring at his mother through a thick glass window. He still wore his basketball uniform and had Sam's jacket draped over his shoulders.

Maxine lay on a gurney inside the room. An oxygen mask covered most of her face and what skin he could see was bruised and cut. IV lines snaked into her arms, and other tubes and wires stretched to banks of beeping machines. A doctor and a nurse tended to her, studying the readouts on the monitors and making notes on a chart. The doctor saw Max watching and walked out to meet him.

The man took off his gloves as he talked. "You're Max, right?"

"Yes, sir." Max's voice was flat, emotionless.

"I'm Doctor Rivera. Your mother has suffered some serious injuries."

"Is she going to live?"

"It's touch and go right now. I'm sorry."

Max turned to face him. "Tell me the details."

The doctor hesitated. "Maybe we should wait for your father."

"I don't care about my father," Max said. "He's the reason she's in here. Now please tell me what's wrong with my mom."

Dr. River cleared his throat and started the rundown. "All right. She's lost her spleen, her liver is bruised, and she's got some broken ribs. She's got a concussion and some minor swelling of the brain that's causing the coma, but it seems to be receding. That's a good sign. But the bad part is her spine. We think it's partially severed, but until the inflammation goes down we can't tell for sure. To be honest, it doesn't look good."

Max stared at his mother through the window. "When will you know?"

"We're doing more tests, and once she wakes up, she can help us with the diagnosis."

He expected Max to cry at this point, like most people would. But the young man's face was blank. The doctor suspected shock. He suspected wrong.

"You should go check on your dad. He's back in the reception area. If you need anything, page me at this number. I'll be here all night." He held out a business card.

Max took the card and studied it before putting it in his pocket. "Thank you." He turned away and walked down the hall.

Joshua stood between two policemen in the emergency room lobby. His hands were cuffed behind his back. Other than a Band-Aid on his chin it didn't look like he'd been in an accident at all. The officers traded paperwork with a nurse and dragged him toward the exit.

Max didn't know he was angry until he saw his father. As he walked toward the man he flexed his fists, rage rising with every step. Years of hatred boiled up from the depths of his soul and coursed through his veins. And for the first time, he didn't force it back down inside.

Joshua Brown wouldn't make it to the jail that night. He was destined to stay in the hospital for a while longer.

The first blow was a fist to his father's nose. Cartilage crunched and blood exploded from Joshua's face. Max followed with a forearm to the jaw, and his teeth cracked against each other and shattered along with the jawbone. The police fell on the boy then, trying to protect the defenseless prisoner from the attack. They pulled Max back, but he was young and fast and slipped out of their grip. He slammed his shoulder into Joshua's abdomen and cracked a few of his dad's ribs before he was pulled off again and wrestled to the floor. One of the policemen held Max down while his partner and a nurse led Joshua away.

"Arrest the little fucker!" Joshua wailed through his ruined face. "Arrest him!"

The cop shoved him forward. "Shut the fuck up. For what you did tonight I should let him finish the job." They disappeared through a pair of swinging doors.

The cop on top of Max rose to his knees but kept a wary hand on the boy's chest. "You gonna cause any more trouble if I let you up?" he asked.

Max lay on the floor, feeling the cold linoleum seep through his clothes. It calmed him somehow. He searched his feelings and found the anger was gone. "No. I'm done."

They both got to their feet.

"Look, kid. I'm sorry about your mom. But you can't just attack people like that," the cop said.

Max held out his hands to be cuffed. "Are you going to arrest me now?"

"For what? All I saw was a drunk asshole trip over his own feet."

"Thank you."

"Not needed," the cop said. "I gotta go find my partner. You keep cool. And good luck with your mom." The cop walked down the hallway.

Max stood in the center of the empty lobby. He had spent most of his life by himself, but now, for the first time, he was alone.

Sam burst through the emergency room door an hour later and saw Max sitting on a hard orange bench. The boy's eyes were glassy and his face was slack. Sam wondered if he had been tranquilized.

"Max, are you okay?"

He stared up at his coach. "What happened at the game?"

The question caught Sam off guard, and he stammered an answer. "What? We won by six points."

"Good for the guys."

"Yeah, it was. But how's your mom?"

"Alive. Breathing. But they think she's—" Tears burst from his eyes and great heaving sobs ripped through his body. He collapsed into his coach's arms. "She's—she's—" he choked, the tears drenching the coach's shirt.

Sam hugged the boy and tried to soothe him. "It's going to be all right."

It wasn't all right, and Sam knew it. But you do what you can for the people you love. And that meant holding Max in his arms as he cried his life out instead of going to a bar with his wife and friends and celebrating the biggest win of his career.

There was no place Sam would rather be.

NOW

"You were something back then," Sam says to Max.

Max snaps out of his memory and turns to see his boss standing behind him. He jerks his head toward the picture. "The team was something."

"Yeah. And I was a good coach. Face it, hotshot. You carried us all the way."

"Halfway, maybe."

"That's more like it. Now, did you just come in to remind me of my losing record, or did you need something?

"Just dropping off the bank recs."

"Gee, thanks. Can't wait to look them over. It's the highlight of my week."

"Glad to help. And hey, I got all caught up for a change. Do you mind if I take off early tonight?

"What, do you have a date or something?" Sam jokes.

"Kinda."

Sam's eyes light up. "With a real live girl?"

"Yes, you asshole."

"That's great! Where did you meet her?"

"Uh, at the park. We shot some hoops."

"You did? Been a while, hasn't it?"

"Yeah. My shot was a little off."

"I was talking about the girl."

Max blushes. "I'm a little rusty there too."

"And...?"

"It feels good. Though I have to admit, I kind of like playing with the girl more than the ball."

Sam claps Max on the back. "You're growing up, kid. If you ever want the birds and the bees speech, just let me know."

"I think I'll pass."

"Your loss. But just remember to wear a condom. Maybe two these days."

"I'm going to pretend I didn't hear that."

Sam holds up his hands in defeat. "All right, I quit. But tell me about her. Does she work in accounting? A lawyer maybe...?"

"She's a trapeze artist with a traveling circus," Max says, and when he sees the dubious expression on his boss's face, he piles on, "and a knife thrower."

"Sounds like a nice girl," Sam says, playing along with the obvious joke. "Where are you planning on taking her?"

"I thought we'd go somewhere nice for dinner, then a movie or something. Then maybe we'll hit the shooting range if we have time. I've got a new machine gun I want to try out."

Sam stares in disbelief, then he chuckles. "You almost had me there. Now go on and get out of here. And if things work out between you two, I'd like to meet her someday. Maybe we can have you over for dinner."

"Sure. If things work out," Max says, and walks out the door. But what he thinks as he heads for the parking lot is, if both he and Deb are still alive in a few weeks, he'd be happy to introduce her to Sam and Cindy. Though the chances of that happening are pretty slim.

❧

"You take me to the nicest places," Deb says, and shoves a forkful of syrup-drenched pancakes into her mouth.

Max looks around the greasy spoon's dining room and grins. "Only the best for my girl." He digs into his plate of food, a giant strawberry and whipped cream-covered waffle with a ham steak side, complemented by a large Diet Coke.

Deb nods in agreement as she chews. "I like it. Really. It's good to know some things haven't changed."

"Are you doing all right? With all the new stuff, I mean."

"Yes and no. I mean, you were right about the music. But so many things are better and easier these days, like cars and computers. And what the hell did we ever do without the Internet? Still, I miss things the way they were sometimes, you know?"

"Yeah," he says. "Everyone gets a little nostalgic, even me. But for you, the past was yesterday, so it's a lot more intense."

"What do you miss about the good old days?"

"I miss my mom," he says with a wistful smile. "Wrong thing to say on a date?"

Deb touches his arm. "No. The absolute right thing. Tell me about her."

"She was the sweetest woman I ever knew, and the best mom ever. But she's gone and I'll never get her back no matter how many games I win."

"I'm sorry."

'Thanks. Can we, um, talk about something else?"

"Sure. Why don't you tell me how you got the house?"

"I was hoping for something a little less painful."

"You asked."

Max swallows a lump of ham before he replies. "Ed left his entire estate to me. I guess he made the will up before... before we got into a big argument. Then he disappeared for long enough to be declared legally dead."

"That's really a thing?"

"I guess so."

"What was the argument about?"

"We just disagreed about some family stuff. It got pretty heated, but I left and never saw him again after that."

"Do you think he's really gone?"

"He has to be. If he wasn't, he'd be hanging around the house making my life miserable."

Deb almost buys his answer. Almost. "More miserable than you already are, you mean?"

"That's right. But who cares? He made me rich. So, the joke's on him.

"How rich?"

"I knew it," he says. "You're after the money."

"You didn't think I was interested in your personality, did you?"

"I figured it was the car."

Deb laughs. "Definitely the car. You had me at 'rusty Chevy.' Was that part of the inheritance too?"

"No, I got that from a friend. But Ed left me everything else. I didn't want the house at first, you know. There were so many bad memories in the place, but I was stuck in a crappy apartment and couldn't afford to move, and all of a sudden I had the keys to this cool old mansion. So I moved in, and the rest is history."

"It must have been strange for you."

"It got stranger after I found the books. I'm sure you've noticed."

"Yeah. But it's a good thing no one else ran across them."

"Oh, he hid them pretty well. But to be honest, I don't think I found *them* as much as they found *me*. It was like they called out somehow. The spell book did, at least. But anyway, they led me to the basement, and to the door. A lot of stuff came back to me then. Stuff I'd forgotten."

"Like what?"

Max struggles before answering, tortured by his memories. "Ed used to take me down to the cave when I was a kid and made me watch some of the games. I didn't know what was going on, but I knew it was wrong. It scared the hell out of me but he just laughed. I forgot all about it until my first time down as an adult. Which was almost my last time."

"What happened?"

"Oh, I read the books, got all curious, and went down on the full moon. Like you already know, it was simpler then, just a blank cave. No nightmare illusions. But I waded into the mist and got attacked by a demon. It ripped the hell out of me, and I panicked and ran away up the stairs, but the door wouldn't open. It took me a while, but I figured out I couldn't leave until one of us won. House rules. So I broke a chair leg off an old table Ed had moved down there and used it as a weapon to score my first win."

"You got lucky."

"Very. The demon turned into a woman, and I took her upstairs. She didn't wake up for a week. And when she did, she started raving like a lunatic and ran out into the street and got hit by a car. Somebody called the cops, and I told them she was a homeless person I found living in my garage. I didn't know what else to do. It was all so new to me then. Luckily, they believed me. And she couldn't tell them anything different."

"What happened to her?"

"Her body healed up, but her mind never did. They were going to dump her in a state home, but I found a doctor and made arrangements to keep her in a private facility near here. She's been there ever since."

Deb looks down at the table, then back up at Max. "Do they allow visitors?"

"Yeah, why?"

"I want to meet her."

He frowns. "She's out of it all the time. And she gets, well, agitated at some visitors. Like me."

"You can stay in the lobby," she says. "Please. It's just something I need to do."

"If you really want to," Max says with a sigh, and motions to the waitress. "Check please."

"Hi, Doc. How's things with you?" Max says to the white-coated woman standing in the lobby of a private psychiatric hospital. Everything in the place, her gentle smile, the carpet, the wallpaper, the bubbling water feature, whispers *relax*.

"Everything is good, Max. It's been a while since you visited. Which to be honest, isn't a bad thing. No offense."

"None taken. I'm just glad I haven't had any new clients for you in a while."

The doctor's eyes flicker over his shoulder to Deb.

Max shakes his head. "This is Deb. She's just a friend, not a patient. Not yet anyway."

Deb elbows him in the ribs.

"Nice to meet you," the doctor says as she shakes Deb's hand. "If you want me to sedate him, just let me know."

"I'll keep that in mind."

The doctor turns back to Max. "I assume you're here to see Jane?"

"Yes. It's been a while, like you said."

"She did have a rather violent episode the last time you were here, as I'm sure you remember. So it might not be a good idea."

He rubs a scar on his forearm. "I remember. And I don't want that to happen again. But if it's possible, Deb would like to see her."

"Are you working for Max's foundation?"

Deb is caught off guard. "Um, yes. I just started. So far it looks like he does good work with lost people."

"Yes, he does."

Max blushes. "Just trying to help."

"You do more than most. Anyway, we can check on Miss Doe if you want. She should be in the rec room now. Just in case, do you mind staying out of sight, Max? She's been very quiet and comfortable for some time."

"I understand," he says.

The doctor leads them down the hallway. She motions toward a door and Deb steps toward it. Max hangs behind, leaning against the wall.

The doctor leads Deb into a large room where two orderlies and a nurse watch over ten patients. Some play board games, others read, and a few watch TV. One man just sits in a chair and looks into space.

Deb sees a woman in the far corner, sitting in a rocking chair. She stares at the floor in front of her and mindlessly rocks back and forth. And but for a few years, red hair instead of brown, and the sunken features of the damned, Deb could be looking in a mirror.

The doctor nods toward the woman. "I don't know how much Max has told you about us, but we're a nonprofit recovery center for the mentally disabled. We specialize in the homeless and other people society would just rather forget about. A lot of our guests are recovering addicts, both drugs and alcohol. A few combat PTSD cases here and there, but the VA usually handles those. All of them suffer from mental issues, from severe depression to schizophrenia and more. And some, like Jane, are a total mystery."

"You mean, where she came from?"

"That, and what's wrong with her. She's an enigma. We've never identified her or found any family. She was catatonic for the first couple of years. Then, as you heard, she had an outburst one day when Max visited. We never found out why, or what caused her mental state. I assume it was some form of violent trauma, but we have no way of knowing. We just keep her comfortable and do what therapy we can."

"It must be expensive," Deb says, trying to find something neutral to say.

"A lot of us donate our time, but yes. It is. Thankfully, donors like Max don't just find people who need help; they write big checks to help keep the lights on, too. He's a blessing. But I'm sure you already know that."

While Deb absorbs this, she watches Jane rocking in her chair. When another patient walks by, she stops and shrinks back in fear. After the patient moves on, Jane uncurls and starts rocking again.

"We'll get through to her someday, I hope," the doctor says. "Until then, at least she's in a safe place."

"Thanks for your time," Deb says, fighting back tears. She walks out of the room.

Max waits in the hallway.

"Take me home," she whispers to him.

"Sure," he says. "Thanks, Doc, I'll be in touch."

The doctor waves goodbye, and Max follows Deb to the car.

Deb is silent for the whole ride home. Max keeps quiet, letting her work through her thoughts. He pulls up at the house and puts the car in park, but she doesn't get out. She just sits there, staring out over the lawn, to the streetlights, and the road beyond. After a few minutes, she wipes a tear from her cheek and speaks.

"That could have been me."

"Could have been, yes. But it isn't."

"And why not? We're not so different."

"You don't know that. Maybe she had mental problems to start with. Maybe the game messed her up. Maybe Ed tortured her. We just don't know."

"I know why she attacked you."

"Why is that?"

"She hates you."

"Why would she hate *me*?"

"Because she never came all the way back from the other side. She still remembers being a demon."

"Do you remember that too?"

"Yes," Deb whispers.

"Okay," Max says. "Let's start at the beginning. Tell me. What was turning into a demon like for you?"

An amazing parade of emotions ripples over Deb's face at the question, from fear to lust to anger and beyond. She shifts in her seat, struggling with the memories racing through her mind.

He sees her struggling. "Forget I said anything."

"Too late," she says, taking a deep breath. "It's the ultimate violation. Rape on a molecular level. You want to scream and run but you're paralyzed and all you can do is lie there and let it come inside you. And it hurts. A lot. You lose all control over your body, kind of like shitting and pissing and puking all at once. Then your bones turn to jelly and, hell, I don't know, slither is the best word I can think of. Your bones slither into a new shape. Then... oh, Christ. Then you're one of them."

Though goose bumps cover Max's skin, he is fascinated by her tale. "What do you remember from the other side?"

"Hate. It grows until it consumes your every thought. You hate everything around you and just want to rip things apart. Somehow you know the only way to make it ease off is to claim another soul. And later—I guess you could call it later because time isn't the same down there—I hated you. I didn't even know who you were, but I had this vision of me killing you burned into my head. When I woke up it was still there. And to be honest, it was hard to figure out my real feelings for a while."

"I'm the bad guy. Funny."

"Not funny at all."

"Do you still hate me?"

"Only when you eat the last piece of pizza."

They share a tension-relieving laugh, and he asks another question. "What did it feel like when I won? When your side lost a soul?"

Deb trembles. She crosses her hands around her stomach to control the shaking. "It—it's hard to describe. Just call it rage. Pure primal rage. Again, all directed at Max Brown. You must have royally pissed somebody off in another life."

"I did my best," he says. It's his turn to tremble. "But that makes sense. Sandy must still be feeling residual hate from when she was a demon."

"That's her real name…?"

"Yes. She's in Ed's scrapbook. With you and all the others. I just never told the doc."

"Why not?"

"She'd just look up her family and they'd have to relive the horror of losing her all over again. And how could they explain the missing years? I figured everyone was better off not knowing."

"Are you sure?"

"No," Max says, his voice breaking. He lets his emotions bubble to the surface and continues. "I'm just a guy, you know? I have to deal with life and death and I don't know what to call it, un-death, for all these people and I have no fucking idea if I'm doing the right thing or not. But someone has to make the decisions. And I'm the only one who can. So, I do it. Right or wrong, I do it. For them—for you—the ones still down there. It's all up to me. And do you know what the real kick in the teeth is? I want to walk into that room and hug Sandy and tell her how sorry I was about what happened and help get her life back together, but she just wants to rip my throat out with her teeth."

Deb grabs his hand. He grabs back, hard, holding on as if his sanity is slipping away and she is his only lifeline. And at this moment, she is.

"It's not really her, you know."

"I know. Somehow, it's Uncle Ed. He's long gone and he's still fucking things up." He takes a breath. "Sorry to go off like that. It just hit me all at once."

"It's all right."

"No, it's not. You're the one who got your life destroyed. You and the others. I can't even imagine what it was like."

"Stop that."

"Stop what?"

"Stop taking yourself out of the equation," Deb says. "You've suffered as much as any of us. Maybe more. You've got the right to be upset just like the rest of us."

Max chuckles. "You sound like the doc."

"Why, did she tell you the same thing?"

"A time or two."

"And did you listen?"

"Of course not."

"Well, maybe you should start opening up."

"Or what?"

"Or I'll kick your ass."

He sighs. "I'll try, but I won't promise anything."

"Just remember, you're not alone in this. You just think you are."

He stares out the window. They sit in silence for a while longer, then Deb lets go of his hand and gets out of the car. Max gets out on his side. They look at each other across the faded roof.

"I want to see Ed's books," she says.

Max hesitates. He has kept the books locked in a steel safe for years, afraid to let anyone discover the deadly secrets inside them. But like the emotions he keeps hidden in his personal lockbox, he wants to share them with Deb for some strange reason. So he decides to let her see them. And besides, he knows she'll just wheedle them out of him anyway.

"All right," he says. "But please don't try any spells. I haven't paid the insurance yet."

Max sits at a large wooden desk in his bedroom. The top of the desk is covered with tablets of paper, reference books, empty coffee mugs, and parts of guns. He cleans the inner workings of his .45.

Fleabag slumbers on a pillow next to Deb, who lies on her stomach on the bed, half under the covers. She has two books in front of her. One is a dated but ordinary scrapbook, but the other one is anything but normal.

The cover on Edward's book of magic is made of battered leather, stained by a long-dried fluid. Metal clasps and sewn bindings hold the thick tome together. Deb flips through the dense text and arcane drawings; some are pictures of skeletons and human anatomy, and many are of demons and other creatures. Mathematical formulas litter the pages, along with graphs and charts. There is an architectural blow-up of the door in the basement, with a series of numbers and words scribbled in the margin next to it. She frowns in disgust at the pictures, unable to decipher the writing—it's all Greek to her. And Latin and Sanskrit.

"This is unbelievable," Deb says. "I wonder where he got it?"

"His diary says he and a colleague—a Professor Heath—found it in India in 1939. It was in a secret chamber of a haunted fort called Bhangarh or something like that. I checked, and the fort is real. And there was a Professor Heath who taught ancient languages at Cambridge in the thirties, and he did make a trip to India searching for manuscripts. But he never came back. His party was lost in the jungle."

"I can guess what happened to them."

"Yeah."

"But—1939? That's pretty much impossible. That would make Ed, what, seventy or eighty when he kidnapped me? He didn't look a day over forty.

"And there can't be a house with a basement full of monsters, either. Impossible is relative around here."

"I suppose."

Deb lays the magic book aside and picks up the scrapbook. She flips through the pages, reading the yellowed print and studying pictures of people who disappeared in the area. With each page turned, her thoughts grow darker. Tears well up in her eyes. She slams the book shut and buries her face in her hands.

"We were just lab animals to him," she says.

"Worse. I don't think most scientists enjoy torturing their subjects."

"Did he take everyone to the basement?"

"Not all," Max says, his voice thickening. "Ed had other games he liked to play."

"Sick bastard."

"You don't know the half of it."

"How many did he make play the game?"

"Around sixty. He's not that clear on a few of them. The diary says he opened the door in 1942 and created the game about a year after that. He probably would have played every month if he could have gotten away with it, but for a long while he only managed two or three a year. And for almost a decade didn't play at all, so I figure he either stopped to let the heat die down or went on another vacation. He traveled a lot."

"How many people have you gotten back?"

Max clicks the slide back on the pistol and wipes his hands on a cotton rag. "Counting you?"

"Only if I count."

"You do," he says. "And you're number forty-two."

"Jesus. How long have you been doing this?"

"I've been going down there every month for almost five years. I take every chance I can to save someone. And I was winning most of the time until this year, so it ain't all bad."

Max lays the gun down on the desk. He moves to the bed and lies down next to her. He dumps Fleabag off the pillow before propping it under his head and stares into the shadowy ceiling. Fleabag yowls, gives up on his nap, and trots out of the room.

"You ever think about taking a vacation yourself?" Deb asks.

"Never had time. I've been wrapped up in the game ever since I discovered the cave. And I like my day job. It keeps me grounded. And gives me an alibi."

"What about before the game? Did you travel then?"

"I had to work to support the family."

"Didn't your dad work for Ed?"

"Joshua drank away every penny he made. My mom had to pay for everything until—" Max catches himself.

"Until what?"

"I'd rather not talk about it."

Deb rolls over next to him. "You said you were going to open up more."

"I said I'd try."

"Try harder. You've got to talk about it sooner or later or it's going to kill you."

Max chuckles. "I can pretty much guarantee I'm going to die from being ripped into little pieces by a monster, not by unresolved issues in my personal life."

"You know what I mean. Talk to me."

She moves closer, snuggling up under his arm and putting her head on his chest. His hand falls on her waist. He lies there for a long time, listening to her breathing, feeling the warmth of her body against his. The scent of her hair washes into his nostrils and sends his brain reeling. His emotions roil but they are less ragged and raw than usual.

"All right," he says at last. "If you really want to know..."

THEN

The whirring sound coming from deep inside the machine coupled with the hypnotic hiss of air it pumped into and out of the massage bags hugging his mother's legs lulled Max into a stupor. His lack of sleep helped; he had snatched three or four hours a night in the week since the accident, on uncomfortable couches and chairs in a series of hospital rooms. But he didn't care. He refused to leave her side.

"Max? Can I talk to you for a minute?"

Max snapped awake. He stared at Doctor Rivera, orienting himself, then glanced over at his mother. She was still unconscious from the wreck but her bruises were fading. Aside from the machine, she seemed almost normal.

"Yeah, sure. Be right back, Mom."

She didn't answer.

Max and the doctor sat down on a couch in the hallway.

"I know the machine might seem strange," the doctor said, "but it's important to keep the blood flowing for when she—"

"She's never going to walk again," Max said, interrupting him. "You can stop treating me like a child and tell the truth."

"You can't say that. A positive state of mind is the most important thing you two have."

Max glared at the man. "I saw the X-rays. There's nothing left down there. You can have all the fantasies you want about her muscle tone but it won't make any difference. She's going to be in a wheelchair for the rest of her life. You know it, and I know it. And when she wakes up, she'll know it."

The doctor searched for the right thing to say, but there wasn't one. "Okay, I admit it. Her chances of walking again are slim."

"Then why are we wasting our time with this stuff?"

"Because she's going to live, Max. Maybe not like before, but she can still have a good life. The machines help keep her blood flowing. That keeps her heart healthy and helps minimize the formation of blood clots. If she doesn't exercise, she could have a stroke. And quite frankly, that could be worse than the accident."

"Thank you."

"For what?"

"For being honest."

"Well, don't thank me yet. It gets worse. She's going to need a lot of medicine and round-the-clock care until she's learned how to help herself. On top of the therapy. And..." He glanced down at a chart.

"And what?"

"We've got to figure out how to pay for all of this."

Max frowned. "Doesn't the insurance cover most of it?"

The doctor shuffled through the papers in front of him before he spoke. "Your dad stopped paying the premiums sometime last year."

A brief flash of anger roared through Max, white-hot, all-consuming, then he shoved it away into the fire-proof safe at the bottom of his soul where he kept such emotions, slammed the door shut, and spun the combination. He'd gotten so good at this the doctor didn't even notice.

"What do we do?" He asked.

"The state will pay for some of it, and I think we can get the hospital and some of the doctors to waive part of their fees. I've already done that. But the ongoing care will be expensive."

"Nobody has to waive anything. I'll pay for it somehow," he said defiantly.

"I know this is touchy, but maybe your dad could help?"

Max didn't try to hide his anger. "We don't need his help. And if he comes near my mom again I'll kill him."

The doctor nodded. "I understand. For the record, what he did was reprehensible. Everyone here knows it."

"Thank you."

"Well. I've got to go make my rounds. I'll talk to you later."

Max watched the man walk away, then turned to see a nurse checking the readings on a monitor. A new feeling surged through him as he watched her. He felt like running out of the hospital, onto the street, and away from the nightmare that had claimed his mother. He wanted to run forever and leave everything behind. But he knew he would never abandon her. So he banished that loathsome feeling and went to be with his mom.

∽

Max set a box down with a *thump* and stretched his back. It didn't hurt as much as when he had started working at the warehouse at the beginning of summer. He'd grown stronger each week, his upper body filling out to match his basketball-toned legs.

He wiped sweat from his face and glanced at his watch. Quitting time. The other workers were already heading to punch out. It was Friday, and everyone was in the usual rush to get a head start on the weekend. Max finished emptying the pallet he was working on and followed them to the time clock across the dock.

As he slid his timecard into the slot and heard the machine *chunk* as it was marked, one of the workers called to him. "Hey, Maxie. We're going to The Station for some beers later. You wanna come?"

Max shook his head as he swapped his card for the paycheck waiting in the metal rack. "No, thanks. Got to get home."

"Come on. Your mom will be all right for another couple hours by herself."

Max shook his head no. "Sorry. Maybe next week."

The worker shrugged in defeat; Max said the same thing every week, like a broken record. He waved goodbye and headed for the parking lot. Max ripped open the envelope, frowned at the numbers on his check, and followed.

☙

Sam glanced up from his desk and saw Max standing in the doorway. He shoved his papers aside. He was always happy to get a visit from his star player, and even more so when it saved him from grading tests.

"Hey. Haven't seen much of you lately. How have you been?"

Max stared at the floor and didn't move. "Okay."

"Glad to hear it. How's your mom doing?"

"All right I guess. She's getting around pretty good now. The new chair helps a lot."

"Good. Good. Tell her I said hi."

"Sure." Max still avoided the coach's gaze.

Sam slumped back in his chair, trying his best to act calm. "We missed you in the summer league. The team wasn't the same without you."

"Sorry."

"You still in shape?"

"I don't know. Probably can't run a mile right now. Getting pretty big arms, though."

"Lifting boxes does that for you. I worked in a warehouse to put myself through college. Gained ten pounds of muscle in the first month. Then I ate on twenty pounds of fat after I quit."

Max didn't respond.

Sam frowned. "Seriously, are you all right?"

Max looked up for the first time. His lips quivered as he forced out what he came to say. "I'm not going to play ball this year."

It was Sam's turn to fall silent. His brain couldn't grasp the concept of the boy not playing basketball. He searched for something to say, and failed.

Max continued. "I'm going to move to second shift at the warehouse when school starts. Might even pick up some Saturdays."

Sam found some words. "It's your senior year. There's going to be college scouts at every game..."

"I know. But I don't have a choice."

"You could get a full ride to any school you want. Think about that."

Max's eyes reddened. "I've been thinking about it every night for the last three months. College is... well, it's just a dream now. And I don't have time for dreams. I've got bills to pay."

"Are you sure? We could work around practices without you. I could talk to your boss and see about getting game nights off."

"No."

"The team needs you. I need you."

Max spilled his anger and frustration out on his coach. "Are you thinking about me or your record?"

"That's a shitty thing to say," Sam growled. "Of course I'm thinking about you. You've got a chance to get out of here and do something with your life."

"Other than wasting it taking care of my mom?"

"That's not what I meant."

"It sounds like it."

"Listen to me, goddammit. Your mother needs you, but she's going to get better. Pretty soon she'll be able to do things by herself. I just don't want to see you throw away your best shot at a good life. For you and your mom. You've got to think about the future."

Max was silent for a long time, then he whispered, "I can barely handle the present right now. I'm sorry."

Sam nodded. "You have to do what you think is best. It's your life. Just remember I'll help you any way I can."

"I know. Thanks for everything."

"You don't have to thank me, son. Ever."

Max turned and walked away to hide the tears streaming down his face. And when he sneaked a look back over his shoulder, he saw Sam was crying too.

NOW

Years later, Max cries again at the memory. "...So I walked away from the team, from Sam, from everything but my mom. I stayed with her until the day she died. And he did end up helping me. He quit teaching a couple of years later and got a job as an accounting supervisor. He hired me as soon as he could, taught me the job, and got me out of that damn warehouse. The money was a lot better, and that helped with everything."

"He sounds like a great guy."

"He is," Max says, wiping his eyes. "I never would have made it without him. Those first few years with mom in the wheelchair were tough."

"You did what you had to do."

"I kept telling myself that. And most of the time it was true. But sometimes I wondered what would have happened if I could have kept playing. If I got a scholarship and went to college. Then I realized it wouldn't have mattered. No matter where I went, I would have wound up right back here at the house. Right where I'm supposed to be."

"You think this is fate?"

"Fate is too impersonal. I like 'curse' better," Max says. "Uncle Ed created it, and it's up to me to break it."

"You and your friends, you mean."

"They help, yeah. But they can leave anytime. I have to stay"

"You have to, or you want to?"

"I don't even know the difference anymore."

Deb squeezes his hand.

He closes his eyes, taking strength from her calming touch, then looks up at her and forces a smile. "In the end, I'm just like any other kid who grew up and went to work in the family business. Just so happens my business is fighting demons."

"The company is in good hands. Not many people would take on this kind of responsibility and not ask for anything in return."

"I'm just doing what I have to do, whether anyone notices or not," he says. "That's from a book I read."

"*I* noticed." Deb props herself up on one elbow and stares at him. "And now it's my turn to tell you something."

"Okay..." Max says, wary of the serious tone in her voice.

"I want to play the game with you next time."

Her statement catches him off guard. "I appreciate the offer, but you might not be ready to go back down there. Maybe you should think it over a little longer."

"There's nothing to think about. I want to help. And besides— Edward stole my life from me, and I want revenge. For me, for you, for everyone he took. I might still be a little cloudy about some things, but I'm crystal clear on that."

"You could die. Become one of them again. And I can't guarantee I can get you back this time."

"I know. But I can't just walk away from this without giving back a little. And we both know you need the help."

Max rubs his face with his hands. Deb is right, he does need the help. She is level-headed and a fighter, qualities that make her more valuable than the average person. But the General in him is tired of ordering his troops to the slaughter. And even though he's only known her for a few short weeks, she is more than just another piece of cannon fodder. Something deep inside he doesn't quite understand makes him want to protect her more than anyone since his mother. But in the end, he knows what he has to do.

"It's your choice," he says. "House rules."

"Then I choose to fight."

"I almost feel sorry for the demons."

Deb smiles and gives him a quick kiss on the lips. "So that's settled. What do you want to do now?"

"I dunno, play chess?"

"Wrong answer."

Before Max knows what is happening she kisses him again, a soft peck that turns into something far more warm, wet, and intense. Heat rises from deep inside and bursts through every pore as their mouths and hands explore each other's bodies, their desperate embrace fusing them into one being. Through the haze of mutual desire they know it is something more than just sex, though there is a raw animal quality to it that would make even Marlin Perkins blush. No, Max and Deb make love. Hungry, lonely, passionate love that goes on far longer and with more intensity than either could have imagined.

Afterward, they lie in his bed, twisted in the sheets, sweat cooling on their skin. Deb's arm drapes across Max's chest as she slumbers. He stares at the ceiling, thinking about the strange creature lying next to him. He thinks she is vibrant and alive, a ray of sunshine in his gloomy world. He thinks she is smoking hot and fun and astonishing in bed. He thinks it is remarkable how she has worked her way into his life in a way no one ever has before, and it is even more remarkable that he likes it. He thinks being with her calms him down and excites him at the same time. He thinks his heart aches at the thought of losing her. He thinks he could spend the rest of his life with her, though since his life might be over in a week that isn't as much of a commitment as it seems. He thinks he has figured out what the warm feeling deep inside him is, and why he wants to protect her; it's because he loves her. He thinks for a moment that calling it love is premature. But when he considers it, they have shared more meaningful experiences in the past few weeks than most couples do in a lifetime. So love doesn't seem too far off the mark. And with that final thought, he closes his eyes and for the first time in years drifts into a nightmare-free sleep.

‿

The blue mist fades away and reveals a steaming jungle covering the cavern. The frightened expression on Tommy's face and his anguished whisper confirm what Max and the others are thinking:

"The 'Nam..."

"Are you going to be all right?" Max asks.

Tommy nods. His normally ruddy face is pale.

Walter steps close to the man-child and puts a calming hand on his thick arm. "It's okay to be scared. I should know. Just take some deep breaths and try to relax. It will pass."

Tommy takes the advice, and a few deep breaths bring the color back to his cheeks. His crooked grin returns and he claps Walter on the shoulder.

"Thanks, man. Let's go find your girl."

Tommy leads the way down the steps to the cavern floor. Walter, Max, and Deb follow. Everyone is in full battle dress. Deb carries a pump-action shotgun and has bandoliers of throwing knives crossed over her body armor. They stop in a line at the edge of the jungle. Max glances over and sees Deb's eyes wide with astonishment.

"Don't let it get to you. Just think of it like a giant video game."

"This doesn't look anything like Ms. Pac-Man," she says. "I just didn't expect it to be so real."

"It *is* real. Maybe more than real. Just don't forget it can kill you."

"As long as I can kill it back," she says.

"You'll get your chance," Max says. "Any pointers, Tommy?"

"Go slow, pay attention. They can be standing right in front of you and you can't see them," he says, then looks at Deb. "And watch out for snakes."

"All right let's do this," Max says. "You want to take point?"

"Absofuckinglutely," Tommy growls.

The sound of guns cocking covers the animal sounds echoing from the dense foliage, then the team moves out.

The sweltering jungle heat and stinging insects add even more stress to the already tense patrol. Max wipes sweat from his forehead as he brings up the rear. Tommy walks through the brush as if land mines are waiting underfoot. Because there just might be. They reach a small clearing and without a word they go back-to-back, each covering a section of the jungle with their guns.

"What do you think?" Max asks.

"It's too easy," Tommy says. "They should have jumped us already."

"They're afraid of Deborah," Walter jokes. "I know I am."

She smiles at the compliment but knows it isn't true. The demons aren't afraid of anything. She wrinkles her nose and sniffs the air. "You smell that?"

"Smoke," Max says. He sees a faint breeze swirling the leaves on a tree and turns upwind. "Let's check it out."

Tommy follows the scent into the brush.

After winding through the thick foliage for longer than should be possible given the dimensions of the cave, Tommy stops and holds up a fist. The others come to a stop behind him. Max motions for Walter to cover the rear, then creeps up next to the point man. A burned-out village is spread out before them. Smoke drifts from four ruined bamboo huts and a smoldering pile of bodies. Tommy's hands tremble at the sight.

"What happened here?" Max asks.

"We—we were up by the border, near Laos. We stopped here for a little R and R, and the villagers were really nice. We went out on recon, a couple of clicks away. Heard shots and ran back. The VC had showed up, and killed everyone for just fucking talking to us..."

"It wasn't your fault, Tommy."

He nods, unconvinced. Max studies the area for a minute and doesn't see any signs of demons, so he creeps forward and inspects the gruesome pile of corpses. Deb inches up next to him. She gags at the smell.

"God..."

"Stay cool. It's just the game getting inside Tommy's head."

"It's getting in mine too."

"Let's check the hut," he says. "Cover me."

She raises her shotgun and follows him toward the only structure still standing. Max leads with his AK, sweeping the interior and finding—nothing. He turns back to the others.

"Dammit. This is too much like last month. What did we miss?"

A hissing sound reaches everyone's ears at the same time, but Tommy reacts first. "Run!" he bellows, and shoves Max and Deb toward the brush.

Walter follows close behind. An instant later, a rain of wooden spears slashes into the dirt where they were just standing.

"Spears!?" Max yells as he runs. "How did they get spears?"

"Who cares?" Tommy yells back. He twists around, running backward long enough to unleash a booming shotgun barrage to guard their retreat. "Just find some cover."

As they run through the jungle more wooden javelins lash out, sticking into trees and the ground all around them. As Max darts through the greenery, he sees a giant fallen tree ahead and runs for it. "Over here!"

The other three follow, and everyone dives over the log. Spears slam into the wood, then they all pop up and return fire.

Their concentrated bullets rip the foliage to shreds—but miss the monsters hiding behind them. As they reload, they can see the demons leaping from tree to tree as they close in.

"We're pinned down," Walter says.

"They're going to flank us!" Tommy yells as he sees a couple of demons running to the side. He shoots a wild barrage in that direction.

"We have to move," Max says, but as he rises above the log to look around, a spear thunks into the bark right in front of his face. He ducks back down. "Shit!"

Deb scans the jungle behind them, focusing on a towering tree and the plant life hanging from it. She claps Max on the shoulder. "I have an idea—get their attention!"

He turns to Tommy and Walter. "Covering fire!" he yells, and all three aim over the log and blast away. As the creatures jump for safety, Deb runs away from the fight and scrambles up a tree. She disappears into the leafy heights.

Max glances over his shoulder in confusion. Then Deb breaks through the green canopy, swinging through the air on a twisted vine. She arcs over the fallen tree, and even the demons are stunned as she soars high above, releases the vine, and drops to the ground behind them. She slaps her shotgun up and opens fire.

The monsters screech and scatter. Buckshot rips into two of them, spraying gore all around, but they are only injured; one darts into the undergrowth, and the other charges right at the fallen log. Still reloading, Max and the others duck as it leaps over their heads.

Deb takes another shot. She misses. The injured demon scrambles into the brush and disappears.

"All right, Deb!" Tommy yells as he jumps up and chases after it. "We got them on the run!"

Max rolls to his feet and follows him. "Here we go again."

Tommy rushes through the dense brush, following the blood trail left by the demon. He goes slower than he did in the cornfield, more cautious. But like before, he is focused on the chase and has forgotten the squad behind him.

Max runs hard to catch up, and this time runs right into Tommy as he rounds a tree. The huge man stands still, glaring at the mind-numbing sight before him.

Above another clearing, three bamboo cages are strung out on the ground. Two of them hold the corpses of American soldiers, their green fatigues shredded and stained with blood. The GI prisoner in the third cage is still alive, but a demon in a shabby Viet Cong officer's uniform dances in front of the cage, back to Tommy, jabbing a spear through the bars to stab the prisoner. The soldier cowers in the shadowy back of the cage, just out of reach of the sharp point.

Tommy raises his gun to shoot but sees the demon is right in line with the cage. He throws the gun aside and draws his machete as he charges, leaving Max behind.

"Leave him alone!" Tommy screams when he is halfway to the cage.

The creature hears him and spins around, opening its fang-filled mouth and snarling. And to his horror, Tommy sees the man in the cage do the same thing; he's not a prisoner, he's a demon like all the others, and the fiend leaps at the bars with a triumphant growl.

Max sees it all happen in slow motion. He raises his machine gun and yells. "Tommy! Get down!"

The man drops, but not how Max intended; the thin bamboo poles and leaves camouflaging the pit under him give way and he tumbles into it. He twists as he falls, trying to grab the edge, but it is too late. Fate and gravity grab him tight and pull him down.

"Max!" he yells, and disappears from view.

There is a pained grunt from the pit, and the two monsters throw their heads back and cackle before cartwheeling away into the jungle. Max trudges forward just as Walter and Deb break out of the brush behind him. They see his gun hanging loose in his hand and the tendrils of blue mist puffing through the trees and realize that can only mean one thing.

The match is over.

The demons have won.

Max stops at the edge of the pit, tears streaming down his face. He looks down and sees Tommy lying at the bottom, impaled on four long, barbed spikes. Max slides into the hole and falls to his knees. He crawls over and cradles Tommy's head in his lap.

Blood bubbles from Tommy's mouth as he struggles to talk. "I fucked up and... ran off again, Max. I'm sorry..."

"No, Tommy. You did good."

"I just wanted to be like you. To save people..."

Max's guts twist in agony. "You did. You always did."

Tommy coughs up a blob of red spit. "Tell Walter—don't give up... get... get her back..."

"I will, Tommy. I'll get you *all* back. I swear."

"I know you will..." Tommy smiles as the light in his eyes fades out. "I know..." he says, then his body goes limp and he dies.

Max moans and holds his friend's body until it starts to transform. He sees the blue mist pouring into the pit like a waterfall, and Deb and Walter staring down at him. He drags himself to his feet and crawls up the side. They help him out and together they start the long walk back to what passes for reality.

Upstairs.

Max strips off his gear and leaves it in a pile on the floor. He trudges to the bathroom and turns on the shower. When the water turns hot he steps in and stands under the scalding flow. He tries to wash away the pain wracking his mind and body. He fails. He puts his head against the tiles and sobs for his fallen friend. The shower door opens and Deb steps under the stream. She puts her arms around Max and rests her head on his slick back. He grabs her hands and they weep together, two lost souls floating on a sea of pain. Steam rises and mercifully blots out the world.

Downstairs.

Walter is passed out on the couch. An empty bottle of whiskey sits on the table next to him. He still wears his fatigues, and tears have cut streaks through the grime on his face. He clutches a chess piece in a limp hand, a white knight. The rest of the pieces are scattered around the room where he threw them in a fury powered by impotent rage. He and Tommy were not friends, and at times they were bitter rivals. But they were brothers-in-arms who fought a deadly war against a common enemy.

And tonight, the enemy won.

Checkmate.

స్

The next morning Max calls in sick for the first time in years. He has gone to the office with a broken arm, shattered ribs, crushed organs, and an addled brain. But this time it's not angry bruises or lines of stitches that keep him in bed for the rest of the week. It's the rotting evil gnawing at his soul.

స్

A week later Max returns to work. He shows up on time, goes straight to his desk, and starts digging through the backlog of papers on his desk. He doesn't speak to anyone. That would have gone unnoticed on any other day, as he never makes small talk anyway, but today the cloud over his head is more stormy than usual and he is the talk of everyone on the floor.

Sam hears the rumblings and ignores them at first. It's just Max, he thinks, and people like to gossip. But when he passes his troubled employee's desk on the way to the bathroom, he sees what everyone is talking about.

Max works, but his movements are robotic. He processes paper like the copier in the other room—a cold, unfeeling machine. He stares at the ledgers before him with glassy eyes. He ignores everything and everyone around him.

Sam knows Max was sick the previous week, but whatever has a hold on him is nothing like the flu. He looks up at the clock and sees it's almost lunchtime. He and Max eat together more often than not, so he figures a lunch invite is the perfect excuse to be a good manager. And a friend.

Ten minutes later in the cafeteria, they sit on opposite sides of a table. Sam wolfs down his sandwich, but Max hasn't touched his food. Sam tries to break the ice.

"How are the TPS reports coming along?"

"Okay, I guess," Max says.

"You find that trillion-dollar overage yet?"

"Not yet."

"Cindy and I got picked up by aliens last night. She's pregnant with Bigfoot's love child."

"That's nice. You guys always wanted a kid."

Sam studies Max's face to see if he is joking. Not one bit; he is in a total stupor. Sam smacks his hand down on the table. Their trays jump and clatter and everyone else in the room stares. He takes a stern glance around the room and they go back to their lunches. When he turns back, he sees Max's eyes are clearer.

"I'm sorry, what were you saying?"

"That sandwich cost fifteen bucks," Sam says, pointing at Max's plate. "I don't pay you enough to let it go to waste."

"I'm not hungry."

"What? No crack about giving you a raise? You *must* be sick."

Max manages a thin smile. "The last time you gave someone a raise was when Bob in Records thought you were coming on to him."

"That's more like it. And I *was* coming on to him. Don't tell HR. Hey, you want your pickle?

"All yours."

Sam grabs the pickle and bites off the end. He points the remainder at Max like a cigar. "What was wrong with you, anyway? Anything contagious?"

"No. I mean, I hope not."

"Good, because you still look like shit. And don't forget, you kind of set the bar for that around here."

"It's a gift," Max says, then turns serious again. "Can I ask you a question?"

"Shoot."

"Do you ever think about God?"

"Yeah. Every time I eat here I pray the mayo won't kill me."

"Seriously. Do you ever wonder if God is real or not?"

"My wife and the pope say he is. C'mon, don't you want to talk about the playoffs or something?"

Max ignores the question. "How about the devil?"

"You take one, you gotta take them both I guess."

"How do you know for sure? That they're real, I mean."

"I don't know. I guess you just have to have faith."

"Do you believe in Heaven?"

"Yeah, of course. It's all part of the same grand plan."

"But what's the point of it all? I mean, are we just a bunch of mice in a maze? Are God and the devil watching us and making bets on who winds up where?"

"You're wondering if we're just cheap entertainment?"

"Something like that."

"Look," Sam says, "I don't know what God has in store for us, or why the world is like it is. Lots of people say they do, and I call bullshit on that. But I do think there's a purpose to life. There has to be."

"Then why do bad people never seem to get punished?"

"I believe everyone gets what's coming to them. Good or bad. If you want to call that Heaven and Hell, karma, just desserts, poetic justice, or whatever, go right ahead. But trust me. The bad people will get what's coming to them. It just takes a while. Same for the good ones."

"Doesn't seem that way sometimes."

"No, it doesn't. But sooner or later the ship rights itself."

"They sink, too."

Sam shrugs. "If it does, you keep paddling. Why are we talking about all this, anyway? Aren't you an atheist or something?

"Agnostic."

"Ah, an atheist without balls. Listen, is there something I should know? Are you thinking about converting? I could call a priest for you."

"No, I just—" He comes close to telling his boss about Tommy, about the game, about everything, just as he has come close many times before. But like before, he stops himself and keeps the truth buried in his bulging vault of secrets. "I just had a lot of time to think while I was lying in bed sick this week, that's all."

Sam nods as Max's behavior starts to make sense. "The flu can make you think you're about to die."

"Yeah," Max says, and finally takes a bite of his sandwich. "And thanks for letting me talk. As usual."

"Anytime, kid. You know that. I'm always here for you."

"I know. But I can't open up too much—it'd be bad for my image."

"You blew that a long time ago," Sam says, then motions toward Max's plate with his fork. "You want your slaw?

☙

Deb soars high above the clouds when a bouncing sound echoes through the air. She tucks her arms to her side and dives through the billowing white mist, and when she breaks out of the bottom of the cloud the sound gets louder. She twists her neck to look behind and sees something chasing her, a shadow with jagged wings. It slashes at her as it rushes past, and she twists out of the way. The motion sends her into an out-of-control spin. She falls faster and faster, and as the ground rushes up to meet her she realizes she is having a nightmare.

She wakes and jumps to her feet, fists up in defense. When she sees there is nothing more threatening in the room than a lethal build-up of dust on the ceiling fan, she relaxes. The bouncing sound is coming from outside. She pads over to the window to see what is making it.

Deb looks down and sees Max behind the house, playing basketball by himself in the evening light. Bare-chested, he has dragged a portable goal in front of the garage. Sweat pours off him; he has been playing for a long time and doesn't know she is watching from above. He shoots the ball from long distance and misses. He grabs it and dribbles it between his legs before popping up and releasing another shot. He misses again. Frustrated, he chases the ball down and takes an easy shot—and the ball bounces off the rim and flies toward the half-dead grass.

As he chases the ball down, she studies his face; he is focused on the goal to the exclusion of everything around him. There is a lethal intensity in his gaze, and she recognizes it as the same one he gets when he talks about beating Uncle Ed's vicious game. A bomb could go off in the garage and Max wouldn't notice.

In spite of that focus, he misses yet again. He curses as he catches the rebound and changes direction, dribbling toward the hoop with such aggression she realizes he is attacking the net. And though she doesn't know much about basketball, she knows men of Max's height would have a hard time dunking the ball. So when he leaps into the air and slams the ball through the hoop with bone-rattling force she is reminded once again he is far from normal.

He lands on the ground as light as a cat, knees bending to absorb the fall. He lets the ball bounce away and stands under the goal, staring at the fat full moon hanging low in the evening sky. He glares at the silvery orb as if it's his mortal enemy. Then, as if sensing her watching, he glances over his shoulder and locks eyes with Deb three stories up. His familiar casual smile wipes the fierce expression from his face. He waves, grabs his shirt, and heads into the house.

Max steps out of the shower and grabs a towel. When he walks into his room he sees Deb sitting on his bed. Her face is neutral, but for some reason her demeanor makes him nervous.

"Hi," he says. "You ready for tonight?"

"We need to talk," she says, avoiding the question.

"That sounds a little ominous, but okay. Let's talk." He dries himself off and pulls on a pair of sweatpants and a clean shirt.

"You need to take a break from the game."

"Why? You saw me playing. I'm good to go."

"Your body might be okay, but your head is a mess."

"What the hell are you talking about?"

"I watch you, Max. I see that crazy look in your eyes. And I listen to you talk in your sleep. It's scary sometimes."

"So I have nightmares. That doesn't mean anything."

"Really. Tell me, how many shots did you miss down there tonight?"

"A few."

"Right."

"Okay, I missed some baskets. I told you I was rusty."

"You're not rusty, you're one step away from a rocking chair at the clinic."

He glowers at her. "I've been one step away since I inherited this place. But that doesn't change the fact there are people down there who need me to save them."

"They'll still be there next month. And you'll be down there with them if you slip up and get yourself killed."

"I won't slip up," Max snaps, feeling the heat rising to his cheeks. "And I won't skip a chance to win someone back."

"They'll forgive you."

"How the hell do you know?"

"I think I know what I'm talking about."

"Are you speaking for all of them now?"

Deb stands and faces him. "I'm speaking for *you*, Max. Because you can't, or you won't. You've been doing this for years and you're about to break. Just admit it, for Christ's sake."

"I've never denied it," he says, waving his hands in frustration. "What do you want me to do? Lose a chance to get Tommy back? To save Elizabeth? Walter has been putting his life on the line for months to find her and you want me to stop?"

"That's exactly what I want. Just take a month off. Let the full moon go by for once and see what happens."

He stares at her, unable to believe what she is saying. When he sees the genuine concern on her face, his anger fades, and a feeling of helplessness washes over him. "I can't," he whispers.

"Yes, you can," Walter says.

Max sees the man standing at the door. He looks as concerned as Deb, and as haunted as Max.

"Deborah is right," he says. "You're pushing too hard. You're breaking down. We both are."

Tears well up in Max's eyes. "What about Elizabeth..."

Walter walks over and puts his hands on his friend's shoulder. "She'll understand."

Max studies their faces and sees their minds are made up. His brain protests, as every fiber of his being is wired to play, to fight, to win. But he has hit a wall even he can't break through or climb over. He slumps in defeat.

"All right. We take tonight off."

Relief floods through Deb. "Thank you," She says, and hugs Max tight.

He buries his face in the crook of her neck. Walter walks out of the room and leaves the two alone.

☙

It is a beautiful Saturday in the park. The sloping grass is bright green and the trees are as full of life as the children playing among them. Engaged in a mindless game with made-up rules, they toss around a bright red ball.

Above them on a small hill, Max hovers close to his mother, who relaxes in a lawn chair. Two other women sit nearby, chatting about adult things he doesn't care about or understand. Maxine nudges him toward the kids below.

"You should go down there and play."

"But Mom..." his protest is almost a whine.

"No buts. You need to make some new friends and you won't do it sitting up here with me."

He thinks it over, then comes to a decision. "I won't be far away if you need me," he says.

"I'll call if I do. Now go on and have fun."

Max doesn't want to leave his mother. He has a feeling something isn't right, and he wants to be near her if something happens. But he follows her orders and trudges down the hill to the group of kids. They stop playing as he nears. The leader, a pony-tailed girl holding a red kickball, stares at him without blinking. The others whisper and share conspiratorial giggles.

He is used to this. He's been the new kid often enough to understand the ritual. The group will stick together, pretending they want nothing to do with him until he defers to their superiority. It is the same in every city, every time. A very clear, very adult thought goes through his young head: children act like the packs of wild hyenas he saw on *National Geographic* one night.

Max glances up the hill at his mother. He waves to her. She waves back, then returns to her conversation with the other women.

With a knot in his stomach, he walks up to the girl holding the ball. The other children gather behind her, the playground version of an angry mob. Angry with him for interrupting their game. Things are going right on track; he can't wait to get beat up and get this over with.

"Hi," he says.

The girl doesn't answer.

"My name's Max."

The girl gives him a snotty look. "So what?"

He considers this, knowing whatever he says will be wrong. "Can I play with you?"

The girl turns to her friends, then back to Max. "Do you have a ball?" she asks. More cruel giggles from the mob.

"No."

"If you don't have a ball, you can't play."

He points at the other kids. "They don't have a ball. How come you let them play?" As if logic will help.

"It's my ball, and I make the rules. And I say you can't." She sneers and walks away. The other children follow her and they go back to playing their nonsensical game.

He sinks to the grass and watches them play, his feelings hurt despite knowing it was going to happen in advance. And feelings, he knows from experience, take much longer to heal than bruises. This is much worse than getting beat up.

Max waves at his mother again, but she doesn't see him. He looks back to the children but sees just empty grass and trees. They are all gone. The park is quiet except for the wind rustling through the leaves. The ball sits abandoned in the grass, a bright red blot on the green lawn. He spins around and sees the park is empty except for him and his mother. He tries again to get her attention, but she stares into the distance, ignoring him.

Frustrated, Max turns back to the park and sees a man standing in a small patch of trees nearby. He holds the red ball. The man's face is dark; Max can't make out any distinct features. Goosebumps rise on the back of his arms at the strange sight. He backs up the slope, keeping his eyes on the man. He makes it about twenty feet when he trips on a rock and falls to the dirt. Panicking, he searches for the man, but he is gone. Max looks back up the hill.

The shadowy man stands behind his mother. Her lawn chair has turned into a wheelchair, and his hands are on the handles. He smiles, and a line of white teeth breaks through the darkness of his face, the only detail visible. The smile is wrong somehow, the teeth misshapen, the mouth too big for his head.

Even though he can't see his eyes, Max knows the man is staring at him.

When he speaks, his voice is a hoarse whisper that carries to the bottom of the hill. "It's my game, and I make the rules..."

Max scrambles to his feet and runs to help his mother. Before he gets to her, the man pushes the wheelchair down the incline. Maxine panics and tries to hold on.

"MOMMMMMYYYYY!!!!" Max screams as he watches the wheelchair career down the slope. He is horrified but confused now as well; his mother is no longer in the hurtling chair. Just the red ball.

The wheelchair smashes into a tree. The ball bounces in the grass, landing at Max's feet. He looks down at it, then back up at the top of the hill. The shadowy man is gone. The hilltop is bare. Max is alone. Alone except for the chilling voice echoing through the trees.

"I make the rules..."

"Jesus!" Max yelps as he wakes from his latest nightmare. As usual, he looks around until he remembers where he is—safe in bed. He checks the clock and sees it is 11:01 p.m. He hears residual creaking in the rafters and realizes he has slept through the forming of the cavern. Wiping sweat from his face, he gets up and heads downstairs.

Deb, Walter, and Fleabag sit in their usual places in the kitchen. The usual bottle of whiskey has been replaced by Deb's favorite: tequila. It is half empty as usual. And as usual at this time of night, they are well on the way to being sloshed. She pours him a large shot. He downs it in a long gulp, and as his eyes mist over from the intoxicating fumes wafting through his sinuses, he slams the glass down for a refill.

"Hit me."

Deb pours. "Nice nap?"

"Killer," he replies.

"Here's to the park," she says with a grin, and clinks glasses with Walter before gulping the liquor down.

Max glares at her. "The park," he toasts, then drains his glass and holds it out for more.

"You're drinking pretty fast, aren't you?"

"You had a head start. And besides, I plan to be numb by midnight."

"Good plan," she says, and all three drink again.

As Max sits down across from her, Walter pushes his chair back and staggers to his feet. He weaves and grabs the table for support.

"If you will pardon me," he says with the exaggerated enunciation drunks use to try and cover the fact they are wasted but only succeed in drawing more attention to their inebriated state than if they had just slurred their words, "I am retiring to the living room to do some reading. You two have a most pleasant evening."

They toast him as he wobbles out the door. After he is gone, Max swirls the caramel-colored fluid in his glass and looks at Deb.

"So this is it? We just sit here tonight?"

"Beats getting our throats ripped out."

"Good point. But it's hard to just do nothing."

"Then do something."

"Like what?"

"Drink more, for one."

"No problem there." He drains the glass again and shivers as the alcohol eases into his system. "Now what?"

"Tell me a story."

"What do you want to hear?"

She slams her glass down and stares him straight in the eyes. "Whatever happened to Uncle Ed?"

Max stares back, a deer caught in high-beam headlights. He breaks her gaze and reaches for the bottle. "The last thing he wrote in his diary was about his plan for a trip to Haiti to study Voodoo rituals. That's all anyone knows."

"Anyone but you."

"What do you mean?"

"Don't bullshit me, Max. I was on the other side, remember? The whole game centers around making your life hell. And since the game is a reflection of its creator..."

"I'm telling you, I don't know."

"You want me to believe he just headed for parts unknown and left everything here? Including his diary and spell book?"

"Yes."

"You're a terrible liar."

"I'm not lying. I came over the day he left. I was looking for my dad, but he wasn't around."

"And you and Ed had a 'falling out' I think you said? Tell me about it."

He grits his teeth, fighting back a tide of painful memories. "Why do you do this to me?"

"Because you've been living with this for too long, and you're going to explode if you don't talk about it. And we've got nothing else to do tonight."

Max jerks his chin up toward the bedroom to try and change the subject. "We could—"

"Oh no. That's done until you tell me what's in that thick head of yours."

"You're evil."

"Not as evil as Ed was. Now talk."

He sighs. "All right, you win. But payback's gonna be a bitch."

"Looking forward to it."

He leans back and takes another drink. "It was the longest day of my life..."

THEN

Max stood at the edge of the grave and stared down at his mother's coffin. He was a boy no longer, now taller, harder, with muscles filled out from years of labor at the warehouse. He was old enough to drink, old enough to fight for his country, and old enough to bury his mother. But he was not old enough to let her go. His face was blank, the only sign of emotion his red, raw eyes.

A small group of people chatted behind him—a preacher, Sam and his wife Cindy, a couple of maids from the hotel Maxine worked at before her accident, and Doctor Rivera from the emergency room. Max ignored them all. He bent down and grabbed a handful of dirt and tossed it into the hole. It hit the top of the cheap casket and skittered away.

"I love you, Mom," he said, and with a mournful glance at the sky, turned to walk for his car.

Sam saw him leaving and trotted to catch up. "Max. Wait. Hey, Max!"

He turned around and greeted his former coach. "Hey. Thanks for coming."

"Of course. Glad to be here. I mean, not glad, but…"

"I know. My mom really liked you, you know."

"She did?"

"Yeah. She told me how you came over and asked her to come to the game that night."

Sam's face flushed with shame. "If I would have known..."

"You did a good thing, no matter how it turned out. Sorry I never told you before. This..." he waved a hand back toward the grave, "this is Joshua's fault. No one else. And she would have been so proud to see me play."

Sam choked back tears. "Thanks for that. It means a lot."

The two men stood in awkward silence for a sad moment, watching the low clouds blowing by in the overcast sky. Then Sam spoke up again.

"I didn't see your dad here."

"Don't call him that, please," Max said as rage roared up from his gut at the mention of the word. He slammed the emotion back down before the other man noticed. "He's not my dad. He's a man I share blood with. No more, no less."

Sam studied him, marveling at the easy way the young man could dismiss his father. He knew Max was a loving person; he had proved that often enough with his mother and his teammates. But there had always been a hard edge to him, even as a boy, an ability to stifle his emotions and stay in control no matter how trying the circumstances. On the basketball court, players like Max were akin to assassins, cold-blooded playmakers who reveled in taking big shots at critical moments with no fear of the consequences. On the court, having no conscience could be a useful skill. But off of it, at times like this, the ability to suppress emotion was frightening. He shuddered as he realized Max scared him.

Sensing Sam's discomfort, Max broke into a smile. "Sorry. I didn't mean to sound so intense. But Joshua didn't even bother to show up today, so as far as I'm concerned he's as dead as my mom."

"Fair enough," Sam said. "Well, we've got to get going. We're having pot roast later if you want to come over for dinner. There'll be plenty to go around."

Max shook his head. "Thanks, but I've got some stuff to do. Maybe another time."

Sam nodded, and the two men embraced. When they touched, the dam broke, the assassin melted, and Max cried in Sam's arms. The hug lasted longer than either of them would ever admit.

⁓

Max parked in front of Uncle Ed's mansion and got out of the car. He stared up at the house, seeing for the first time how the front resembled a ghoulish face. The vines climbing the trellis on either side were like wiry hair, the second-story windows were glaring eyes, and the doorway was a sneering mouth open and ready to devour him. Then he blinked. It was just an illusion. It was just a house. And he hoped the man he came to find was inside.

He walked in without knocking and wandered through the rooms searching for Joshua. As he searched, he saw all the furniture was covered in dust cloths and the window shutters were closed; it looked like Ed was going away for a while. As far as Max was concerned, the man could go away forever. He heard a noise deeper in the house and followed it down the hallway to the study.

Uncle Ed glanced up from packing a box on top of his desk and grinned when he saw his great-nephew come into the room. "Max! What a pleasant surprise. Come in, come in."

Max took a wary step into the room and glanced around before looking at Ed. He marveled at how his uncle was still young and vibrant even though he knew the man had to be at least seventy years old.

"Where's Joshua?" Max asked, not bothering with pleasantries.

Uncle Ed came around the desk; he moved with sinuous grace for such a large person. He stopped in front of the younger man and peered down at him.

"I'm sorry, but he's not here. He's taken my bags to the train station. I'm off on another extended adventure, you see. Haiti, this time."

"Good for you," Max said. "When is he coming back?"

"He won't be, I'm afraid. After he drops my things, he is a free man until I return in October. I'm planning a special Halloween party to celebrate my return."

Max turned to leave. "I won't keep you then."

Ed clamped a large hand on Max's shoulder. "Please don't rush off. I've got hours before the car comes for me and I haven't seen you for so long. We've so much to catch up on. Your mother, for instance. A tragic loss. You have my condolences."

Max trembled, then shrugged the hand off. "I've got to go."

"It might help if you talked about her death, my boy."

"Let's cut the bullshit, Ed. You didn't give a damn about my mom. And I'd give everything I have to see you in the ground instead of her."

Uncle Ed smiled. "You *have* grown up, haven't you?"

"A long time ago."

"Grown indeed. Into a beautiful young man..." Ed touched Max's cheek.

He closed his eyes as horrific memories flashed through him. He tried to move but couldn't find the strength. Just like when he was a child, power seemed to flow from Ed. It rooted him to the spot and rendered him helpless.

"Don't—"

Ed pulled Max close and started to embrace him. And as his great uncle's arms folded around him, the rage he had kept buried so deep vomited to the surface, sending a white-hot surge of energy through his veins. His eyes snapped open, full of hate.

"I'm not a little kid you can play with anymore," Max growled. He grabbed his uncle's hand and twisted it backward. Wrist bones snapped. Ed howled in pain. He clubbed at Max's face with his good hand, but Max ducked the blow and drove a powerful punch into his stomach. Air woofed out of Ed's mouth and he fell to the floor.

Max jumped on top of Uncle Ed and the beating began. Years of fear and pain and anger were channeled into each savage blow. He beat and beat and beat until his hands were numb and bleeding wrecks. A detached part of his mind noted it felt good to inflict the pain, to render his uncle as helpless as he had been as a child. When his rage was spent he crawled off, leaving the loathsome man a bloody, whimpering wreck. Max wiped his trembling hands on his shirt and turned to the door.

Behind him, the broken thing that was Uncle Ed croaked out to him. "You will pay for this, Max... pay worse... than you can ever imagine..."

Max looked back. "Try it. If I ever see you again, I'll kill you. Do you understand me? And if I ever catch you around another kid, I'll do worse. You're done here, Ed. Go find a rock to die under and leave the world alone."

He turned his back on his uncle and walked out of the house.

NOW

"...And that was the last I ever saw of him. Years later a lawyer tracked me down. Like I told you before, Ed had been declared legally dead, and he left me everything."

"Do you think he died from the beating?"

"They never found a body. I figure he cleaned himself up and took his trip to Haiti after all and got messed up in something even he couldn't handle."

"Good for him."

"Yeah. Well, now you know everything there is to know about me and this screwed-up thing I call my life," Max lies.

It's a lie because he has not told Deb everything. Even though he loves her, and she has an uncanny ability to make him talk about himself and tell his deepest secrets when he'd much rather be pulling his teeth out with a pair of rusty pliers, he keeps part of his story from her, a part he will take to the grave without telling another soul.

THEN

Max sat in his car in a shadowy spot on the side of the street, watching the outside of a rundown tavern on the edge of town. He still wore the bloody clothes from beating Uncle Ed. He sat there for hours, watching people go in and out of the bar. The radio was off, leaving him alone with a freight train full of thoughts. One was that Joshua must have been a good person at some point in his life for his mom to have married him, making her a victim of time, place, and circumstance as much as Max was. She was just human and fell for the wrong guy. Or maybe she just wasn't as smart as he remembered her being. He adored his mother, but he knew people often built a mythology around the ones they loved and imagined them incapable of making the same poor choices they made themselves every day. As soon as he had that thought, he rejected it. Even in a meaningless intellectual discussion with himself in the parking lot of a bar, he wouldn't let anything stain her memory. And her memory *was* stained by the fact she had died suffering while her wife-beating, child-endangering, drunken husband went on with his life as if nothing had happened. This was unacceptable to Max, and like any good avenging angel, the time had come for him to do something about it.

Something biblical.

At closing time the front door banged open and a drunken man stumbled out onto the sidewalk. Max started the car and pulled up next to him. He rolled down the window and called out.

"Hey. You want a ride?"

Joshua leaned down and looked in the car with bleary eyes. "Who's that...?" he slurred.

"It's me. Max."

A hint of clarity came onto the drunk's face as he recognized his son. "Boy? What're you... doing 'ere...?"

"Taking you home. Get in."

Joshua stumbled but managed to fall into the front seat before passing out. Max leaned over the prostrate body and closed the door. He put the car in drive and took off into the night.

He drove deep into the country, taking an occasional glance at the man sleeping in the passenger seat. There was no anger left in him. He had spent all of his rage earlier on Uncle Ed. No, his calm demeanor came from channeling the assassin Sam had recognized and feared. Max looked at his father with no more feeling than a garbage man had for the bags of trash he took away to the dump. For that was how Max saw Joshua—garbage that needed to be disposed of.

Miles later he turned onto a narrow dirt trail that ended in a fallow field. He stopped the car and got out, then went around to get something out of the trunk.

Joshua woke up and climbed out of the passenger door. Using the car to support himself, he stumbled to the back and growled at his son. "Where the hell are we, boy?"

"At the end of the line," Max said, and he raised a shovel and bashed Joshua's head in with a cartoon *clang*.

As he watched the twitching body, Max's thoughts drifted. He thought about right and wrong, about good and evil. He realized even though they were opposite sides of a bloody coin, true judgment depended on your perspective. By all legal and most moral definitions he had just performed a heinous act that should send him to prison for life, or condemn him to death. But he knew in his heart he had done the right thing.

And if God and Satan were real after all, and happened to stop by this particular field on this particular night at this particular time and saw this particular act, he was sure they would both give him a cosmic high five before they wandered down to the closest bar and shared a pitcher of margaritas and talked about what strange creatures these humans were.

A cold wind snapped Max out of his reverie. It was late, and he had miles to go before he could sleep. So he started digging Joshua's grave. When he was done he buried the body deep, and along with it, the last remnants of his childhood.

NOW

Max looks at Deb from across the table and tries to put the memory away. It fights to stay out of the vault, to leap from his lips, but even in his wasted state, he manages to wrestle it into submission and lock it back where it belongs. With his past shut away again, he glances at the clock.

"Looks like we made it."

"What...?" Deb asks.

"Twelve thirty. No door. No cave. No game." Max feels equally sad and relieved.

Deb grabs his hand. "I told you everything would be all right."

He squeezes back, and they sit in drunken silence for a while. Then a sound from the living room filters into their consciousness, the low rumble of the television set. Both become aware of it at the same time, then realize they've been hearing it for quite a while but didn't notice. There is something wrong about the noise, and Max can't put his finger on it. But with the amount of alcohol in his bloodstream he has trouble putting his finger on the table, so he ignores it. Deb's digits, and her brain, are working a little better than his. She turns her head, trying to figure out what's wrong, and scowls.

"Max."

"Yeah?"

"Why is the television on?"

"I don't know. Nothing worth watching this late other than *Sammy Terry* reruns."

"That's not what I mean. Walter is in there."

"So...?" Max says, and a sick expression floods onto his face when he realizes what she means. "What the hell?"

He gets to his feet, motioning Deb to do the same.

Together they creep out of the kitchen, careful not to make any sound. They sneak across the hallway and pause outside the half-open living room door. The dim light from the television and a table lamp illuminates their drunken faces as they peek through the crack and take in the scene.

A fire has died to embers in the fireplace. *The Twilight Zone* flickers across the TV screen. They see it's not Walter watching the show—he's stone-cold passed out on the couch.

It's something else.

A pair of glowing red eyes glare from behind the furnace grating on the wall across from the fireplace.

Max and Deb stumble into the kitchen.

"It's watching TV? Oh, Jesus!" Deb says, trembling with rising panic.

"Fuck, fuck, fuckity fuck. I knew we shouldn't have skipped the game. When we didn't show up in the cave, it came looking for us."

"Okay, but how did it get into the living room?"

"You got me," Max says. "This never happened before."

"Great. Just great. What the hell are we going to do?"

"I don't fucking know, but we can't let it watch horror movies all night. It could pick up all kinds of scary ideas."

"So we just change the channel to Mr. Rogers?"

"Hell no. We've got to get it out of there."

"How are we going to do that? It's in the goddamn furnace vent."

"Maybe we can shut off the flue from the basement and trap it in the pipe."

"Then what? Call an exterminator?"

"We scare it into the open and kill it."

"What happens if it dies outside of the cave?"

"We're going to find out."

Deb shakes her head. "That's a terrible plan."

"Do you have a better one?"

"No."

"Fine then. Now go down to the basement and find the pipe. When I yell, you close the flue and bang like hell on it. That should scare it into the living room."

"Then what?" Deb asks. "Are you going to wrestle it?"

Max shakes his head. "I'm going to go upstairs and get some guns."

"Someone will call the cops if we shoot up the living room."

"Shit. Yeah. I'll get a knife or something."

"A knife? I don't want to go up against that thing with a fucking knife!"

"Then stay in the basement and let me kill it!"

Max's anger bites through her hysteria. She rubs her face with her hands and collects herself. "I'm sorry."

"Me too. Just give me a few minutes. I'll yell when I'm ready."

"All right. But be careful."

Max heads for the stairs, leaving Deb searching for a flashlight in the kitchen drawers.

Max staggers up the stairway, moving as fast as he can without making noise. At the top, he stumbles on the last step and grabs the banister to keep from falling. He runs down the hall to his room, throws the door open, and rushes inside. Leaping over the bed, his feet catch on a pillow and he tumbles to the floor. He uses the closet door handle to pull himself back up.

"Fucking tequila," he growls.

He slides into the closet, pulls the chain on the overhead light, and tosses boxes and clothes aside to uncover a huge black steamer trunk.

After misdialing the combination on the lock three times, he finally gets the numbers right and heaves the lid open. The trunk is filled with neat rows of weapons. Pistols, shotguns, and assault rifles are stored next to their respective clips and ammunition. An assortment of knives is bound to the lid, along with his trusty machete in a long sheath. A Louisville Slugger rests next to Max's bulletproof vest and a pair of hockey gloves.

He reaches for a shotgun, but stops. Deb is right. Shooting in the cave is one thing. Blasting up the front room is another. The noise is bound to bring unwanted attention. So he weighs the bat in one hand and the machete in the other, trying to make up his mind. He can't, so he shrugs and takes them both. For a day off from fighting, it's shaping up to be quite a night.

Deb flips on the basement light and creeps down the stairs. She crouches when she reaches the landing, shining the flashlight back under the step to see if any monsters are lurking below, but there is nothing but dust.

As she inches through the main room she sees the service door standing open on the belly of the furnace. She realizes the thing must have crawled through the flames to get into the pipes. But where did it come from? A yellow glow from the back room catches her eye. She looks in and sees the bookshelf has been pushed out, and the door is open behind it. The yellow glow spills into the room from the tunnel beyond; something obviously forced its way out from the cavern. Deb's guts knot up. They had never thought to lock the portal. And why would they? That wasn't how the game worked. But, she thinks, the rules have changed.

A noise sounds behind her. She whips around and shines the flashlight beam at the source. Fleabag sits on the bottom step, tail swishing, nonchalantly licking his paw.

"You scared the crap out of me," Deb hisses at the cat.

It shoots her a 'get that light out of my face' look and trots back up the stairs.

After the cat leaves she shines the light on the tangle of furnace pipes snaking under the ceiling, searching for the one leading to the living room.

Max sneaks into the living room by the television light. Walter snores on the couch, oblivious to the drama unfolding around him. The demonic eyes still watch the TV from the grating. An infomercial plays now, Max notes, with an excited host blathering about a high-tech rotating oven that cooks meat in half the time as a conventional stove. He smiles as he pictures the demon on a spit, skin crackling as it roasts, and vows to buy one of the stoves if he lives through the night.

He drops to all fours and slips behind the couch. When he's in a good position, he lays the baseball bat on the floor and slides the machete out of the sheath with a faint swishing sound. He peeks out from the other end of the couch and gets an oblong view of the furnace grating; the creature is still absorbed in the program.

Max rises to a crouch, waits for a sound spike from the commercial, and scurries for the wall. A floorboard *squeaks* as he passes. The demon glances in his direction, but seeing nothing in the shadowy room, it goes back to the television set.

Deb locates the furnace pipe and follows it back to a tangle of ducts above the furnace. A painted lever marks the flue control. She puts her hand on it and waits.

Max takes a deep breath, tightens his sweaty grip on the machete, and leans over the grate. He is inches away from the demon, the iron mesh the only thing separating them.

"Boo," he says.

The imp shrieks in surprise and scrambles back down the pipe toward the furnace.

"*Now! Shut it now!*" Max yells through the floor.

Deb hears the demon scuttling down the pipe toward her and the distorted echo of Max's yell. She pulls the lever—and her hand slips off; it's stuck. She struggles with the handle as the scrambling sounds get closer. She drops the flashlight, puts both hands on the knob, and pulls as hard as she can.

The pipe magically bulges as the monster approaches, looking like a ball being forced through a hose. Adrenaline surges through her blood and she pulls even harder. The flue slams shut just before the demon scrambles by.

A dull *thump* sounds inside the pipe as the creature smashes headfirst into the closed gate. The tube shakes. Dust falls in her eyes.

She coughs and beats on the metal duct with her hands. There is a startled screech from inside, the scrambling sound starts again, and the bulge zips back up the pipe toward the living room.

"It's coming your way!" she yells, and runs for the stairs.

Max uses his blade to pry the grate from the wall. The painted metal clatters to the floor. Walter groans at the sound, almost waking, but turns on his side instead and starts to snore.

The hole in the wall looms dark and dangerous. Max waits in front of it, weapon ready to strike. The scrambling sound gets closer, then a whirlwind of teeth and claws bursts out of the hole and lands in front of him. He slashes down—a total miss—and the machete cuts deep into the floor and sticks. He struggles to pull it free.

The two-foot-tall beast blasts across the room, running for the hallway. Deb steps through right as the creature leaps to escape. She yelps and jumps out of the way, slamming the door behind her. The demon bounces off the wood with another squeal and rockets back to the center of the room. It stops its frantic flight in the middle of the floor and its blazing eyes flash from the closed door to Max, to Deb, then to Walter. It hisses when it sees it is trapped in the living room with them. Then it cackles when it realizes they are trapped with *it*.

Deb spots the baseball bat on the floor and jumps for it.

Max frees his blade and spins around just as the imp scrambles toward him. He aims another cut as it rushes by but misses again, cutting a lamp in two with a spark and killing half the light in the room.

The monster slides under the coffee table with Deb in hot pursuit. She swings an overhead blow with the ball bat and smashes the table. The demon jumps from the wreckage, aiming straight at her face. She jerks back and dodges its slashing claws but falls sideways onto an end table. The table collapses and she hits her head on the floor. The bat slips from her limp hands.

The demon claws over the couch. Max slashes at it but misses, and the machete cuts deep into the cushion and stops a few inches above Walter's head. The imp scrambles away. Stuffing flies as Max yanks the blade free, vaults over the couch, and gives chase. He lands on the baseball bat and it rolls underneath his foot. He slips, drops the machete, and crashes to the floor. He lies on his back, stunned.

The demon stops running and takes stock of the situation. Max and Deb are down and out, and the living room is trashed. It smiles wickedly, huge teeth splitting its scaly red face, and stalks toward Max. A forked tongue licks swollen lips in anticipation.

Max groans as he comes around. He opens his eyes and sees the demon a few feet away, giggling as it creeps toward him. He grabs for the machete but can't reach it. The imp stalks between his legs. He churns his feet and tries to escape, but he slips on the floor and goes nowhere. The demon opens wide to deliver a terrible bite. Venomous saliva drips to the floor and hisses where it burns the wood. Max gets ready to die.

"S'cuse me," Walter says.

The beast whirls around and sees Walter standing behind it, baseball bat cocked back on his shoulder in a stance that would make the Babe proud. The drunk man swings and slugs the demon in the stomach and catapults it through the front window.

Glass sprays outward.

The demon bounces across the porch.

Dogs bark around the neighborhood.

A light comes on in the house next door.

Max gets to his feet and runs to the front door. He throws it open and scrambles outside. Walter and Deb quickly follow. A trail of greenish gore leads from off of the porch and into the bushes. Max vaults the railing, searching the undergrowth for the injured creature. He follows the gruesome trail to the wooden lattice covering the area under the porch to where the thing has ripped a hole through the slats. Deb shines her flashlight into the dark space and they see a smashed window; the demon has slipped back into the basement.

The three exchange frustrated glances.

"It's probably back in the cave by now," Max says.

"I'm not going to sleep tonight until I know for sure," Walter says.

Max crawls under the porch and stops at the foundation, shining his flashlight through the broken pane. The beam follows the trail of blood across the basement floor, to where it disappears behind the ancient door. He clicks off the light and creeps back into the open.

"You can take a nap now. It's gone."

"You should go shut it to make sure."

"And get a freaking lock while you're at it," Deb says.

As they head back for the porch they are blinded by the glare of another flashlight. Max squints into the beam and sees his elderly next door neighbor watching them. Mrs. Johnson has a Maglite in one hand and a broom in the other. A flower print nightgown complements the plastic curlers in her hair, and she jabs a broom in his direction.

"Who's in the bushes?"

Max smiles like a choirboy as he pushes into the yard. "Hi, Mrs. Johnson. It's just me, Max."

Deb and Walter step into view from behind him.

"Hi," Deb says, and waves.

Mrs. Johnson snaps her light off. "I should have figured it was you. What the hell are you doing out here at this time of night?"

"Um, we were just looking for my cat."

෴

Max pushes his plate back with a satisfied groan and smiles across the table to his hostess. "That was delicious, Cindy. Now I know how Sam stays so fat."

Cindy smiles back. "It helps that he doesn't exercise."

"Knock it off, you two," Sam says around a forkful of food.

"Or what?" Max asks.

"Or I tell everyone how old you were when you quit wetting the bed."

"He still does," Deb says. "So that's not much of a threat."

"Hey! We're bagging on Sam, not me."

"All's fair in love and war."

Max groans again when Cindy sets a slice of chocolate cake in front of him. "Are you trying to kill me?"

"Just fattening you up like Sam. You look like you've missed a few meals."

"Well, I do drink my lunch more often than I should. But when you work for a slave driver like him it's easy to get stressed out."

"All right, all right. I give up." Sam laughs and pushes his plate back as well. He turns to Deb. "I'm just glad you turned out to be real. With all the stories Max tells, it's hard to know when he's making things up."

"Like what?" Deb asks.

"For one thing, he told me you worked for a traveling circus, throwing knives or something stupid like that."

"I do."

"You do what?"

"Throw knives. And swing from a trapeze. In a circus."

Sam blushes, embarrassed. "Really."

Deb smiles, enjoying his pain.

"Told you, jackass," Max says.

"Well, don't I feel like a jerk."

"It's okay. It *is* a pretty weird job. And to be fair, I'm technically not with them anymore. I, um, took some time off and they moved on without me."

"That's too bad," Cindy says. "What are you going to do now?"

Deb grabs Max's hand. "For now, I'm enjoying being a gold digger and spending all the money he embezzles from the office. Beats the hell out of sleeping in a carnie trailer."

Everyone laughs but Sam. He gives Max a serious look. "We're back to the jokes now, right?"

"Absolutely," Max says. "Just like your career."

After dinner is over, Max and Sam do the dishes while Cindy does the thing people do when company comes over; she shows Deb around the house.

Sam smiles at the women talking in the living room. "She seems like a great girl, Max," he says while drying a plate.

"Yeah, she is. I'm lucky I found her."

"So, is it serious?"

Max considers his and Deb's unconventional relationship for a moment, then says, "I think so, yeah. I mean, we haven't known each other for very long, but it's going pretty damn well. Still, there's always the chance she'll leave again."

"Back to the circus?"

"Maybe. Or just take off. She spent her life traveling around, and I've spent mine rooted in one place. Who knows what might happen."

"You can travel too, you know. Take some time off, get the hell out of here. You've got the money."

"I wouldn't get far on what you pay me."

Sam shakes his head. "Cut the crap. Everyone knows you're rich. How much did your weird old uncle leave you, anyway?"

"Not much, other than a moldy old house with a leaky roof and a giant hole in the basement full of really mean rats."

"Sounds nice. I can see why you stay there."

"It's got character."

"Well, if you're *not* made of money, why the hell is a girl like Deb going out with you?"

"It's either my stunning good looks or my dazzling personality."

"Now I know you're rich," Sam says with an eye roll. Then he turns serious. "I don't know her very well, but from the way she's been staring at you tonight I get the feeling that woman would stand by your side even if you spent the rest of your life living in your basement with those rats."

"We'll see," Max says. And in his heart, he hopes his boss is right.

❧

The rest of the month passes in much the same fashion as the dinner at Sam's place did; totally normal. Walter spends his time in the library reading piles of books. Late one night, when everyone else is asleep, he watches an episode of *Magnum P.I.* And though he enjoys it far more than he would have imagined, he cries at the end. Max and Deb go on actual dates, to movies and dinners. They take walks in the park. Nothing attacks them, nothing tries to eat them, and nothing goes wrong. He even says a surprisingly small number of stupid things. So, for a few weeks, he is happy. He doesn't worry about the future, he doesn't care about the past. He just enjoys being alive and spending time with someone he loves.

But as the saying goes, all good things must come to an end. As the moon waxes fatter the pull of the game returns, creeping into his consciousness like a slow leak in the hull of a ship that the bilge pumps handle with ease at first, but slowly turns into a raging fountain of stress that floods the passageways of the S.S. Happiness and threatens to drag Captain Max to the bottom of a turbulent sea.

᠅

Max dials a combination on a shiny new padlock and clicks it open. The chain holding the bookcase to the wall falls away with a clatter, and he pushes the shelf out of the way to reveal the door.

"The vacation was fun while it lasted," he says. "Now we have to get back to work."

Max, Deb, and Walter walk down the narrow stairs onto the landing and are greeted with an unnerving surprise; the cave is already covered in blue mist.

"Never seen that before," Max says.

"What?" Deb asks.

"The mist. It never forms this early," Walter says. "It always waits for us to arrive."

"Ignore it. It's just another trick to throw us off."

Max heads for the steps. Deb and Walter follow. They stop at the top of the steps and wait for the roiling fog to fade. When it dissipates it reveals a warehouse loading dock. On the left is the edge of the dock, with an open white semi-trailer waiting to be filled. Idle forklifts sit in the wide lane in the middle, and past them is a maze of wooden pallets stacked high with cardboard boxes and wooden crates. Where the back wall of the cave would be, a two-story office looms over the cardboard labyrinth, dark windows looking for all the world like soulless eyes watching over the space. There are no demons in sight.

"Come on," Max yells to the empty arena. "Is this the best you can do? You could at least throw in some fire and brimstone or something."

"What is this place?" Deb asks.

"This is the warehouse I worked in after I quit playing ball."

"Do you remember anything that might help us win?"

"Just that I hated every freaking second."

Max walks down to the warehouse floor. He moves across the yellow stripes marking each trailer's loading lane, then stops by a forklift. Deb and Walter catch up and see him looking through the high metal racks and stacks of cardboard boxes to the second-story office windows in the distance.

"I've got a bad feeling about the office up there. Let's go check it out."

"Any particular reason?"

He shrugs. "My boss was a dick."

Max takes point and leads the way into the pallet maze, with Walter right behind him and Deb in the rear. They walk with agonizing slowness, sweat running down their faces as they pause at each corner and peek around to make sure the path is free of traps or demons. Max marks each turn with a piece of chalk. Like fighter pilots, they keep their heads on swivels, checking ahead and behind and up to the rim of the box canyon towering above for any sign of the enemy. They are ready to shoot anything that moves. But nothing does.

Ten minutes of creeping takes them halfway across the warehouse. The office structure looms closer. Max peeks around a corner and sees the path beyond is monster-free and runs for another fifty feet before ending in a T-intersection. He marks a box and turns the corner. Walter follows.

Deb trails behind. After a few feet, she hears a soft scraping sound behind her, coming from around the last corner they turned. She hesitates for a second, watching the guys moving forward. Then curiosity overrides common sense and she slips back to take a quick look.

Unaware she has stopped, Max and Walter walk on and turn left at the intersection.

Deb looks back around the stack of boxes and sees nothing but an empty pathway. Frustrated, she turns back the way she came—and her heart lurches when she sees the guys are gone.

"Shit," she whispers to herself and rushes to catch up. At the intersection, she glances left but the path is empty. When she looks to the right, she sees their backs as they walk away from her.

"Hey guys, wait up," she whispers, and in her haste to catch up she misses the chalk mark and goes in the wrong direction.

Max checks behind and sees Deb is gone. "Dammit."

Walter turns and sees the empty path. "She was with us a few seconds ago. Where did she go?

"I don't know. But we had better find her before they do."

Max and Walter run back the way they came.

Deb breathes a sigh of relief as she catches up to Max and Walter and falls in line behind them. They don't turn around, and she figures they didn't even know she was gone. Even though she is new to the game, she should know you can't take anything for granted in a magic cavern designed to shatter your mind and rip your body to shreds and suck your soul down screaming through all nine circles of hell.

Never assume, Deb.

The figures in front of her are very aware of her actions, but the problem is, they are not Max and Walter. From her vantage point behind them, they seem identical to her companions, but if she could see them from the front she would see they are red-eyed, slavering demons dressed to mimic her teammates. Their scaly red faces and thick necks bulge from the collars of their work shirts, and their clawed-tipped hands clutch sticks instead of guns. But like the chalk mark, she doesn't see this. So she tramps along behind them, unaware.

Max and Walter throw caution to the wind as they backtrack through the warren of boxes. They skid around a corner and stumble on a nightmare scene: Deb lies face down on the floor with a demon hunched over her, the creature's long fingers choking her from behind. Rage flares in Max's brain. Without breaking stride, he channels his inner Dick Butkus and tackles the monster at full speed, slamming it off her. He tumbles to the concrete floor in one direction, and the beast flies the other way. It rolls to the floor in a tangle of limbs and comes up running.

"Shoot it!" he screams at Walter.

Walter opens up with his Uzi, spraying a line of fire inches behind the fleeing demon. The bullets rip dozens of boxes to shreds but miss the target.

He runs out of bullets and the creature scuttles around the corner.

As the gun smoke clears, both men rush over to help her. She lies face down, gasping for air. Max grabs her shoulder.

"Deb! Are you all right?"

She twists her head around and glares at him with glowing red eyes. "I'm just fine," the doppelganger croaks from a throat that has never spoken human words before.

Max is too startled to move as he stares at Deb's twisted twin. The thing's hair and clothes are identical to hers, but the bestial, horned-tipped face and jutting fangs are pure demon. As Demon Deb flips over she drives an elbow into his groin. With a pained grunt he staggers back, crashes into a pile of boxes, and rolls around in agony.

Demon Deb growls and leaps for Walter's throat. He pulls his Uzi in front of his neck and her snarling jaws slam shut around it. The gun bends under the pressure. Walter is pushed back by the force of the attack; the demon claws at him, ripping his clothes and skin but it can't quite reach far enough for a killing blow. He screams, twisting the gun to the side like a strange bit in the mouth of an even stranger horse, leading the creature's head around with it. Her muscles bulge, but there's no way he can break the thick neck. It is a stalemate as they stumble around the warehouse floor, Demon Deb pushing and slashing, Walter backing and dodging.

"Help me, Max!" Walter cries.

Max groans and struggles to breathe, still pale and helpless from the perfect shot to the family jewels.

Deb hears gunshots echoing from somewhere in the maze. She pauses, craning her neck to listen, but the two figures ahead of her keep walking.

"Guys, wait. Did you hear that?"

The two demons stop, but don't turn around or answer. A cold feeling creeps into her gut.

"Guys?"

She sees something move in the back of Walter's pants. The fabric bulges, there is a ripping sound, and a bright red tail tears through the cloth and swishes back and forth.

"Shit."

She tries to aim her shotgun, but Demon Walter is quicker; he spins and leaps at her in the same motion, leading with wicked claws. Deb ducks and the claws whiff over her head and shred the box where her face was an instant before. A rain of packing peanuts floats to the floor.

She ducks under the blow and comes to her feet in front of another stack of boxes. She brings her shotgun for a blast, but Demon Max is already in motion. He rushes at her head-first with long horns sticking out to gut her like a raging bull.

Ka-blam!

Deb gets off an errant shot as she leaps to the side. Buckshot rips a deep furrow down Demon Max's back before he crashes into the boxes and buries his horns deep in a crate of toys. He groans and tries to pull free, but is stuck.

She rolls to her feet, once again in range of Demon Walter's claws. He rips at her face, but she twists away, and the talons tear a bloody swath across her shoulder instead.

Deb grunts in pain as blood spurts. She ignores the wound and strikes back, smashing the shotgun butt across the demon's jaw. It falls backward, off balance. She racks the slide and aims at his back and pulls the trigger—and nothing happens. A shell is jammed in the gun's chamber.

Demon Max manages to pull his head out of the crate. A Hello Kitty doll is impaled on his horns and blocks his vision, but there is nothing funny about the image to Deb. Not because she has no idea what Hello Kitty is, but because the creature's mouth spits out a howl of such indescribable rage she can't help but panic.

She takes stock in an instant. Her gun is jammed, her shoulder is shredded, and she is facing two enraged monsters that are faster and tougher than she could ever imagine. So she lets discretion prove the greater part of valor and gets the fuck out of there.

Demon Walter crawls to his feet and helps pull the doll from his partner's horns. With his vision clear, Demon Max sees Deb is gone. He looks at his fiendish partner and whines. Their toy is gone and he still wants to play.

Deb holds her shotgun close to her chest as she backs into a shadowy cul-de-sac. She tries to clear the gun, but her hands are slick with sweat and blood and she can't free the shell. She hears a noise and peers out to the corridor. Two misshapen shadows fall on the boxes across the way, growing larger as they near her position. The demons are on her trail. She is trapped. Fighting down panic, she looks for a place to run, but she is surrounded by a canyon of crates. Then she glances toward the ceiling and sees salvation. Slinging the shotgun over her good shoulder, she starts to climb.

She reaches the top of the wall of boxes just as the two creatures round the corner and see her high above. They screech and give chase. Deb runs along the top of the box maze, staying just ahead of the pursuers below. She keeps one eye on the path as she runs. Here and there the piles of crates dip lower, and as she hurries over those sections the demons leap up and rip at her legs. Time and time again she jumps over them but a growing thicket of scratches leaks blood into her boots.

"Come back and play!" Demon Max cackles.

Deb sees a stack of boxes ahead. She slams into them with her good shoulder. The crates teeter, then avalanche down on top of the monsters. With the road blocked, she sprints ahead and loses them. She runs another hundred feet, then slows down and looks on either side of the ridge of boxes; there is nothing but an empty floor and deep shadows. She catches her breath, dries her hands on her pants, and works on the jammed shell. She works it free and cocks the slide to slam a new round home. She searches for a target. There is nothing in sight, but then she hears the sound of a battle from a few lanes over. Pissed, she heads in the direction of the fight.

"Payback time..."

Venom from Demon Deb's fangs sizzles down the length of Walter's Uzi, etching the dented metal. He pushes back with all his might but can't get the monster away from him. She drives him backward, and he knows it is only a matter of time before he trips on something or gets backed into a wall and then he will be watching TV with Tommy in hell.

Like all things inevitable, the inevitable happens; the raging beast pushes him back over Max, and Walter tumbles to the floor and loses his grip on the gun.

Demon Deb spits out the ruined weapon and jumps forward for the killing blow. As her claws slash down, she sees a flash of metal and realizes in some dim part of her bestial brain that maybe she shouldn't have ignored Max.

Rising machete meets falling arm and Demon Deb's gnarled hand leaps away from her wrist in a fountain of green blood. She roars in pain, then lunges at her attacker with snapping jaws. Max dives to the side and takes another swipe with the blade but only whacks off one of her horns.

Howling, Demon Deb scrambles for a gap in the boxes just as Max finally gets his pistol out of its holster. He aims at a trail of green gore but the monster has escaped.

"Dammit!" he yells.

With his free hand still covering his crotch, he limps over and helps Walter to his feet. "Are you all right?" Max asks in a voice an octave higher than usual.

He sees Walter is a mess; the front of his clothes and armor are shredded, and dozens of oozing scratches cover his arms and body. But as Max calculates his friend's damage through the dull nausea still wracking his body, he concludes he would trade injuries with him any day.

"I think so," Walter says. "How did they do that?"

"I don't know. And I don't like it. I never saw anything like it before—"

A sound from above and behind cuts Max off. He spins and points his .45 at the source.

As Deb works her way along the top of the wall, the sounds of the fight grow louder. She hears a demon screech in pain, then the scraping of clawed feet as something runs away. Leading with her shaking gun barrel, she moves toward the edge of the boxes and points her shotgun down at what seems to be Max and Walter.

"Drop the gun!" she barks.

"You drop yours," the thing that looks like Max replies.

Deb hears something off about his voice, his skin is pasty white instead of just being pale, and he is hunched over like Quasimodo having a bad day in the belfry. She has learned her lesson and doesn't assume this is Max.

"Fuck you! Drop the goddamn gun or I'll cut you in two."

"Deb, knock it off. There's no reason to shoot us."

"I can think of one," she says and jerks her chin toward her bloody shoulder.

"All right. All right. I'll put it down."

As he starts to lay his pistol on the floor, the thing that looks like Walter stops him.

"What if that's not her?"

Max tightens his finger on the trigger and studies the woman on the box wall. "How do I know you're really Deb?"

"How do I know you're really Max?"

"You don't."

"That's right, I don't! So put the fucking gun down now!"

"I'm not putting it down."

"I'll shoot you, goddamn it!"

"Then shoot me!"

Sweat drips into Deb's eyes as she considers the proposition. If he is a demon, one shot will win the game and save a soul. If not, she might kill her teammate and lose. But there is no way to be sure if this Max is real, and she is too shaken up to decide.

"There has to be a way to figure this out," he says. His pistol barrel trembles. He can't keep it aimed forever.

Deb can't keep her shotgun on target much longer either. "What do you have in mind?"

"Look. I don't know what you saw, but the ones that attacked us weren't perfect. They were just crude replicas. And you seem like the real Deb to me."

"The two chasing me weren't perfect either," she says. "But you might just be a better version."

"Same for you."

"Fuck." She lets the gun barrel slip a little. It does look like Max, and the longer he talks, the more normal his voice sounds. And his cheeks are turning back to their usual shade of pale.

"All right. Let me see your hand."

He raises his left hand and shows it off. "And...?"

"No claws," Deb says. "That's good. Now open your mouth."

"Why?" he asks.

Her finger tightens on the trigger. "Because I said so."

Max shrugs and opens his mouth wide. Deb examines his human-looking teeth.

"Ahhhh."

"You need braces. But at least you don't have fangs."

"Your turn."

She shows her teeth. Human teeth. "What do you think?"

"You've got some nice choppers for a 70-year-old," Max says with a grin.

They break into nervous laughter and lower their guns. Deb climbs down from her perch atop the boxes and stands in front of Max. They each wait for the other to morph into a demon and tear the other apart, but nothing happens.

"I guess you're you," Deb says.

"Sometimes I wonder."

They hug each other, and wince at their various wounds.

"Are you all right?" Deb asks.

Max shakes his head. "Let's just say if we win tonight, the celebration will be pretty boring."

The door to the office creaks open, pushed by an AK-47 barrel. Max follows his weapon into the room with Deb and Walter right behind. They do a quick search of the room and find nothing but dusty furniture and paperwork.

Max shakes his head. "I could have sworn there'd be something up here. Doesn't make sense."

"It makes perfect sense. It's like the magician we had at the circus. Everything was about misdirection, making you look one way while the trick happened right in front of you."

"Okay, then what did we miss?"

Walter points out the window with the barrel of his backup 9mm pistol, over the warehouse spread before them to the gaping white semi-trailer backed up at the dock by the steps.

"That."

The three walk out of the maze of pallets and step onto the open loading dock. Max leans against a low pile of boxes and wipes the sweat from his face. He nods to the trailer across the way.

"Let's take five. If they're in there, we have them trapped."

They share swigs from a canteen. As they rest, Deb looks around the vast room.

"This place looks huge. Is the cavern really this big?"

"No. It's about half this size. The arena ends on the other side of the dock."

"Are you sure about that? Have you ever tried to go past the edge?"

"No," Walter says. "We never—"

"I did," Max says, cutting him off. "Before your time, Walter. When I was younger and stupider."

"And...?" Deb asks.

"We were out in the desert, or at least that's what it looked like. At an old gas station on Route 666."

"Don't you mean sixty-six?"

"No," Max says. A dark expression passes over his face as he thinks back. "We couldn't find the demons, so I thought I'd walk down the road past the edge of the wall and see if they were hiding somewhere."

"What was out there?" Deb asks.

"Nothing. Everything. Monsters and angels, or things that looked like angels anyway. There was light, dark, color, gray. Life, death, love, and hate. Screams so loud they almost drove me insane. And silence so hard and deep my heartbeat sounded louder than a rock concert. Then Troy grabbed me—he was a Marine like Tommy—and he was smart enough to tie a rope around himself before he followed me in. The others pulled us out. It felt like I was in there for a year, but they said it was about ten seconds.

"Holy shit."

"Yeah. So if you want to take a trip down the highway to hell, be my guest. I'm going for coffee somewhere."

"No thanks."

Max stands up and checks his AK. "All right, let's do this. Time to stop messing around and—"

The roar of a motor hits their ears and a forklift blasts out of the maze. They have a quick view of the demon driver, a fanged creature dressed in a work shirt, blue jeans, and with a baseball cap pulled down between its horns. The metal forks are raised and aimed right at Max.

"Look out!" Walter yells.

He tackles Max before the lift truck can run him over, but not before a jutting fork rips into his right thigh. The two men tumble to the ground on one side, and Deb dives in the other direction.

The driver lays rubber and motors away from them, heading across the dock. Deb blasts away at the back of the machine. Bullets ricochet off of the safety cage. The driver ducks, and against all odds, every shot misses. The forklift roars into the open mouth of the trailer and vanishes in the darkness.

Max rolls around on the floor, holding his leg to stop the bleeding. "Great," he moans through gritted teeth. "Now they can drive."

"Keep the pressure on," Deb says as she pulls a thick bandage out of her pack. Walter keeps watch as she wraps Max's leg. Blood seeps through the white cloth.

"How bad is it?" Max asks, afraid to look down.

"You'll live," she says, and rolls another layer around and ties off the dressing. "But your leg is really messed up."

"Just like Willis Reed," he says. Then he stands up, grits his teeth against the pain shooting from his leg, and limps back into the game.

As they approach the trailer they see the side wall is painted with cartoon demons wearing trucker hats. They stop near the open rear doors, guns pointed at the dark mouth.

"Could this be another diversion?" Walter asks with a nervous glance over his shoulder.

"No," Max says. "It's still in there. And it looks like we have to go in after it."

Max's leg buckles as he starts toward the trailer, and he stumbles. Walter grabs his shoulder and props him up.

"I'll do it, Max."

"Walter, no."

"You're both hurt worse than me," Walter says. "And besides. I'm expendable."

Max sees a glimmer of fear in the man's eyes, the same terror that has dogged him since the day he was rescued. But now there is a glint of steel in his gaze as well.

"Okay," General Max says to the soldier who has become a friend, a friend he now agrees to send to certain death. "Just be careful."

"I will indeed."

Deb hands over her shotgun. "A little more firepower just in case."

Walter takes the weapon in trade for his 9mm and turns to the trailer. With the others covering him, he steps forward and flips on a yellow work light at the edge of the dock. The lamp casts a harsh glow down the forty-eight-foot container and reveals the forklift jammed into the wall on one side, and three large wooden crates in a line beyond it.

"If anything goes wrong, hit the floor," Deb says. "We'll waste it."

Walter walks into the trailer. He casts a long shadow as he creeps along, each step on the hard wooden floor echoing back onto the dock. Moving around the forklift, he reaches the first crate and pokes the shotgun barrel under the lid. He flips it open, steps back, and aims the gun at the opening. Nothing jumps out. He leans forward and peers inside.

Empty.

The second crate's lid is gone, showing another vacant interior.

Walter trembles as he approaches the last box, the only hiding place left. He kicks it, but there is no response. He puts the shotgun barrel under the cover and prepares to lift it, then looks back past the glaring light to Max and Deb.

"Aim high," he says, and flips the lid. He jumps back, ready to shoot, but there is no target. Walter shrugs. "Strike three."

Max and Deb exhale together.

"Shit," she says. "Where the hell did it go?"

Max rubs his forehead in frustration. "It's got to be in there."

Walter backs away from the crates, then turns to his companions. Relief and hope flood his face. "I'm starting to think they're afraid of me."

"They should be," Max says, then a tearing sound makes him glance up.

Jagged fangs sprout from the top and bottom of the trailer's mouth, ripping through the metal. The running lights on either side change into eyes shining with a hellish red glare. The floorboards wriggle and twist and turn into a giant forked tongue. The container has morphed into a giant demon, and Walter stands in its mouth. Max gets one last look at his horrified face before the monstrous jaws slam shut and the unearthly thing begins to chew.

Horrified, Max and Deb stumble back across the dock.

"Walter..." Max moans.

Then a sound comes from inside the creature—a muffled *bang*—and they are filled with wild hope. A shotgun blast punches out through the scaly skin. Gore spatters the dock. Another shot rings out, then another, and gooey green holes tear through the trailer demon's torso as Walter blows the monster apart from deep in its gut.

The demon's mouth opens and emits a bellowing roar followed by a deluge of dark green bile. Walter rides the wave, spitting and choking as he splashes down on the warehouse floor. Behind him, the dying monstrosity collapses into a pile of scaly skin that bloats and quivers in the unnatural light.

The transformation has begun.

Max and Deb rush forward and grab Walter. All three slip and slide in the gore, laughing and hugging each other.

"We thought you were dead!" Max says.

Walter coughs a mouthful of gunk onto the concrete and grins at his companions. "I think I am."

A wisp of blue fog floats by. They look back at the monstrous corpse and see the creature has been magically replaced by a young woman lying on the floor.

Walter squints through the mist. "I wonder who we saved—" His face freezes as he recognizes her.

"Elizabeth…"

He crawls over and reaches out to touch her face, but stops short, afraid she might be a dream. She stirs, drifting into consciousness. Her eyelids flutter, then open, and her eyes focus on the man kneeling over her.

"Walter…?"

He groans and grabs her in his arms, crushing her in a fierce embrace. "Oh, Elizabeth. I love you so much."

"I love you… too…" Her voice drifts off and she falls back asleep.

Deb puts her head on Max's shoulder and cries. He spills a bucket of tears himself. Then the blue mist thickens and the loading dock fades away.

කෘ

"So, tell me how this happened again?" a gray-haired Doctor Rivera asks as he stitches the cut on Max's leg. The doctor wears silk pajamas and seems more than a little annoyed to be binding wounds in his kitchen at four in the morning. Deb sits beside them, her shoulder already dressed in a large bandage. A pile of bloody cloths and an array of medical equipment are spread out on the table under the overhead lamp.

"We were out camping, and somehow a bobcat snuck into the tent. We woke up and it freaked out on us. Damndest thing I ever saw."

The doctor pulls the next stitch harder than needed, and Max winces.

"The last time this happened, you said it was a mountain lion. And we don't have any mountains around here." Rivera gives Deb an accusing look through his thick glasses. "Or lions."

She shrugs. "Damndest thing."

The doctor ties off the last stitch and lays his tools down. He wraps a clean bandage around the wound, leans back in his chair, and gives the banged-up couple a hard look.

"I take it you don't want me to call animal control?"

"Gosh, no," Max says, the picture of innocence. "I mean, it wasn't the cat's fault. We shouldn't have left the tent open like that."

"Right. And why didn't you go to the Emergency Room?"

"You know me, Doc. I hate paperwork. And besides," Max says, tossing a fat green roll of hundred-dollar bills onto the table, "why should County General get my money when a hard-working doctor like you needs a new car?"

The doctor counts the money in his head but doesn't touch it. Yet. "One more time, for the record. Is there anything illegal about all this?"

"On my mother's grave, no."

Rivera nods and the money disappears into his pocket. "I've been meaning to check out a new Lexus anyway. I'll call some prescriptions in to the pharmacy, and make sure you keep the wounds clean and dry for a couple of weeks. I'd tell you to come back so I can remove the stitches, but I have a feeling you'll get an alligator to chew them out for you or something."

"Thanks, Doc," Max says as he and Deb limp to the door.

"No problem. And do me a favor? Ditch the tent and buy a camper."

⌒

Elizabeth sleeps on the living room couch. Walter has pulled his chair close and sits by her. Fleabag naps on his lap. He pets the cat, but all his attention is on his fiancée. He brushes a stray hair from her face and touches her cheek with the back of his hand. Tears have reddened his eyes, but unlike the rivers of rage and frustration he has spilled many times before in this room, these are tears of hope.

"I love you," he whispers, then kisses her forehead.

Fleabag purrs.

∽

Max and Deb sleep curled in each other's arms. Deep, relaxed, nightmare-free sleep. Max rolls over and the morning sunlight hits his face. He yawns and squints at the alarm clock. It's 9:30 a.m.

"Oh, crap."

Max limps into the office over an hour late. He is a total mess. His hair is uncombed, his shirt half-buttoned, and his face is bruised and scratched. Coworkers give him a wide berth as they edge past. Shane the bagel guy takes a quick look and wheels his cart in the other direction.

Max ignores them all as he hurries to his desk. When he arrives, he sees his boss sitting in his chair, drinking coffee. But this is not jovial, self-deprecating Sam. This is pissed-off boss Sam.

Max cringes. "Um, good morning."

"Same to you. No one was using your desk, so I thought I'd try it out."

"Sorry I'm late."

"Must have been quite a party."

Max tries to straighten his rumpled clothes. And fails. "Uh, yeah. Late night last night. I forgot to set the alarm."

"Take a few minutes to clean yourself up, then come see me in my office."

"Sure."

Sam gets up and walks away. Max sees a few co-workers looking at him. Staring is more like it. Judgmental staring. He realizes he may get the vacation everyone keeps telling him to take. And he may not come back from it.

In the bathroom, he washes his face in the bathroom sink. As he dries himself off, Max studies himself in the mirror. Messy doesn't quite cut it. But there's a light in his eyes that hasn't shined for a long time. A good light. The game is far from over, but he feels like it has turned a corner. He heads for Sam's office with a bent spring in his step.

Sam glances up from a report when a knock sounds on the door.

"Come in."

Max shuffles in and stands in front of the desk. Sam looks him up and down, then waves him toward a chair.

"Have a seat. Looks like you need it."

"Thanks." Max eases into the chair. He waits for Sam to say something, but the man doesn't speak. He just stares. After an uncomfortable moment, Max blushes under the strain and starts talking.

"Look, I'm sorry for being late."

"I believed you the first hundred times."

"You're right. I don't know what to say."

"You better think of something, because we need to talk."

"What are we doing now?"

"I don't know about you, but I'm watching somebody piss their life away."

"Oh. You mean *talk*."

"Forgive me for being blunt. I just don't know quite how to say this, but what is it? Heroin? Coke? Meth?"

This is the last thing Max expected Sam to say. "You think I'm a drug addict?"

"What am I supposed to think? You come in late half the time, and you fall asleep at your desk the other half."

"Sam—"

"Let me finish. Your work is piling up and you've made more mistakes in the last two months than you did in the last two years combined. Simple lunch talks turn into conversations about life and death. The police come by and ask questions about you because your neighbors say you stay up all night with strange people and play with guns and smash up your house. After dinner the other night I thought you had it all figured out and had gotten your life together. But now you come in looking like the wrong end of a train wreck. So, you tell me, Max. What the hell should I think?"

"It's not drugs. That's all I can tell you."

Sam rises out of his chair, face flushing with anger. "That's all you can tell *me*? I've been there for you every single day since you were twelve years old. I was with you when your mom got hurt. I got you a job to buy her medicine. I paid your rent when you didn't make enough at work. I gave you the car you drove her to rehab in. And I picked up the phone at three in the morning every goddamn night for years when you called and didn't have the guts to say anything. But I answered every time, just so you'd know someone who cared was on the other end of the line. Yeah, I knew it was you. And after all that, you can't tell me what's going on?!"

"Sam, please..."

"No. I've got a lot to say and I'm going to say it. I know this is tough on you. You always were an independent little bastard. Nothing got to you. It like to killed me when you quit basketball and went to work to take care of your mom. You could have gone to college and been a star, but you just smiled and let it go because she needed you."

"I was too short anyway."

"That's what I mean right there!" Sam explodes. "Just once I wish you'd admit something hurts instead of making a joke and swallowing it."

The vault in Max's gut bursts open and raw emotions spill out—and this time he doesn't try to shove them back in. "All right, it hurts! I admit it! I could have gotten out of this stupid town and done something with my life instead of watching my mom die a little more every day. It hurt like hell to give up my life for her, but I did it anyway. And do you know why? Because I loved her, and she would have done the same thing for me. And I'd do it all again in a heartbeat. I'd put *myself* in that fucking wheelchair if it meant I could see her walk through the park and laugh one more time. So there, I said it. Are you happy? What do you want me to do now?"

Sam leans back, stunned by Max's admission. But now that the door is open, he's not about to close it. "I just want you to tell me what's going on. Hell, I wish I had half your balls. But you can't be that tough forever. Sometimes you have to hold out your hand and ask for help. Whatever is going on with you, let me help."

Max slumps in his seat, face clouded with anger and shame as a flood of painful thoughts flash through his head. He knows Sam is right about everything. He always was. He wonders for the thousandth time why life screwed him out of a dad like him. Then a lightning bolt crashes into his brain and lights up the fact he has been staring at for decades but somehow never noticed.

Sam has done everything for him for years and never asked for anything in return. Whatever God or devil dropped Joshua and Uncle Ed in his lap also gave him Sam to balance the scales. Max's anger fades, and for the first time he understands; for everything that counts, for everything that matters, Sam is his father. He has been since the day they met. He just never got the credit.

Sam sees comprehension creep onto Max's face. "Are you okay?" he asks.

"Yes. I am. Thanks to you."

"What?"

"You're right. You've always been there for me. And I've treated you like shit in return. But it stops now. You deserve an explanation."

Sam sits back in his chair. "I'm listening."

"You're not going to believe this."

"Try me."

"Okay, but I warned you," Max says. "Remember how you said once there was no real good or evil, just faith there were forces out there we couldn't understand?"

"Yeah, I said something like that. What's the point?"

"The point is, you were wrong. There is evil. Real walking-down-the-street-in-a-dinner-jacket-and-tails evil. I was related to him. Uncle Ed."

Sam's face crinkles in disgust. "I never liked that guy. I only met him a few times, but he always seemed kind of creepy."

"Creepy doesn't begin to describe him. He was into black magic and demon worship."

"No shock there."

"No, you don't get it. He was *really* into it. The demons are as real as you and me, and a lot more dangerous. And Ed was the most dangerous thing of all. He used his spell book to create a magic cave under the house, and every full moon I go down there and hunt people he kidnapped and turned into monsters. When I kill them, they turn back into people, and I use them as soldiers to help me hunt again on the next full moon."

Sam's mouth hangs open.

Max smiles at his boss' expression. "Told you that you wouldn't believe me."

"Jesus. I know a guy who runs a rehab clinic. He could—"

"He could piss-test me until he's blue in the face and he wouldn't find anything stronger than Nyquil and tequila."

Sam shuffles papers on his desk. "You're serious."

"Dead serious."

"For the sake of argument, let's say this is all true, and you're not having a psychotic break or an acid flashback or something."

"I'm not, but go on."

"Do you have any proof?"

"You met her."

"Deb...?"

"She's over seventy years old. Ed kidnapped her almost forty years ago and turned her into a giant snake thing. I saved her two months ago and pulled her out of the cave. She didn't age the whole time she was down in the hole in my basement. She'll tell you the same story if you want to call her. And that guy Walter I've been hanging out with? He was taken in 1946. You can Google him and have him over for dinner, so he can fill you in on what he's been doing for the last eighty years. There are dozens more Ed wrote about in his diary."

"I thought he was just a dirty old man or something."

"He was that too," Max says.

The comment hangs in the air.

"Jesus," Sam says.

"Jesus wasn't around. I know. I called for him a lot and he never showed up."

Anger thickens Sam's voice. "Did your parents know about this?"

"Mom never really liked Ed, but there was no way she could have known what he was up to. He was a world-class con artist on top of being a sorcerer."

"And your dad?"

"You know," Max shrugs. "He mowed the grass, fixed the gutters, watched the house while Ed was gone, and every month brought him... things."

"Like people."

"Mostly."

"How could this go on without anyone noticing?"

"Every town has a haunted house and strange old man everyone talks about but never checks on. And people disappear all the time—thousands of them, all over the country. Ed just hid it all in plain sight."

A clock on the desk ticks away as Sam absorbs Max's horrific tale. He gets control of his churning thoughts and speaks. "You know, if this was anyone but you, I'd have you in a straitjacket by now."

"As long as I don't have to wear a tie."

Sam takes a deep breath, then blows it out. "I don't know what to say."

"I'd appreciate it if you didn't say anything. I don't want anyone wandering into my house and getting killed by one of Ed's pet monsters."

"Including me."

"Especially you."

"Is it that dangerous?"

Max considers lying, because he knows Sam's reaction will be to protect him, and that might end with a brave but foolhardy attempt to go into the cave. Which is the exact kind of thing *he* does every month, of course. But by his own admission he's the hero of the story, and that's what heroes do. He sees it as his burden and no one else's. So with the time for lies long gone, he tells the truth.

"Yes. It is dangerous. More than you can imagine. So please, promise me you'll stay away."

Sam hesitates, then nods. "I promise."

The two men stare at each other for a long time, Sam searching for even a hint of insanity, and Max just baring his soul to the man who raised him. After a minute, Max clears his throat and speaks again.

"So that's why strange people are always staying with me. And why I come to work late, beat to crap, and fall asleep all the time. And for the record, I *am* rich. Ed left me over eight million dollars."

"Eight million...?"

"That was *before* I bought the Apple stock. But don't worry. You're in my will. And you might get to retire sooner than you think."

"I don't want your money. Well, I do, but not like that."

"I know."

"So if you're rich, why the hell do you come to work?"

"I need the routine, you know? Even if it's just for eight hours a day. If I didn't have you and this stupid job, I would have fallen apart a long time ago."

"I can see that. But you could at least get a new car."

"I like the old one. It reminds me of the man who gave it to me."

Tears well up in Sam's eyes.

"Any more questions?" Max asks.

"You want some time off to get your head screwed on straight?"

"It's about as straight as it's ever going to get."

"Are you sure you're going to be all right? Really sure?"

"Someday. I'm still working through it. And Deb is helping a lot."

"She's good for you. I can tell. Hang on to her."

"As long as I can."

They stand up. There is an awkward moment where they almost hug, but it passes and Sam claps him on the shoulder instead.

"If you need anything..."

"Thanks. For everything. And sorry for waking you up all those nights."

"I'm still there if you need me."

"I know," Max says, and limps out the door.

୧୬

After work, Max drives aimlessly through his normal town, gazing through the Impala's cracked windshield at normal people going about their normal lives. He sees two little kids help their parents unload boxes from the back of their minivan. He sees a teenage couple sitting on a bench outside of an ice cream store sharing a frozen dessert. He sees a prostitute on a corner waiting to give her next customer a different kind of treat. He sees a police car cruising in the other direction with the cop inside scanning the streets for trouble. He sees a homeless woman push her overloaded grocery cart down the street with a mangy dog trotting at her heels. He sees people waiting at the bus stop with their heads lowered to their phones. He sees the bus pull up and the weary driver open the door to let the human tide embark. He sees an attractive blonde woman jogging down the sidewalk and wishes her a beautiful life as she turns a corner and disappears. He sees them all, but no one sees him. He is a specter cruising the roads, a ghost floating through their lives just as he floats through his own. A ghost in a rusty old car. And for once, a ghost who has told the truth and found absolution in the telling. A ghost who, if just for a little while, feels normal too.

But old habits die hard, even for the temporarily normal. So he pulls the car to a stop in the grocery store parking lot and walks inside the building. He grabs a sack of Meow Mix without checking the label and takes it to the checkout stand. The girl behind the register notes his disheveled state and gives him a funny look. He smiles at her.

"Hey, Amber. What's up?"

"Hey, Max. Did you get in a car wreck or something?"

"No, I fell off a ladder trying to paint the ceiling. They're really high in my house."

"I can imagine. That place is gigantic."

"Yeah, it is."

"So, just the cat food again?"

"Yeah."

"Can I ask you a question?" she says as she rings up the purchase.

He realizes her funny look hasn't gone away. And it's more serious than funny. He hands over a twenty and waits for the change. "Shoot."

"I was just wondering how many cats you have."

"Just one, why?"

"You buy an awful lot of cat food."

"He, uh, eats a lot. And I feed some strays."

"I guess that explains it then," she says, and hands him the change.

"I guess it does. See you later."

❧

Max walks through the front door and hears laughter. He follows the sound to the kitchen and sees a heartwarming scene. Deb takes pieces of pizza from a stack of boxes and arranges them on plates, while Walter sets the silverware, and when he is done, returns to doting on the woman sitting at the table.

Elizabeth.

Fleabag flops before her, batting at a piece of string she dangles for him. She laughs as he plays, and the sound is light and clear and innocent. In that instant Max understands the depths of Walter's despair over losing her as profoundly as he understands the pure joy lighting the man's face now.

An unfamiliar feeling floods through Max as he watches the domestic scene; total happiness. It is a strange sensation, and he feels his body and mind trying to reject it. He is an old hand at battling his emotions, so he quickly negotiates a truce and the sentiment retreats to an acceptable level of general contentment.

Deb sees him watching them. She smiles and the feeling blossoms in him again. He surrenders and lets himself enjoy it.

"You're late," she says.

"I took a drive. And got some cat food," he says, and sets the bag of food on the counter. He smiles at Elizabeth. "Hi."

"Hello. You must be Max," she says, extending her hand. "I'm Elizabeth."

"Very pleased to meet you, Elizabeth," He says, taking her hand and sitting next to her.

"I've only been awake for a few hours, but Walter has told me a lot about you."

"The good stuff, I hope."

"Of course," she says with a smile that crinkles her eyes in a way that melts his heart, the ice in her glass, and a few cubes in the freezer. "I still don't understand what happened, but Walter assures me that I will in time, and for now I'm safe from those... things. And we have you to thank."

"Don't thank me. If it wasn't for Walter, you'd still be—asleep down there."

"I'm sure you had more than a little to do with it."

Elizabeth leans forward and kisses Max on the cheek. He blushes. Walter beams. Deb grins. Fleabag yowls. And for one precious night, everything is right with the world.

∽

A week later, Max plays ball by the garage. He drains shot after perfect shot as he dribbles around the concrete. After playing for an hour he hears the back screen door shut and sees Deb come out of the house. He grabs the ball and walks over to meet her.

"Hey," he says.

"Hey."

"Everything all right?"

"We need to talk."

"I hate it when you say that."

Her eyes dart away as she struggles to say what is on her mind.

He makes it easy on her. "You're leaving."

She slumps as the tension floods out of her body. Most of it. "Yes. I've decided to go with Walter and Elizabeth to California. I'm going to help them get set up in a new place, then try to track down my family and see how they turned out."

He sighs and rubs his face. "I understand. Everyone leaves eventually. One way or the other."

"I'm not everyone."

"No, you're not."

The words hang in the air as they stare at each other.

"Are you mad?" Deb asks.

"No. I'm actually relieved. It's good to have you in the game, but at the same time, I'm scared to death that something is going to happen to you."

"It was my choice to fight."

"I know, but I'll sleep a hell of a lot easier knowing you'll be somewhere safe."

"This isn't how I expected you to react."

"What was I supposed to do?"

"You're supposed to beg me to stay."

"And that wouldn't work, would it?"

"No," she says. "But I hoped you'd try."

He struggles to speak. "Sorry. The truth is, I want you to stay so bad it hurts. But I don't want you to die again even more. So I'm not going to argue with you."

She nods. "Do you even want to know why I'm going?"

"I can guess. You saw how close we came to dying and you don't want to take another chance, right?"

Deb gets a distant look as she remembers the last fight. "I was an inch away from having my head torn off. You almost bought it, and Walter *did*. He was dead, Max. That thing was chewing him up and he got lucky. Hell, he probably pulled the trigger by accident. And if he hadn't, he'd be back down there with the rest of them."

"That's the chance we take."

"It's not a chance anymore. They're stacking the deck. Don't you see it? Throwing spears, imitating people, driving, *talking* for crying out loud. What the hell is next? They figure out how to make guns? The game is too hard now. We can't beat them anymore."

"Yes, we can."

"You really believe that, don't you?"

"I have to. The second I stop thinking I can win, this whole thing comes crashing down."

"Stop acting like it's a game."

"It *is* a game. A totally fucked up game I have to play to the end."

She marvels at the mad gleam in his eyes. "You like it, don't you?"

"What?"

"You like the thrill of the hunt. Making the big shot. Winning the game at the last second."

"It's not like that."

"It's exactly like that. I can see it now. You were alive out on the court, more alive than you've been before or since. And when it got taken away something died inside of you. Ed gave you a chance to get that feeling back and you can't give it up."

"You think I *like* risking my life every month? Seriously?"

"Yes, I do," she says. "I'm not saying you don't do it to help the people trapped down there. I know you care about them. And I can't ever thank you enough for saving me. But if you think about it, you'll see I'm right."

"I love to win, I'm not going to lie about that. Almost more than anything in the world."

"Even more than me?"

"That's not fair," he says as hot shame burns through him. "It's not just about us. It's about ending the curse."

"Whatever you need to believe," she says, and winces when she sees how much it stings him. She grabs his arm. "You can come with me, you know. We could just leave this place. Burn it down, fill in the cellar, something."

"I can't do that. I have to get them all back. I owe it to them."

"Jesus, Max—this isn't your fault. You didn't create the game, you inherited it from your sick uncle. It's his fault, not yours!"

"It's my problem now."

"You've got a life to live too."

He pictures himself far away from the house, sitting on the porch of a cabin in the woods overlooking a pristine lake. It is a nice dream until the tortured spirits of the damned rise up from the dark water and plead with him to save them.

"I won't leave."

"I know. But I had to try."

They flow together then, two desperate people clinging to what little reality they have left.

༃

Max stands under the canopy of the downtown bus terminal. Deb stands nearby, achingly close yet a million miles away. Walter and Elizabeth are there. They wear new clothes and carry luggage. Elizabeth struggles with her bag, still weak from her ordeal, but her eyes are strong and clear when she looks at Max.

"Are you sure you won't come with us?"

"I can't, Elizabeth. I have a job to finish here."

"Walter says it's dangerous. And that you shouldn't do it alone."

"I promise I'll be careful."

"I'll hold you to it." She steps away, leaving the two men alone.

"Deb has everything you'll need for the trip," Max says. "Your IDs are solid and the credit cards are good as gold. Patrick is going to meet you in LA and take good care of you. You can trust him."

"I will," Walter says, choking back tears. "I—Thank you, Max."

"You know how to thank me. Live your life and forget all this ever happened."

"We'll try."

The two men start to shake hands, but the gesture turns into a hug. When they break away, Walter puts his arm around Elizabeth and they head for the bus. Max watches them board, then he holds up a beaten leather satchel.

Deb raises an eyebrow. "What, no flowers?"

"Not my style. Yours either, for that matter. I figured you'd like this better anyway."

She peers into the bag and sees the leather-bound tome inside. "Ed's spell book?"

"I want to know it's with someone I trust in case something happens to me."

He holds out the satchel.

Deb reaches as if to take it, but grabs him instead. "If you don't come find me when this is over, I'll hunt you down and kill you," she says.

"I will. And Deb—I love you."

She grabs the back of his head and pulls him into a hard kiss, then breaks away without another word. She takes the bag and boards the bus. The door closes behind her, and after a moment the motor revs and the Greyhound pulls away.

Deb's haunted face peers out the side window. Max stares into her eyes until she disappears around the corner.

❧

Max cruises the streets again. After crisscrossing the town a dozen times, he pulls the car into the park. He stops underneath a burned-out streetlight and surveys his domain. It is back to being a run-down city park now, far from the nightmare field of his dreams or the happy spot he shared with Deb. It is just a place to kill time and keep him away from the loneliness and horror of the house. He is once again the king of the past and a slave to the future, but he feels a certain freedom in having his fate laid out before him, his path so crystal clear. Whether the path leads to victory or loss is irrelevant; he will follow it to the end without hesitation.

He grabs a basketball from the back seat and walks over to the court. As he dribbles the ball around, warming up, he once again notes the decay strangling the place. Weeds push through cracks in the pavement, the white lines are faded, and the net hangs from the hoop by a few remaining threads. He chuckles to himself as he recognizes the metaphor for his life.

He takes a shot. Swish. Retrieving the ball, he dribbles, fakes to the left, and shoots to the right. A smile crosses his face as the ball goes through the hoop again. Just like old times. He dribbles some more, looser now. When he spins around to make another shot he sees a ten-year-old boy sitting on a bench watching him play. Max searches for the kid's parents, but he's alone. Max knows the look on the boy's face well; he's seen it in the mirror a thousand times.

"Hi," Max calls out.

"Hey."

"Want to shoot a few?"

The boy shrugs. "My mom says I'm not supposed to play with strangers."

"So did mine. And she was mostly right."

"I don't know..."

"Come on. You afraid I'll beat you?"

"Are you kidding? You're an old man."

"I'm not that old."

"You sure?"

"That does it," he growls. "Get out here and play."

Max throws him the ball. A grin lights the boy's face as he dribbles over. Max grabs for the ball, but the kid blows past him and makes an easy layup.

"You ever done this before?" the boy taunts.

Max checks the ball and tosses it back. "Just play, smartass."

The kid charges for the hoop. A short, wonderful game follows, the two forgetting their sadness for a while and running and playing and laughing in spite of themselves. The kid is good, but not good enough, so Max takes it easy on him. When the game is tied at nine points each, the boy takes a shot from the three-point line. He misses, and the ball bounces off the rim and into the weeds. Max chases after it. He picks it up and turns back to the court.

"My ball, you little creep. Now you're gonna go down—"

The court is empty. The boy is gone, as if he was never there.

Max smiles and walks to the car.

☙

The full moon rises above the house, casting an ominous shadow across the yard. A single light shines from an upstairs window.

In his bedroom, Max gets ready for the game. An amazing array of weapons is spread out before him on the mattress. He picks each one up, examines it, then straps on the ones he wants with practiced ease and lays the rest back down. Fleabag snoozes among a pile of shotgun shells. He pets his cat's head. It nuzzles his hand and purrs.

Checking the clock, he sees it is almost midnight. He turns to leave and catches a glimpse of himself in the mirror. He is a frightening visage, not so much from the guns, knives, machete, and spare magazines fastened to his body armor, but from the deadly light in his eyes. For a second he doesn't recognize himself. Then he nods to the assassin looking back, for the first time not just acknowledging, but *accepting* the killer inside.

He knows down deep this is the point in the story where he is supposed to realize he can't do it alone and he should pick up the phone and beg someone for help. The police, the Army, Sam, hell, even Mrs. Johnson from next door. But the assassin can't do that any more than a shark can stop swimming and killing. He started the game alone and he will finish it alone. And death will come to anything that tries to stop him. Kind of poetic in a violent and screwed-up way.

Dante would be proud.

He hits the light and walks down the cellar stairs. At the bottom, he marches past the furnace and goes into the back room. The cavern calls to him like a siren and he follows the call. The chain falls away and he shoves the bookshelf aside to reveal the door. He grabs the handle, opens it to the ill wind, and steps into hell.

Max walks down the ancient wooden steps to the cavern. His face is emotionless, resigned. He steps onto the landing and sees the cave is already obscured by the mist. He stops by the rotten chair and calls into the blue.

"It's you and me again, just like old times. So let's play."

The mist obliges. It fades and reveals his darkest nightmare.

Braun Manor looms before him under a leering red moon. The driveway starts at the bottom of the platform and leads to the porch of the three-story mansion. The subtle evil permeating the house now oozes from the stained wooden siding, and the face that had always been suggested by the door and windows now resembles a grinning skull. The tree in the front yard is twisted and black, the shrubs dead. A burned-out replica of his car is parked by the steps.

On any other day Max's knees would grow weak and he would tremble in fear at the sight. Today, he barks a laugh. He draws his pistol, racks a bullet into the chamber, and walks down the stone steps and onto the imaginary driveway. Avoiding the cracks in the pavement, he walks up the stairs to the porch. The wood gives and threatens to break with each footfall. The front door swings open of its own accord, inviting him in. Max pauses to spit on the swirling patterns carved into the wood before he crosses the threshold.

"Fuck you," he says.

The house growls.

And the door slams shut behind him.

An Al Jolson tune warbles through the air as Max walks through the nightmare party filling the house. People wearing clothes from the thirties to the present mill about. Some he recognizes, others he has never seen before. Violence has been done to them all. Great bleeding wounds are gashed through a few people, some are missing limbs, and rotting flesh on others makes them look like zombies. They all stare, but don't touch him. He can't tell if he is the ghost, or they are.

Walter sits in his chair in the living room. His body is mangled. Splintered bones jut from his limbs. His lips twist into a shattered-tooth smile. Deb lies on the floor in a pool of blood, curled around a wooden spear jabbed through her stomach. She moans in agony. Tommy sits on the couch. His decapitated head sits next to him on the cushion.

"Welcome home, Max," Tommy's head says. "We've been waiting for you."

Max turns from them and sees Fleabag hanging from a cord tied to the chandelier. He takes out a knife, cuts the cat down, and lays him on the floor. He pets the animal's head like he did to the real one minutes before.

He feels his iron control slipping and grits his teeth as he walks down the hallway. A zombie brushes against him. He moves to avoid the touch. The crowd parts in front of him and fills in behind, herding him down the hall to the basement door. His hand trembles as he reaches for the handle. The door swings open the instant before he touches it. Max walks down the cellar steps in forty-watt silhouette.

Max steps into the basement and sees the furnace pipes writhing and twisting like demonic serpents trying to break free of their brackets. The grate at the bottom of the furnace body is open, revealing gnashing fangs and a slurping tongue. A *creak* sounds from behind him, and he turns, leading with the .45. He sees Walter and Deb and Tommy have shuffled down the steps, Tommy carrying his head by the hair. Max looks down at their feet and sees Fleabag. The cat's neck is broken and his head hangs at a disgusting angle. He cries a pathetic, broken meow.

Max vomits on the concrete floor. As he wipes his mouth, a quiet voice catches his ears. A voice he hasn't heard in half a lifetime.

"Are you all right, Max?"

He looks up and sees a woman standing inside the doorway to the back room. She is partially hidden in shadows. He straightens up and stares in disbelief at the woman from his memory. The woman from his dreams. The woman who gave everything for him, and to whom he gave everything back.

"Mom?"

Maxine's grim face lights up in a smile. "It's so good to see you again."

"Is nothing sacred down here?"

"Hush. We don't have much time..."

"Time for what."

"Time to escape. There's still a chance if we hurry."

She steps forward.

He raises the gun and points it at her face. His hand quivers. "Don't."

Maxine moves back into the shadows and frowns. "You think I'm one of them? One of these monsters?"

"What else would you be?"

"It's me, Max. I swear. I've been trapped down here since—"

"Since you died?" he snarls, cutting her off. "I remember. I buried you."

"You buried my body. But Edward took my soul."

"No. This is just another goddamn trick."

Tears spring from her eyes as she pleads with him. "You've got to believe me. You have to. You were always there when I needed you before. Has this game turned you against everything?"

His face twists in agony. He lowers the gun an inch. Maxine keeps walking backward, luring Max into the back room. He shuffles forward, hypnotized by her words and movement.

"You're not my mother."

"I brought you into the world. I fed you from my own breasts."

"Shut up."

"I gave you everything. And now I need you and you're turning your back on me again."

"I never left you."

"You did. You left me to die while you snuck over to play with your uncle."

He stops just short of entering the back room. He stares through the door frame, into the shadows, past his mother, and to the cavern portal beyond.

"No. That's not what happened."

"Yes. You left me to waste away. But I forgive you, Max. I love you. I always have. Now come here and let me hug you one more time."

He raises his foot to take a final step, then snaps out of his trance. His hand stops trembling and he raises the gun again. "I was sitting next to my mother when she died."

"No. Please, I'm real—" she begs, but there is an angry tone to her voice now. A tone his mother would never take with him.

"You're nothing but a twisted memory."

A shadow looms over her from behind. Max flinches as a clawed hand reaches out and grabs her by the throat. It picks her off the floor and her feet dangle as she gasps for air.

Max whips the pistol to the new threat and sees something beyond his comprehension. Standing before him, holding his struggling mother like a toy, is the ultimate demon. He looks up from the thick, muscular legs to the ill-fitting evening coat, past the swishing forked tail and the vicious claws to the monster's evil, red-tinted, fang-split, oh-so-familiar face. It speaks in a guttural voice that hasn't been used in ages.

"Mother and pup together again. How sweet."

When Max hears the booming words, the last shred of his sanity snaps.

"Uncle Ed...?"

"You should have killed me when you had the chance, boy."

Demon Ed squeezes, strangling Maxine.

"Help me..." she gurgles.

"Let her go!" Max yells, no longer caring that she is just a replica of his mom. She is a soul in pain and that's all that matters.

"Of course. But let me fix her for you first."

Ed grabs one of Maxine's legs with his free claw and pulls it sideways. There is a brutal *snap* as the leg breaks.

She shrieks.

"That sounds like it hurt!" Ed booms. "Hope you brought the wheelchair. She's going to need it."

Ed throws the body across the room. Max catches the hurtling figure and the two fall to the floor. His gun clatters to the pavement beside them. He cradles the thing in his arms. Her broken leg flops to the side at a sick angle. Max turns her over and sees she is now a long-decayed corpse. Horrified, he shoves it away.

"You don't like your present?" Demon Ed laughs.

Like it did that day in the study so many years ago, the vault in Max's gut opens wide and decades of boiling hate spews out. It flashes through his mind and body and erupts from his mouth in a bestial roar. He explodes off the floor, lunging at Ed, forgetting his gun, forgetting his knives, forgetting anything but pure blinding hate and the need to kill.

He slams against the monster, driving Ed backward despite his awesome bulk, and pounds at him with his fists. Ed tries to fight back but his attacker is a revenge-fueled wolverine who hits and kicks and bites until bones break and green gore and spit splash the floor. It is hard to tell which one is human and which is the demon.

Ed gets his balance and grabs Max on either side of his head, long claws overlapping in the back. He picks the struggling man off the floor and booms another laugh.

"You are a pathetic worm!"

Max kicks and screams under the awful pressure but manages to plant his feet in Ed's chest. He shoves hard and slips through Ed's grasp, the claws slicing his scalp. He flies across the room and crashes into a pile of boxes. Ed rushes across the floor and slams into him before he can pull the shotgun free from the holster on his back. Max tumbles again, hitting an old wooden desk with a painful crunch. The shotgun flies into a dark corner. He lies stunned on the desk for a second, then a shadow paints over him. He rolls to the side just as a huge fist shatters the desk into firewood. Max hits the ground running.

"Come back and play!" Demon Ed roars.

Max darts behind Ed and stabs him with a hunting knife. The blade sticks deep in the monster's neck and he howls in pain. Ed whirls and charges again. Max dodges and the beast smashes headfirst into the cellar wall. The bricks cave in and a shower of mortar rains down on Ed's shoulders. Max jumps on the creature's back, wraps the scaly neck in a choke hold, and squeezes with all his strength.

"It's time... for you... to die!" Max rages.

Ed struggles, eyes popping, then he reaches over his back and clutches at his attacker. The demon's claws dig bloody furrows in Max's flesh, but he hangs on and chokes harder. With Max riding his back Ed weakens by the second; he staggers and goes down on one knee.

"Noooo..." Ed wheezes and the fire in his eyes dims.

Then his flailing claws find a grip under Max's arm. The demon grabs him and heaves, throwing him across the room. He smashes upside-down against the furnace with a hollow *clang* and collapses in a broken heap, his forgotten .45 lies inches from his outstretched fingers.

Ed bellows and charges.

Max snatches the pistol up and screams as he blasts away. He shoots until the gun is empty and the slide locks open on the empty chamber. The hail of heavy-grain bullets stops Demon Ed in his tracks. He writhes, chest and stomach shredded by the lead. A surge of hope fills Max's heart as he watches Ed paw at his chest and take a stumbling step.

Hope turns to dread as Ed digs a claw under his evening coat and slides it down, ripping the garment open. He pulls the ragged cloth aside and reveals a bulletproof vest with eight sizzling slugs stuck into it. Demon Ed's mouth splits open in a terrible smile.

"It's my game, and I make the rules."

The furnace pipes come alive behind Max, twisting around him and pinning his arms and legs. The metal tentacles hog-tie him as Ed stomps forward, gloating in victory. Max struggles and looks up to see the devil looming over him.

Ed raises a jagged claw for the final blow.

The talon slashes down.

The buzzer sounds.

The game is over.

Max has one last thought as Uncle Ed rips his throat out, as his bones contort and his body melts and his soul merges with the sentient evil surrounding him. One last thought on the edge of a sea of pain and madness.

Who is going to feed the cat?

෬

"Still no answer," Deb says, waving her cell phone in the moist ocean air.

Walter stops reading Edward's spell book and watches her pacing on the beach house deck. "He's probably just sleeping off the battle. You know how beat up we always got in the basement."

She spears him with an accusing look. "No. Something's wrong, I can feel it. And you can too."

Walter stares back at her, his emotions churning. Then his face falls and he nods in grudging acceptance. "You're right. He would have called us if he had won."

She shakes her head in disgust. "He's such an idiot. We have to go back."

He closes the book, stares at the waves crashing on the rocks, and sighs. "I'll have to tell Elizabeth."

"Tell me what?" Elizabeth says as she walks out of the house.

Walter's voice catches in his throat. "Max may be in trouble."

"He *is* in trouble," Deb says.

"Then we have to go back and help him."

"Elizabeth..." Walter starts. "You can't go back down there."

"I have to. Don't you see? I owe him. *We* owe him."

He stares at her, frozen by the thought of losing her again.

"He's right," Deb says. "You shouldn't go. It's nice of you to offer, but you'd be even more of a liability in the fight than Walter was. No offense."

Walter shrugs.

Elizabeth bristles. "I'm sorry, but you're wrong," she says. "I may not be as physically capable as you, but I'm quick and smart and just as driven to stop this madness as anyone."

"Elizabeth—" Walter interrupts.

She whirls and fixes him with a stony stare. "Your vote doesn't count. You're just afraid you'll lose me again."

"That's true, but—"

"Enough. If Max needs help, we all go. I couldn't live with myself if I didn't try. And trust me, you wouldn't want to live with me either."

"Now I know how Tommy felt," Walter chuckles to himself. "I was on the other side of this argument a few months ago. But Max was right to take me along. And we'd be fools to leave you behind."

Deb studies Elizabeth. "You're brave, I'll give you that much."

"Thank you. But from what you've told me, courage might not be enough."

"You're right. We need more firepower if we're going back down there. And I think I know someone who can help."

WHENEVER

Max loses count of the number of times he is hung from a rusty meat hook by a pack of cackling demons, flayed alive by their barbed-wire whips, then hacked apart limb by limb with a dull meat cleaver. The monsters slap his body parts onto a conveyor belt leading to a giant metal roller covered in jagged spikes. The hardest, and most painful part, is his head. He can still think and feel as the creatures pull it off his shoulders with a sickening *pop*, leaving the end of his trachea flopping in the air amidst a tangle of spine and veins and tendons, then drop it on the belt with the rest of his dismembered body.

A demon hits a switch, and Max watches as the conveyor trundles the bloody mess that used to be his body toward the grinder. His feet and legs go under the roller first, crunched flat in an instant with a spurt of blood. Through a bright haze of pain he marvels at how he can feel each part being smashed even though they are severed. His torso follows with a more pronounced liquid *squish* as his organs are pressed out of his rib cage, then his hands and arms, and the grotesque view ends when the metal teeth crush his skull and his eyes pop out of their sockets. He can still *see*, however, and his vision goes wild with each eyeball pointing in different directions, and then, if there were such a thing as mercy in this nightmare, his sight cuts off as they are smashed to paste.

The respite is short, however. At the end of the conveyor, the demons glue his pulverized remnants back together with flaming tar. Once he is reassembled, they jam a tube down his throat and reinflate him by forcing a bag of chunky blood into his ravaged tissues. Then they drag him back to the other side of the grinder over a floor littered with broken glass and razor blades, lift him up, gut him on the hook again, and the process starts anew.

On the $42 \times 10^{666\text{th}}$ time around—and "time" is a relative concept in Max's personal hell that has not only lasted forever, just started, and simultaneously goes sideways so each excruciating moment lasts for infinity—Demon Ed stomps into the room and grins as he watches Max's skull getting crushed. A scattering of teeth and Max's right eye slide off the conveyor and land on the grimy floor.

Ed grabs the eyeball by the dangling nerves, holds it up over his open mouth, and releases it.

Max's detached mind screams as he watches himself fall past Ed's stained fangs, over the bloody tongue, bounce off the epiglottis, and splash into the gurgling acid darkness of the demon's stomach.

"Delicious," Ed says, and walks out of the torture chamber.

Behind him, Max magically reforms once again on the gore-stained conveyor. As the demons put him back together this time, however, a glowing azure mist forms from nowhere. The demons forget him as they cackle with devilish glee and fade into the blue.

Max stands under a brilliant indigo sky, eyes closed, head tilted up, relishing the sunshine warming his face. After a peaceful respite, he looks down to see he is at the end of a line of people he dimly recognizes. He holds an empty paper plate in his hands.

Confused, he looks ahead, and sees the line leads to a picnic table piled with mountains of food. The people ahead fill their plates and laugh and talk. His belly grumbles when the smell of the food tickles his nose. He thinks how good it feels to have his stomach inside his torso for change instead of being spilled out on the demonic butcher's table, and rubs it with cartoonish glee. Bile rises in his throat when the action summons the hellish memory of the torture chamber.

He swallows his nausea and looks around, trying to make sense of where he is and what is happening, but he sees nothing other than a peaceful sunny afternoon in the park. Trees sway in the breeze and dapple the thick grass with swirling shadows. A brightly colored banner hangs above a pavilion with the words *Family Reunion* written on it in a whimsical font. It is surrounded by colorful balloons. His confusion fades as the line moves forward. He doesn't know where he is, or who these people are, but he knows in his heart he is right where he is supposed to be.

With family.

The vague feeling of contentment spreading through Max's mind and body is shattered when he hears a popping sound coming from somewhere in the park: Gunfire. Everyone around him drops their plates and dives for cover. Max stands still, his combat-trained mind seeking the source of the shots, and sees something that rocks him to the core.

A group of heavily armed demons runs down the hill toward the pavilion, moving from cover to cover. They are led by a tall, muscular creature, who is flanked by a wrinkled monster on one side, and a lithe, agile female demon on the other. Two other beasts bring up the rear. One of them carries a book, which is odd in and of itself, but Max doesn't give that much consideration. He is more concerned with what the other attackers carry: A fuckload of guns.

Max groans to himself. *They can shoot now. Shit.*

He freezes at the thought, remembering that demons are evil and at one time he had dedicated his life to killing them. A glimmer of that former life flashes through his mind, a violent life, and he wants nothing more than to never have to kill again. Then he looks down and sees a man beneath the table, covering his frightened wife and children with his body. Is he Max's cousin? Uncle? Brother? Rage flares in his brain as he realizes their relationship doesn't matter. He will do whatever it takes to protect his family from the rampaging monsters.

With a last lament that he never got to try the potato salad, he springs into action. Max leaps over the food table, grabs a butcher knife out of the Roast Beast as he vaults through the air above it, and lands on the other side in a crouch. The demons haven't seen him yet as their attention is occupied by a group of his brethren throwing rocks at them from behind an overturned picnic table. This gives Max an idea. He grabs a small watermelon from the table, runs toward the muscular demon, and tosses the melon in the air.

The beast sees the object flying toward him and raises his gun to shoot it. Too late, the creature realizes the melon is a diversion. Max darts in from behind a tree and slashes it across the stomach with the knife. The demon staggers but doesn't fall. Max curses as he sees the blade has sliced into body armor instead of flesh.

First guns, now body armor, Max thinks as he runs away. *Deb is right. The games are getting too hard.*

Then he thinks: *Who the hell is Deb?*

He jumps behind a dumpster just ahead of a hail of bullets. The green metal tub rattles as bullets punch through, but Max is already gone from the other side, running for the parking lot.

As he ducks behind an SUV, bullets blast the windows out. He rolls away from the falling glass and ducks between two cars. Behind him, he hears the demons barking at each other as they spread out to find him. He searches for a weapon and sees a radio antenna jutting from the hood of an old blue Chevy Nova. He reaches up and snaps it off. An alarm blares from the car.

Max hears the clomping of boots as the creatures run toward him. He backs away, hitting another car, and another alarm goes off. The demons yell again, and his face lights up with another idea. He runs in a pell-mell crouch through the parking lot, banging into every car he can.

The noise coming from all angles confuses the monsters. Stray shots ring out, and random windows blow out around him. All miss their target.

Max pauses to catch his breath amidst the cacophony and sees a demon standing in front of a car ahead of him. It looks the other direction. Max scrambles up on the trunk, runs over the roof, and down the hood, whipping the antenna across the back of its bony skull as he leaps past.

The stinging blow drops the creature to its knees and an almost-human sounding snarl bursts out of its throat. "Goddamn it!"

Max weaves away through a row of cars just ahead of another stitching line of bullets. A demon converges on his location so he drops to the ground and rolls under a truck. He holds his breath as it stomps by, then reaches out and grabs the monster's back leg. The beast trips and smacks its face on the mirror of the next car over and falls with a pained grunt.

The demon's pistol clatters across the pavement and stops in front of Max's face. He grabs at it, but he can barely pick it up. It seems like his hands are swollen, but they aren't. He can see them. They are normal fingers. But they *feel* like fat sausages. He manages to grab the gun in both hands, but when he tries to put his finger through the trigger guard, it won't fit. He jabs at the hole again and again, his brain refusing to accept what he is seeing. His finger is small enough. The hole is big enough. But he can't get it to go in.

He gives up trying to shoot the pistol as the demon shakes its head and claws for another gun on its belt. He throws the weapon as hard as he can into the thing's face. The barrel cracks the beast's nose.

"Ow!" it screeches.

Max rolls away from the creature, and when he is out from under the truck he clambers onto the car in the next spot. The demon blasts away and the bullets just miss the bottom of Max's feet as he pulls them up.

As he runs across the tops of cars to the end of the parking lot the other monsters see him and give chase. He dodges and weaves the bullets ripping through the air around him. Soon he reaches the last line of cars and drops to the ground. A large wooden barn is right in front of him across thirty feet of pavement. A giant cartoon demon is painted on the front of the building.

Max darts across the open space and jumps through the doors. He pushes them shut behind him, then hits the ground just as a demon-fired bullet storm punches dozens of holes in the wood above him. Beams of sunlight stab the inside of the barn through the splintered wood. When the shooting stops he shakes slivers out of his hair and checks out the interior. His mouth drops open when he sees a stunning sight.

His Chevy Impala sits in the middle of the hall, speared by a spotlight from somewhere above. The car is no longer broken down and rusty. It is now shiny and polished and painted red, with stylized yellow flames rippling down the front fenders. Max runs over and opens the door. He slides into the driver's seat and wraps his hands across the steering wheel, turns the key hanging in the ignition, and pushes his foot down on the gas pedal. The motor roars. Smiling wide, he grabs the skull-topped gear shift and slams the car into drive.

The demons spread out and approach the barn, reloading their guns as they come. The muscular one aims its machine gun at the bullet-riddled barn door and nods to the others. They ready their weapons as it steps forward and reaches for the handle. The demon pauses when it hears a roaring sound from inside the barn, and its red-tinged eyes grow wide.

"Look out!" the brawny demon yells and dives to the side just before the door is shattered into a thousand pieces by the Impala crashing out from the inside.

The other pursuers jump aside as Max steers the car toward them through the plank-covered windshield. He narrowly misses running them over. They shoot as he whips by, and bullets ping off the back of the car.

Max whips the Impala around in a tire-screeching U-turn in the parking lot and rockets back toward the monsters. They scatter, and he chases the female demon as it runs away, fishtailing around the barn in chase. Clouds of dust billow from the rear tires as he follows the dodging creature around the far side of the building. He straightens the car on the far side and howls in triumph as the panicked beast runs right in front of him. He centers the hood ornament on her back and floors it. The demon jumps over the hood of a rusty truck and rolls away before he can hit it. The Impala's fender bashes the vehicle as he roars by.

Cursing, he looks ahead and sees three of the demons standing in a line, aiming their guns right at him. He ducks under the dash and punches the accelerator as the windshield blows out and glass sprays everywhere. Hunched down in the seat, he steers blindly back into the parking lot. He rises, slams on the brakes, whips the wheel to the right and punches the gas pedal again. The motor howls and the tires screech as the rear end whips around, and the car points back at the scattering monsters.

"Teach you to mess with my picnic!" he yells as he speeds toward them again.

An SUV rams Max's car in the side. As the Impala crumples around him, he gets a quick glimpse of the old demon grinning at him from behind the cracked windshield of the other vehicle.

The Impala skids to the side and comes to a stop with a hiss of escaping steam and smoking rubber. Roaring in rage, Max tries to get out, but he is stuck behind the wheel. He thrashes, but before he can get free the female demon leaps on the hood and slides to a stop in front of him. She aims a pistol at his face.

"I told you I'd hunt you down and kill you," she barks.

"No! Don't!"

The gun roars, and Max's world explodes into...

Blue?

NOW

Max wakes up with a start. He lies on the couch. His leg is chained to the floor. Fleabag purrs next to him. Morning sunlight streams through the living room windows. The sky outside is deep blue. He is very confused.

"What the fuck...?"

He looks around the room and sees Deb staring at him. She is dressed in combat armor and holds a pistol in one hand. It's not aimed directly at him, but close enough for worry. She turns her head and calls to the kitchen, never taking her eyes off him.

"He's awake," she says.

Walter, Elizabeth, Sam, and Mrs. Johnson walk in. They are all cut and bruised in various ways and carry mugs of steaming coffee.

"That smells good," Max says. "Can I have some?"

"As soon as we're sure you're not insane," Walter says.

"He's insane all right," Deb snorts. "That's the only reason he went down there alone."

"Down where?" Max says, bewildered.

Sam steps closer. But not too close. "You don't remember?"

"I remember getting ready for the game, then—Oh, Jesus..." Max pales as nauseating memories flood his brain. He runs his hands over his body, then up to his face, searching for damage.

He stops probing just below his cheeks. "Do I still have my eyes...?"

"Of course," Elizabeth replies.

"Thank god. I never want to see that stomach again."

The others share a concerned look.

"He sounds crazy to me," Mrs. Johnson says.

As Max stares at her the flood of memories turns into a deluge. He remembers the picnic, the running battle in the parking lot, and the demon driving the SUV that totaled his ride.

"You wrecked my car!"

"Damn right I did. It was fun."

"Not for me," he says, and turns to Deb. "And you—you shot me in the face!"

"You deserved it."

"Yeah, maybe. I was trying to run everyone over. But who did I stab?"

Sam holds up his hand. "That was me, you asshole. You would have gutted me if it wasn't for the Kevlar."

"Sorry," Max says, "and thanks to all of you for coming after me."

"Somebody had to feed the cat," Deb says, frosty.

"Well, thanks for that too."

"That's what friends are for," Walter says, then glances at the others. "He appears to be of sound mind and body."

"That's relative," Deb says, and unlocks the chain around Max's ankle. When it falls free, Sam helps him to his feet.

Max wobbles, then stands on his own. "Nice to have all my body parts attached again."

This garners him a few more odd looks, Deb's the most piercing. Max ignores them and turns to Mrs. Johnson.

"How did you get mixed up in all this?"

"I've been in it longer than you have," she says, her face turning dark. "My husband Harry and I moved in next door right after we got married, years before you and your family showed up. He was an older man, but that didn't matter to me. I loved him at first sight. And he loved me back. We were happy for years, even though we knew strange things were happening over here. Harry tried to find out what was going on, but Edward grew suspicious."

"Oh, no."

"Yes. I told Harry to stay away, but he was headstrong like that. One night he went out for a walk and never came back. I knew Edward had something to do with it, but I couldn't prove it. And no one would listen. The bastard just laughed whenever he saw me after that. I wanted to get back at him, but he left on his trip and I never got the chance. Things were almost normal after that. At least until you moved in. Anyway, your cat showed up a few weeks ago asking for help, so I came over and looked for you, but you were gone. So when your friends showed up and explained everything, I asked them if I could come along."

"It was either that, or she was going to call the cops," Deb says with a guilty shrug.

"That's why you were always watching me and the house, then?" Max asks.

"Yes," Mrs. Johnson replies. "You were a good boy when you were younger, but your father, and Edward..." She trickles off, lost in a terrible memory, then continues. "When you inherited the place I didn't know if you were part of their evil or not."

"And you waited all those years to get revenge."

"Harry was worth it." Tears spill from Mrs. Johnson's eyes. "And now I'm hoping we can get him back."

Max's face falls. "There's no easy way to say this, but there's nothing about Harry in Ed's scrapbook. So I don't think he's down there with the others."

"I—I was afraid of that. I just hope whatever that monster did to him was quick."

"I'm sure it was," Max says, and puts a gentle hand on her shoulder. "And I hope you know by now I never would have helped Uncle Ed."

Mrs. Johnson touches his hand. "I know."

After a quiet moment, he turns to the others. "How did you find me down there, out of all of the demons?"

"I've been doing a little light reading," Walter says, holding up Ed's spell book.

Max jerks upright. "Walter—"

"There's nothing to worry about. I took every reasonable precaution before studying the material. And a few unreasonable ones."

"I'll take your word for it."

"As well you should. It's a rather fascinating read, by the way."

"And very illuminating," Elizabeth adds. "By studying it, we've figured out a way to end the curse."

"That's good to hear, because I've got some bad news."

"Which is...?"

Max looks around the room at the faces of his friends, and locks eyes with Deb. "I found out what *really* happened to Uncle Ed."

Deb follows Max into his bedroom and slams the door shut behind her. He holds out his arms for a hug.

"I knew you'd come back for me," he says.

She slaps his hands away. "Don't you ever, ever, *ever* do something that stupid again."

"What are you so mad about?"

"Oh, I don't know," she growls. "Maybe I'm pissed that you went down to the basement alone and got yourself killed?"

"I was going down there alone for years."

"That was before you had something to lose."

Max stares at her, dumbfounded. Then a wave of emotions breaks over him. Terror. Regret. Anger. And the most overpowering feeling of all: Love.

His shoulders slump in defeat. "You're right. I'm sorry. I don't want to screw up and lose you again."

"Then don't."

She holds out her arms this time, and he stumbles to her.

Bring on the love scene.

Walter flips through Ed's spell book by the yellow light of the kitchen chandelier as Max and the others watch. He stops on a page halfway through and points at a pentagram-based symbol surrounded by dense text.

"...As you can see, the initial spell Edward cast created a rift in between dimensions and juxtaposed the magic realm onto our own. Then he layered in additional incantations that gave the cavern access to our subconscious minds and allowed the demonic transmogrifications to occur. It's quite simple when you understand the underlying theory."

"Simple for you, maybe," Max says.

"And Einstein," Sam adds.

"Funny you should mention Albert," Elizabeth says. "There are direct manipulations of space-time evident in the incantations, though in ways Relativity never could have predicted. There are also elements of Heisenberg's S-Matrix theory at work as well. It seems that magic, like everything else, is all in the arithmetic."

"I almost flunked math," Max says.

Deb grins at him. "Good thing you wound up being an accountant."

He shoots her a dirty look, then turns back to Walter. "That all sounds great, but can you reverse the spell or not?"

"I believe so. The enchantments allow the user to manipulate matter on a quantum level. And anything that can be done, can be undone."

"Sounds dangerous. And incredible."

"It will be, if it works."

"And... will it?"

Walter shuts the book and pushes it away. He takes a deep breath. "It has to be done in the cavern, after the transformation, when and where the magic is strongest. And we'll need everyone to make it happen. But if you can buy us enough time, I am confident we can break the curse."

Max nods at him, then looks at the others. "Deb was right when she said the fights have gotten too hard. And with Ed out in the open now, I don't see how we have much choice. He's too powerful. So I say we go down and buy Walter the time he needs to beat this thing."

"Let's do it," Deb says.

"I'm in," Sam adds.

"I wouldn't miss it for the world," Mrs. Johnson says.

Elizabeth grabs Walter's hand. "We all go together, then."

"I promise I won't let you down," he says to her, to everyone.

Max smiles. "I never thought you would."

Sam studies the complicated scribbles on Elizabeth's notepad and frowns. "So how are we going to distract Uncle Ed?"

"Leave that to me," Max says. "I've got a brilliant plan."

❧

Outside.

The fat, full, gleaming man in the moon gazes down on the house with a knowing smirk.

Inside.

In the basement, Max, Deb, Sam, Walter, Elizabeth, and Mrs. Johnson stand before the ancient door. They have no weapons or armor. Nothing but a bulging athletic bag carried by Max, a satchel by Elizabeth, and the spell book clutched in the crook of Walter's arm.

Max looks back at his friends, staring each one in the eyes. *Not friends*, he realizes. *Family*. The family he never knew he had until it mattered. He speaks to them in a voice thick with emotion.

"I just wanted to thank you again for coming with me. This isn't my private war anymore. Maybe it never was. But if we stick together as a team, we can beat anything."

"Even without the guns?" Sam asks.

"Yeah," Deb says. "We can still go get them."

"No. We stick to the plan. Anyone who wants to stay behind should leave now."

No one moves.

"All right then. Let's go win the game."

He grabs the clammy door handle, and pulls.

Max stands on the landing, staring at the empty cave. He checks his watch and turns to the others.

"This is it. Just remember, don't interfere. No matter what."

Deb grabs his hand as he walks toward the steps. "There's got to be another way to distract him. Something safer."

"I've got to be up close and personal to keep his full attention, no matter how dangerous it is. If he finds out what we're up to, it's all over. And besides," Max says with a smile so vicious it would send a starving tiger running away to hide in the jungle. "I want to beat that son of a bitch more than I want anything in the whole freaking world."

"More than anything?"

A warm feeling swells in his chest as he looks at her, blotting out the hate he has hoarded for so long. "Almost anything."

Deb smiles viciously herself and kisses him. "Kick his ass."

The hate roars back, and this time, Max welcomes it. He nods, goes down the steps, and walks toward the center of the cavern with his vintage Chuck Taylor All Stars clomping on the stone floor. Once there, he opens the bag and pulls out a retro red-white-and-blue ABA basketball. He cups it in both hands and pushes in, flexing the finely pebbled leather, and getting a feel for the ball. He bounces it in a figure eight between his legs.

The sounds reverberate from the craggy walls moments after the ball hits the floor, creating a percussive beat that echoes a death march.

Max stops dribbling when he is warmed up and cradles the ball on one hip. The sound dies away. He calls out to the darkness. "You like games, Ed? I've got a good one for you. So come on out and play."

The blue mist rises in an angry, boiling cloud streaked with crashing lightning and rolling thunder that wipes Max from sight.

On the landing, the others lean forward in anticipation, trying to catch a glimpse of Max through the blue wall. Walter grabs Elizabeth's arm. She grabs back. Deb, Sam, and Mrs. Johnson huddle closer together.

"This had better work," Mrs. Johnson grumbles.

"It will," Sam says. "Max was the best I'd ever seen. But he was even better when the game was on the line."

They look back to the cavern as tentacles of fog pull back, revealing Max standing at center court in his old high-school basketball arena. Empty bleachers stretch up from the landing. A sign indicates Deb and the others are on the visitors side. A demon reporter paces the sidelines in front of them, wearing a tattered fedora with a press pass stuck in it, and holding an old-fashioned camera with a giant flashbulb on top. A gaggle of cackling imps cavorts in the home team section on the opposite side of the court. The creatures roar in defiance at the humans looking at them from across the arena.

"Fuck you too!" Deb yells back.

On the floor, Max's guts churn as a wave of nostalgia washes over him. He studies the replica of the place where his hopes for the future were both born and killed. The place that looks exactly like it did on those faraway nights when he was young, free, and full of fire. The place a younger Max had thought his greatest triumphs and most tragic losses took place, with no way of knowing just how wrong he could be at the time.

Or, he muses now as he thinks his plan over, how *right*.

He squats down and touches the hardwood. The once-bright polish has been worn away by the tread of a thousand players, baring the crimson and white paint of the Red Devil logo to his fingertips. It feels cool, slippery, real. The icon's cartoonish eyes stare back at him. Max's mind reels as it does every time he tries to grasp the unfathomable depths of the cavern's illusions.

While he is distracted, a twinge of doubt creeps into his thoughts. He wonders if Walter can really break Uncle Ed's spell and undo decades of evil. The sense of wrongness here is incalculable, an arcane force no mere mortal should be able to challenge. With a snort, he banishes the thought. If Edward could make this place, Walter can break it. The man has been tested in ways Max's sorcerous uncle never was, and proven his worth time and time again. Max knows his teammate will come through at the final buzzer as surely as he knows the sun will come up tomorrow, and together they will win the game. With that thought he stands tall again, confidence pumping through his veins and filling his heart.

Until the lights go out.

Absolute darkness blankets the arena. Goosebumps ripple up and down Max's arms, caused as much by the frigid air brushing his skin as by the unsettling feeling of being suspended in an endless abyss. His guts churn again, this time driven by cold tendrils of fear that snake through his bowels and tingle his spine. After all he has been through, all he has seen, the unknown is still the most terrifying thing of all. The moment drags on for ages and is over in an instant, so what happens next, though petrifying in its own way, is a relief.

A small spotlight snaps on high above. The feeble yellow light spears Max in place, and he holds a hand up to block the glare. He hears a loud *chunk,* and a far brighter light stabs down in the other direction, casting a blazing circle of white light on the double doors to the home team locker room. Other spotlights swirl around the arena in a kaleidoscope of colors. The demon fans begin to clap and stomp and roar. A bone-rattling *gong* sounds from unseen speakers, then it tolls again. And again. A piercing guitar note and thumping drum join the foreboding knell and Max rolls his eyes as he recognizes the song.

Hell's Bells, he thinks. *Of course...*

As the music and lights shift into a higher gear the locker room doors boom open. Demon Ed struts onto the court in all his hulking, muscle-bound, devilish glory. He raises both arms to the stands and poses for his fans, opening his slavering maw and bellowing a bestial roar that rattles the dingy windows lining the arena as hard as it shakes Max's soul.

Max takes an involuntary step back, stunned by the sheer power radiating from the thing that used to be his uncle. If Goliath had looked like this in the Valley of Elah centuries ago, David might have run away from the battle and crawled under the nearest rock and cried like a baby. Like Max wants to do now.

But he can't.

He won't.

Like the mythical hero, he has a giant to slay.

On the landing, Deb catches her breath as she looks at Ed. "Holy shit," she breathes.

"There's nothing holy about that thing," Sam says. "Are you sure nobody brought a gun?"

"I did. But I don't think it would help."

Behind them, Elizabeth makes a shushing sound. "Quiet. Walter needs to concentrate."

They turn from the spectacle below to see Walter sitting cross-legged on the landing behind them. The spell book is open in his lap. As he reads passages to himself, Elizabeth and Mrs. Johnson spread bags of salt around him in a cryptic circle filled with overlapping lines.

"This better work," Deb says. "You're up."

Sam takes a deep breath, removes his jacket, and walks down the steps.

Back on the court, the demon reporter snaps a picture as Ed finishes his arrogant posing and stomps toward Max. The monster looks like he is going to bowl the smaller man over, but Max holds his ground. Ed stops a foot short and glares down at his foe with a sneer of contempt.

"You won't escape me again," Ed rumbles.

"Don't need to. Because you're going to lose this time."

"Lose?" Demon Ed laughs. "Me? I could strike you down where you stand."

"You could. But then you'd never know if you could beat me at a real game." Max twirls the basketball on a fingertip.

"That's child's play."

"You should be good at it then."

Ed bristles at the insult, rising to his full height and puffing out his muscular chest. Claws spark as they scrape against each other as he fans out his blunt fingers. Smoke smolders from his eyes. His tail swishes in agitation.

Max grins up at the threat. "What do you say? You and me, one on one. Five-point game, and the winner gets the other's soul. I'll even give you the ball to start. Unless you're afraid..."

"I am afraid of *nothing*!" Demon Ed roars, and snatches the ball from Max's hands. Ed tries to dribble and it hits his clawed foot. He snarls, snatches the ball up, and carries it toward the goal.

A whistle *chirps* from behind them.

Demon Ed whips around to find the source.

Sam stands on the edge of the court, wearing a black and white striped referee shirt. He has a silver whistle in his hand. "That's traveling," he says. "You have to dribble the ball when you move. Max's ball."

"Why?" Ed roars again.

Max holds out his hand for the ball. "Because it's my game now, and those are the rules."

Ed trembles with rage and savagely bounces it over to him. Max catches it, dribbles, and darts to the left. Demon Ed follows. Max cuts back to the right, slashing around the monster, and making an easy layup.

"One to zero, for Max," Sam says.

"Your turn," Max says, and tosses the ball to Ed.

The demon dribbles a few times to get the hang of the action, then runs toward the basket. Max cuts in, steals the ball, and shoots over the flustered creature.

Swish.

"Two-zero, Max."

Max shags the ball and sneers at his nemesis. "Come on, Ed. You can do this. I've got faith in you."

Demon Ed snatches the ball away, his claws leaving red slashes across the back of Max's hand. He dribbles again, looking more comfortable with the motion. Max watches, his back to the basket, ready to defend. Ed lunges forward. Max reaches in to steal the ball as the beast whips by, but Ed bounces it from his right side to his left in a perfect crossover dribble, avoiding the groping hand as he twists past. The path to the hoop is clear and the demon takes full advantage. With limbs blurred by speed, he rushes to the goal and lofts the ball toward the backboard. It kisses the glass and bounces down through the hoop.

"One for Uncle Ed!" he yells to the shocked humans.

Max scowls. "You're just lucky I'm out of practice."

Sam grabs the loose ball and tosses it to Max, along with a worried glance.

Max shakes his head in a clear message: *I've got this.*

He dribbles in place, then tries to move around Demon Ed again. But this time Ed darts forward and steals the ball with his long claws. As Max watches in astonishment, the monster spins and launches an off-balance jump shot that swishes through the net. The fiendish fans erupt in wild celebration.

"Two for Ed," he growls. "Tie game."

Sam grabs the loose ball. "You said he didn't know how to play."

"I didn't expect him to go all Reggie Miller on me," Max says. "But I've still got some tricks up my sleeve."

"You better have."

Max scowls and grabs the ball.

Sam steps back and blows his whistle. "Play ball."

Max immediately drives toward the hoop. Demon Ed steps up to block him, but Max pulls up and shoots a long-distance bomb. Ed takes two quick steps and leaps high in the air, blocking the spotlight as he grabs the ball in mid-flight. He lands near the goal, hops up, and rolls it off his claw tips and into the basket. As it falls through the net he glowers at the astonished men.

"And three for me..." Ed rumbles.

"Didn't see that coming," Max says, and takes a nervous look at the stands.

The three women stand in a triangle above Walter, feet placed between the lines of the magic inscriptions. They hold hands as his chant grows more intense. Words foreign and dangerous tumble from his lips. His eyes roll back in his head, showing the whites, but he keeps repeating the arcane mantra. A low hum grows in sound and power, thrumming through the floor, making their bones vibrate like tuning forks on the same frequency as Hell.

Phantasmic energy glows in the air around them. It crackles over their skin and swirls from hand to hand in a growing whirlwind. When it peaks, it shoots down and slams into Walter. He spams as he absorbs the power, and his chant grows stronger.

The women let go of each other's hands and step away from the circle. Deb looks up through the shimmering air above them and sees the illusionary gym roof fading to reveal the natural stone. She catches her breath as she realizes the spell is breaking.

"He's going to do it…" she whispers. Any doubts she had about the mad plan, small though they were, are blown away.

Max faces off against Ed on the court again, dribbling the ball in the middle of the hardwood while Ed blocks the way to the basket. He darts to the left, but Ed dashes over to stop him. He moves back to the center and starts again, trying the right side of the court. The monster cuts him off there as well.

Frustrated with Ed's uncanny speed, Max takes a deep breath, centers himself, and runs straight at the demon. Ten feet away he head-fakes to the left. Ed falls for it and lunges in that direction, but Max keeps moving straight ahead. He drops to the floor and slides feet first between Ed's spread legs, still dribbling the ball. Ed reacts too late, ripping down with his claws, but Max has already slipped behind him. He jumps to his feet, charges the hoop, and rolls in another layup.

"Tied at three," Sam says.

"What was that!?" Demon Ed roars at Max.

"Just a little something I picked up from the Harlem Globetrotters."

Deb's mouth drops open as she watches Max's move. "Damn, he's good."

"He's no Bob Cousy," Mrs. Johnson mutters.

Behind them, Walter's spell, and the hum, grow louder. Air puffs around him, ruffling his hair and fluttering the pages of the book. Grains of salt blow away from the symbol.

The women move closer together, seeking protection from the preternatural forces swirling around them.

Walter chants on.

Sam tosses the ball back to Ed.

"Your ball, ugly."

Ed scowls as he catches the basketball, then bursts into motion. He runs straight at Max without dribbling and bowls the smaller man over.

Sam tweets the whistle. "Foul!"

Demon Ed keeps running. When he nears the goal, he leaps up and shoves the ball into the hoop, then stomps over to Sam. Ed reaches down and slides a claw under the whistle chain and slices it, along with a strip of skin.

The whistle falls to the floor.

Blood drops follow.

"No foul! No traveling! No more rules! Four points for me!" Ed bellows, and shoves Sam aside.

Sam hits the floor hard. Max rushes over and holds out a hand. Sam takes it and pulls himself to his feet. He dusts himself off and looks at a bruise on his forearm.

"Are you okay?" Max asks.

"I'm fine. Just win."

Max turns back to Demon Ed, who bounces the ball to him.

"Let's see what you've got, boy."

"All right. You asked for it."

Max dribbles to the left in a broad arc, talking to Ed the entire time. "You know, I was afraid of you when I was a kid. I could tell there was something evil about you. But I didn't understand what it was."

Ed shifts to keep himself between Max and the basket, so Max moves back the other way.

"When I got older and found out about the game, I thought it was the magic and monsters that made you so scary. But I was wrong."

Ed shifts again, so Max dribbles back toward the center of the court. He eyes the goal behind the demon, calculating the distance.

"No, you were scary because you were bigger than me. Tougher. Meaner. You were a big man, and I was just a little kid. It took me a while, but I figured out you were nothing more than a bully. No more, no less. Once I figured that out, I wasn't afraid of you anymore. I knew I could stand up to you. And do you know the best way to stand up to a bully?"

"How?" Ed sneers.

"You punch them in the fucking mouth."

Max explodes into action, dribbling straight at Demon Ed. This time there are no fakes. No tricks. Just flat-out speed and power.

Ed takes a startled step back and holds up his claws to block the expected shot. But instead of shooting, Max picks up the ball, plants a foot on Ed's massive thigh, and climbs up Monster Mountain. Human torso slams into demonic face as Max leaps between Ed's upraised arms and dunks the ball.

The impish reporter's camera flash *pops*: Demon Ed is posterized. He falls on his back under the basket with a pained grunt.

Max grins wolfishly as he lands next to the prostrate beast. "How you like me now, asshole? That's four to four. The next bucket wins."

Ed springs to his feet. "You are going down!"

"Maybe," Max barks, getting in Ed's face. "But I'll go down shooting."

Ed growls and stomps over to grab the ball. As he does, Max steals a glance at the landing. He sees Deb tilting her chin toward the ceiling. He looks up and sees the roof is obscured by roiling blue clouds spilling down the walls toward the floor.

It's working, she mouths.

Max nods, and turns back to see Ed palming the ball, oblivious to the magic working above him. "You ready to end this, Ed?" Max taunts. "Because I sure the hell am."

"Game point," Ed snarls. "Soon your soul will be mine forever."

"That was the deal, so let's get it over with," Max says, then shoots a surprised look over Ed's shoulder. "Sam! No!" he yells.

Demon Ed whips around to see—

Nothing.

Sam is on the landing, next to Deb.

Max darts forward. He steals the ball from the distracted monster and streaks toward the goal. Demon Ed chases after him with great angry strides. Seeing the creature will catch up before he can get close enough for an easy bucket, Max pulls up his dribble, sets his feet, and launches a rainbow from so far downtown he almost needs Ed's telescope to see the goal.

Time slows as the ball soars high through the air, the breathless moment hanging like a dusty championship banner dangling from the rafters of a fading memory, then flashes back to normal speed as the dagger arcs back down. It reaches the hoop—and bounces off the rim.

Max misses.

Ed rushes by the stunned man and grabs the rebound. He leaps astonishingly high and on the way down dunks the ball so hard it shatters the backboard in a spray of glass and twisted metal.

The demon splits the hardwood as he lands. "Game to Uncle Ed!" he bellows to his screeching fans and bares his glistening fangs at Max. "I win!!"

Max hangs his head in defeat as Ed gloats. Then he looks up with a knowing smile. "You might have won the battle, but you lost the war."

"What!?"

Max points up toward the rafters.

Demon Ed cranes his neck to see a blue-black funnel cloud roaring above him. Lightning flickers out of the maelstrom and cracks the floor. The barrel of the tornado drops down and engulfs the beast as Max dives out of the way. Ed screams as the vortex tries to suck him up, digging his claws into the court and splintering the wood. As it tugs him up feet first, the mist rises all over, defying the gale.

"Noooooooooo!" Ed yells as a strip of floor rips up, costing him half his grip. He flails in the air, holding on by one slipping claw as chunks of wooden shrapnel slash his thrashing body.

The other demons are tossed around like evil chattering tumbleweeds. One rolls past Max and smashes into the wall with a sickening *splat*.

Max's hair and clothes flap as the storm rages. He grabs the goalpost to keep from blowing away.

The ferocious winds buffet the landing, and the mist rises to obscure the view of the court. Deb groans as she loses sight of Max but has to concentrate on keeping herself from tumbling away.

Sam hangs on to the railing for support. "This is getting out of control!" he yells through the roar. He pulls himself along the bar toward the still-chanting Walter, but Elizabeth stops him with a fierce command.

"No! You must not stop him until it is done!"

Sam steps back.

The maelstrom grows and the mist spills onto the landing. Sam puts his arms around Deb, Elizabeth, and Mrs. Johnson, and tightens his grip on the rail. They cling together as the storm grows.

Walter stands up, oblivious to the tempest. He closes the book with a *snap* and drops it to the floor. His eyes glow with

Tanzanite fire as he walks to the edge of the landing and stares into the hurricane. He stands tall and proud and raises his arms to the sky. Stygian lightning cascades up his legs, skitters across his torso, and crackles from his fingertips. He booms an order in a voice that channels the thunder.

"By all the gods of this black place, I command this evil to *END*!!!!"

Max winces as lightning crashes around him. The cavern shakes. Someone—or something—screams. His hands slip as the ethereal goalpost dissolves and the storm grows more intense and the winds howl ever louder.

The clouds pull in from all corners, scouring the illusion away and revealing the stone walls beyond. They converge in the center of the roof and form a ball of purple fire.

The tornado roars like a demon itself, drowning out Ed's protest with the angry sound of innocent souls screaming for vengeance. The vortex spins faster, pulling the monster up with howling force. The floorboard cracks. Ed's claw slips. Muscles bulging, he screams in rage. The wooden anchor gives way. Demon Ed is sucked into the shimmering mass.

It's eating him, Max thinks as he watches it compress. *Eating him alive.*

A roar cuts through the din, a howl so angry, so defiant, *so Uncle Ed* that Max trembles when he hears it. He reverts to a frightened child who buries his face in his arms and tries to hide.

The ball of magic roils as Ed fights back. With one final surge, it crushes him, collapsing into an eldritch singularity that glows white hot then explodes with a soul-shuddering *BANG* that shoots tendrils of fire across the cavern.

The wind stops.

Silence blankets the cave.

Darkness falls.

Walter collapses. Elizabeth crawls to him in the dark and cradles his head in her hands.

Deb, Sam, and Mrs. Johnson switch on flashlights and look to the floor of the cavern, but the feeble beams can't penetrate the black veil.

"Is it over?" Mrs. Johnson whispers.

"I don't know," Sam replies.

Deb bites her lip and takes a step into the dark.

He grabs her arm. "Wait..."

"For what?" She says, pulling away. "Max might be hurt."

Sam nods and follows her. As they feel their way down the steps, the familiar yellow glow returns. In the distance, they see Max sitting on the floor of the cave. A ring of bodies lies around him. Human bodies.

Deb runs.

Max looks at the now very human Edward Braun. The man's eyes are open. He doesn't blink. A line of drool trickles from his open mouth. Max waves his hand in front of the slack face. There is no reaction.

"Game over, Uncle Ed."

Max slumps back. He dreamed of this moment for years, and now that it has arrived he doesn't feel the thrill of victory he had imagined, or savor the sweet taste of revenge. Instead, an overwhelming sense of relief floods through him. He briefly compares the comforting feeling to the jagged emotions that have tortured him for decades and decides relief will do just fine.

He stands up, turns away from his great-uncle, and studies the other people lying around him. They are familiar from the aged scrapbook, and more recently, from the games he lost. He grins when he sees the most familiar one of all.

Tommy's eyes snap open. He sits up and looks around in confusion. "What the fuck happened to the jungle?"

"What do you think happened?" Max says to his friend. "Walter saved the day."

"No fuckin' way."

"Fuckin' way."

"Go Walter!"

Tommy crushes Max in a bear hug as the other people begin to stir around them. Deb crashes into them from behind, wrapping her arms around both men.

"Deb!" Tommy says.

"Hi, Tommy! It's so good to see you again."

"I know, right?"

She pecks his cheek. He blushes.

"And you..." she says, letting go of Tommy and tackling Max. They fall back on the floor in a giggling embrace.

"That was the worst plan ever."

"It worked, didn't it?"

"Barely."

"Come on. Give me some credit."

"I'll give you more than that..." She kisses him. Hard.

Mrs. Johnson walks up with Sam and clears her throat.

"Get a room, you two."

Walter's eyes flicker open, and he sees Elizabeth staring down at him from inches away. "Did we...?"

"Yes. We won."

"Thank God. I wasn't sure our spell would work."

"I was."

He cries as he holds her tight.

Max and Deb get off the floor, and together they haul Tommy to his feet. The huge man eyes Sam.

"Who the hell are you?" Tommy asks.

"I'm Sam. I work with Max. And you have to be Tommy."

"Fuck right, I am. Max says you're a real hard ass."

"Really," Sam says, raising an eyebrow at Max.

"Yeah. But he says you're a good guy too. So, good to meet you."

The two men shake hands, and though there is a brief macho contest to see who can squeeze the hardest, the outcome is never in doubt.

Sam winces and pulls his hand away. "Nice to meet you too."

Tommy grins, then his smile disappears when he sees someone approaching. He pushes past Sam, walks over, and stops in front of the man he tormented for so long. "Walter," Tommy says in a quiet voice.

Walter looks up at his old nemesis and sees the man is trembling. He tenses, expecting the familiar explosion of rage, but realizes Tommy is shaking from what can only be embarrassment.

"Tommy," Walter says. "I'm glad you survived."

"Thanks. Me too. Max told me you saved everyone. Way to go, man."

"Yes, well, it wasn't the easiest task, but I had a lot of help."

"It's good to have a team, right?"

"Yes, it is," Walter says. "Is there something else you'd like to say?"

Tommy grits his teeth, struggling to find the words, then looks Walter in the eyes. "I'm sorry I was such an asshole to you before. It wasn't right. It took a lot of guts to come down here and fight, and you never quit. I hope you'll give me another chance."

Walter is taken aback by the admission, then smiles. "Thank you, Tommy. That means more than you know. Your apology is accepted."

Tommy holds out his hand. Walter takes it. This time there is no competition. They shake politely, then pull each other in for a hug.

Tommy steps back and looks around the room. "Hey, did you ever save your girl?"

"Yes, I did. After a most interesting battle. But that's a tale for another time," Walter says, and gestures to where Elizabeth talks to Max and Deb.

Tommy's face lights up and he runs over to them. He bellows a happy *hello* to Elizabeth, picks her up in his huge arms, and swings her around like a child. She laughs in delight, and everyone joins in.

Sam puts his arm around Max's shoulders. "Good game, sport. Until that last shot, anyway."

"I missed on purpose."

"If you say so."

"It doesn't matter," Deb says. "You won anyway."

"*We* won. It was a team effort. Just like my coach used to tell me."

"It helps if you have a star who can dunk."

They all laugh again, then study the people around them. Crew cuts, afros, and wavy perms top narrow-collared suits, hippie shirts, and ripped jeans on the men and women, marking the decades they were caught in the game.

"The spell saved them all. Every last one," Deb says.

"It saved us all," Max says.

"That was some powerful magic," Sam adds.

"Powerful wasn't the word for it," Mrs. Johnson says. "I thought it was going to—oh my God." Her face pales and she puts a hand to her chest as if to keep her heart from leaping out.

"Are you all right?" Deb asks.

Mrs. Johnson ignores her and rushes toward an older man, who sits up with a bewildered look. She stops short of touching him.

"Harry! Is that you...?"

"I, um, yes. Harry. Yes." the man says. He stares at her for a second, confused, then recognizes the woman in front of him. "Helen?"

She fights for words as he helps him stand up. "Yes. It's me."

"What happened to me? How did I get here? And why do you look so—so different?"

"It's a long story."

Harry nods. "I'm sure you'll tell me all about it later. For now, I just need to know one thing."

"Yes?"

"Are you still my girl?"

Helen's face lights up and the years fall away. "Always," she says, and falls into her husband's arms for the first time in decades.

Max and Deb's eyes well with tears as they watch the scene unfold.

"Your mom would be proud of you," Deb says, and grabs Max's hand.

He squeezes back, and the tears spill over and run down his cheeks in a happy torrent he isn't the least bit ashamed of.

The rest of the people are sitting up and blinking in confusion. Walter does a quick count. "The last of the missing. Well done, Max."

"I'm going to have to open up a lot of guest rooms."

"What about him?" Walter says, nodding at the catatonic Uncle Ed.

Deb's face flushes and she takes an angry step toward the man. "We should kill him right now for everything he did."

Max holds her back. "Yes, we should. But I'm done with killing."

"I'm not," Tommy says. "Let me strangle him."

"No, Tommy. If he wakes up, I promise you he'll pay."

"And if he doesn't?" Elizabeth asks.

"Then I've got the perfect place for him."

"You're the boss."

Max smiles. "Not anymore. I'm just a guy with a creepy old house and a really weird family. Now come on. Let's go make some new friends."

༄

Time passes.

The moon wanes and waxes in its ancient cycle until it once more hangs fat and full over a hulking asylum on the outskirts of town. In a locked and padded room at the end of a shadowy basement hallway, Edward Braun sits in a corner.

Barefoot. Bearded. Broken.

His hair is unkempt.

His face is blank.

His jaw is slack.

His pants are stained.

A straitjacket binds his arms.

The howling screams of black gods shackle his mind.

The once powerful and arrogant sorcerer is now less than an animal in a cage. He stares at the single window set high on the wall, unblinking as he has been since he lost the game.

Lost his mind.

Lost his soul.

As he sits there, the moon slides into view. Hours pass. A beam of silvery light creeps across the floor, over his legs, up his torso, onto his cheek, and finally shines into his eyes. Something flickers deep inside.

And Uncle Ed blinks.

~finis~

ABOUT THE AUTHOR

Eric Miller is the Bram Stoker Award-nominated editor of the horror anthology *Hell Comes to Hollywood*, its imaginatively titled sequel *Hell Comes To Hollywood II*, and the trucking-themed anthologies *18 Wheels of Horror* and *18 Wheels of Science Fiction*. His short fiction has appeared in various magazines, anthologies, and websites. He is a proud member of the Horror Writers Association.

He is the screenwriter of the SyFy Channel hit *Ice Spiders*, the horror films *Night Skies, Swamp Shark,* and *Mask Maker*, and co-writer of the science fiction thriller *The Shadow Men*.

Miller was born in beautiful Portland Oregon, was raised from knee-high to a grasshopper to a full-grown man in Indiana, and eventually moved to Los Angeles, where he has spent over three decades working in various fun-filled, low-stress jobs in the film industry. In his spare time, he reads voraciously, writes occasionally, hangs out in old diners, and hikes when his knees allow it.

This is his first novel. Better late than never.

www.EricMillerWrites.com